No Ordinary Season

by

James V. Jacobs

FATHER & SON

PUBLISHING, INC.

4909 N. Monroe Street
Tallahassee, Florida 32303-7015
www.fatherson.com
800-741-2712

Foreword

When Jim Jacobs handed me the manuscript of *No Ordinary Season* and told me it was a young adult novel, I was surprised. After all, he had spent thirty-six years in elementary classrooms teaching in public schools. He had coached track, boxing, and basketball, but briefly. I wondered what he knew about high school culture, an area I was well acquainted with since I taught high school classes over my whole career.

To add to my curiosity, I puzzled over how his manuscript fit with his own passionate goals to make the world better. Jim has spent his life on the front lines of social issues—concerns about class attitudes and divisions, racial and religious prejudice, and social injustice. He has spoken out about human rights, equity for marginalized children, free speech, and voter rights.

Seriously? A novel about teenage angst? So I read his manuscript.

No Ordinary Season is no ordinary young adult novel. He has realistically captured the world of high school students with all their turmoil, disappointments, hopes, and dreams. However, Jacobs has added a deeper dimension: painting a picture of the human condition while using the very concerns he has spent his life addressing. What results is a story with an underlying narrative that gives it richness and depth.

Jacobs has created the fictional town of River Bend, Indiana and its high school. River Bend is a Midwestern town where kids grow up riding bicycles and hanging around at Elrod's Quick Mart. Like many small towns, its families live for sports and the Friday night football or basketball games. Residents have opinions on the issues of the day, gossip spreads like wildfire, and everyone understands the existing social structure. They have deep-seated beliefs and barely hidden prejudices.

Cassie Garnet, River Bend High School senior, could have been perfectly happy running on her loser cross country team, graduating from high school, getting a job at the local diner, and daydreaming that Jake Nader might notice her. But in fiction, as in real life, unexpected events happen to change all that.

Into Cassie's life—and the normal order of things—comes the exotic Charna Rothstein Simon, a Jewish woman in a gentile world, who exudes self-confidence, intelligence, humanity, and a strict self-discipline. She's hired by the high school to teach chemistry and to coach Cassie's cross country team—a group that is mediocre at best.

Simon's arrival is the event that lifts *No Ordinary Season* above the mundane tale of yet another teenage coming-of-age novel. Suddenly, one season in the story of a sports team provides the backdrop for some of life's most difficult challenges. Simon, as well as Kyesha Hendrix, a new cross country runner from the only black family in town, allow Jacobs to reflect on issues important to all of our lives: integrity, loyalty, guilt, right and wrong, redemption, betrayal, tolerance, hope, jealousy, friendship and trust.

Dating, sex, and the pressures of carrying the town's athletic hopes—in other words, the grist of young adult novels is all here. But Jacobs adds a deeper dimension that follows the work of his own values and life, pointing out issues of social class, racial and religious prejudices, and social injustice. His memorable characters—C.R. Simon, the new coach; Kyesha Hendrix, a heck of a fast runner; Henry Elrod, the school janitor who knows all; "Prissy Butt" McGrady, the school secretary who believes she's in charge; Cassie's parents, a source of both teenage embarrassment and pride; and Jake Nader, the stuff of Cassie's dreams—create the authentic world of a small town, and the people impacting Cassie's life with all of its disappointments and joys.

No Ordinary Season tells the story of Cassie Garnet and the members of River Bend's cross country team, and what a season it is!

Susan Van Kirk
Author of The Endurance Mysteries
(Five Star/Cengage Publishing)

Dedication

No Ordinary Season is dedicated to my daughter Angel, who inspired me by running her hardest and helping her high school cross country team win its conference championship.

Acknowledgments

This book would not have been possible without the help of some talented and kind people, and I express my deep appreciation to all of them. First, I must thank the love of my life, Hattie, my wife of fifty-two years. She encouraged me every step of the way and spent long hours reading the manuscript and giving valuable advice. Trudy Ring, professional copy editor and good friend, scoured the early manuscript. Melinda Jones-Rhoades of the Galesburg (IL) Public Library lent her expertise and gave valuable counsel on young adult literature. Penny Gold, a good friend and fellow congregant at Temple Sholom in Galesburg, IL, advised me on details of Judaism. Rodney Blue, cross country coach at Carl Sandburg Community College in Galesburg, checked the accuracy of the manuscript on the technical aspects of cross county running. I also appreciate the input of my beta readers, who made sure the book would be accurate and appealing to my audience: Sydney

Wright, Jade Wright; my granddaughters, Miya Wright, Hollan Wright, and Bryn Wright; my son-in-law Brian Wright; Angel Wright, my daughter, and my daughter Nikki Jacobs-Inzerillo, and my son-in-law Nathan Inzerillo. Much appreciated is the work of Erin Liles, my editor, who assisted in the wording and development of the book. Finally, I must thank the three people who brought this book to the finish line. Brett Wright provided me with his many years of experience and expertise in the publishing business, representing me as he contacted publishers, as well as making important suggestions to enhance the book. Susan Van Kirk, my friend as well as a wonderful writer, helped in the development of the book, in addition to providing me with advice and contacts to push the project toward fruition. And Lance Coalson, my publisher, who had enough faith in *No Ordinary Season* to put it into print.

Contents

1

A Deadly Practice

When we found Mr. Buchanan's body, I knew things would change for our cross country team. But I never imagined how much they'd change.

A year ago—season before this one—we'd finished the final workout before the sectional and straggled to the gym door. There, all sprawled in the folding chair, was Buchanan, his unblinking eyes staring off at the afternoon sun. Then I noticed chemistry tests scattered over the ground.

"Mr. Buchanan—we're back," I said. He didn't answer.

Of all people, Sherry Dumont sort of tiptoed over and poked him once and then a second time, only harder. Not a muscle twitched—nothing. Sherry jumped back and screeched, "Sweet Jesus!" as her chunky body trembled.

Taylor Meterburg began to sob. Not like Sherry, but quietly. Taylor had Buchanan for chemistry. She idolized him.

While Sherry was screaming up at the fall sky about heaven and hell, God and the Devil, I was screaming at myself, *Cassie, do something!* But my mouth wouldn't work and my feet were frozen to the ground. Destiny Berry took charge. She flung open the side door, sprinted across the gym to the office, and raced back with the principal and a big gang of teachers running behind. Next thing we knew, sirens were blaring.

The River Bend cops got there first. Then an ambulance raced to the curb. Some of the teachers started crying. The principal's eyes shifted from the EMTs loading Mr. Buchanan into the ambulance to us girls. Taylor had her face buried in her hands. Kayla Thomas had faded into the background, pressed stiffly against the outside gym wall like an ice sculpture. Destiny's jaw was set, her lips pressed tightly, like she was in pain but didn't want to show it. Sherry was on her knees by the corner of the building, a couple of women teachers trying to pry her off the ground as she yelped, "Lord, help him!"

My eyes followed as the ambulance crept away. *It's too late for that.*

2

Mediocre
Is A Horrible Word

Now, we're on the bus rumbling south down Interstate 69. My teammates are totally silent. A couple girls have headphones on, eyes closed. Others are gazing out the windows or staring straight ahead. Harvested fields and an occasional billboard streak by. Marion's last exit just shot past.

I don't know why I keep thinking about that day. Maybe it's because the adults made a big deal out of us finding Mr. Buchanan dead. Truth is, his death bothered them a lot more than me. Don't get me wrong. I feel bad about him dying. Sure, he was a terrible cross country coach. But, he was a person—a human being.

Thing is, I had my issues with Buchanan. He really pissed

me off after one meet when he said, "Just a mediocre cross country team—just *mediocre*." He stressed that horrible word as he zipped his jacket over his big belly. Sure, our team wasn't even mediocre, but I despise that word. Mediocre means not special. It means no one cares. The word is for losers. *Ordinary* is a lot better word. Yes, I know they mean the same thing. But at least *ordinary* doesn't sound like something you'd barf up, like *mediocre* does.

I entered River Bend High with big dreams, but Buchanan let me down. It started in eighth grade after I won the 3200 meters—over two miles—in our junior high's all-school track meet. God, it felt great hearing the announcer say, "Winner of the 3200 meter run, Cassie Garnet."

Before winning that race, I had been stuck on ordinary. Nothing except participation ribbons at the county fair, never in the high classes, and always satisfied being a straight C student. So when I won at the track meet, I decided that even if it did make me sweat and smell gross, I'd stick with running. However, when I got up to River Bend High, they didn't have track for girls, only boys.

They'd tried it once a long time ago. Only three girls came out. The school board said it was wasting the taxpayers' money to pay for extra track equipment for less than a half-dozen girls. So they cut girls' track. No one raised a stink, and the board got away with it.

But there's this Title IX law. It makes schools provide girls' sports. Cross country doesn't require any equipment, so River Bend High started cross country for us. I went out my freshman year along with four other girls. Until this season our team sucked.

Oh, I was the best on the team. Doesn't say much, though. It kills me to admit it, but compared to runners from other schools, I was just. . . well, *ordinary*.

4

Even though I wasn't really that good at cross country, there was something about it that I loved. But I wanted to be better than just ordinary at it. I wanted to be good. Maybe even *great*.

Like I said, our team totally stunk. The best we ever did was when I was a sophomore, eighth place out of a nine-team conference. The season before this one we were the worst—last. Our team was so bad the school administration pulled us out of the conference. Buchanan didn't care. We just ran on this half-assed schedule he made up. He never had his heart in cross country. His true love was chemistry. I never took chemistry, but the kids who did said he really knew his stuff. Cool teacher, but a lousy coach. His practices consisted of him plopping his big butt down on a chair and grading tests or planning lessons while we did pretty much what we wanted. The extra thousand bucks they paid him was the only reason he bothered with us.

"Do what you have to, ladies. Run a mile or two, hard as you're able," he'd drawl. Usually the last words he'd utter all practice.

Sure, I tried, or at least thought I was trying. But no one was around to show me what I needed to do to be really good. I would work out during practice by running sort of hard for two or three miles, but come race time it never put me near the front—always toward the middle.

Most of my teammates only jogged a mile or so during practice. And Sherry Dumont—who always blamed her last-place finishes on menstrual cramps—would cheat and only trot as far as Van Winkle's Snacks, where she'd kill time flirting with guys and stuffing her face. After a few minutes passed, Sherry would have one of her lover boys toss a cup of water on her to look like sweat, stroll back to the corner, and then jog the rest of the way. Sherry's workouts added up to a two-hundred yard round trip. Buchanan was none the wiser, and no one ever ratted her out. He wouldn't have cared anyway.

I know it sounds cold-hearted when I say Mr. Buchanan's passing is why I knew this season would be a change from the others. Hey, I'm just being honest. I wish he hadn't suffered that massive stroke. Just quitting as coach would have been enough. His dying did change things, not only for our team, but for all of River Bend. Our high school was left with no chemistry teacher. Must have had a dozen substitutes. Chemistry students said the subs didn't know as much as the kids. The school board hunted and hunted. Internet, ads in school magazines, newspapers and all. After months of looking, they finally came up with a *real* teacher to fill Mr. Buchanan's place. School officials tried to keep it quiet, but word got out. Henry Elrod, the custodian at River Bend High School, overheard the principal tell Betty "Prissy Butt"McGrady, the high school secretary, "I think we've found a man for Mr. Buchanan's job—a C.R. Simon. E-mailed resume and application today."

Henry rushed the news to Clarence, his brother, who owns a convenience store—calls it Elrod's Quick Mart—attached to his vehicle repair garage on the highway running along the south edge of town. Between the Elrod brothers, all North Central Indiana heard that River Bend had found a chemistry teacher. It didn't matter if the license said Outer Mongolia, anyone who pulled in for gas, coffee, or a lube job got the latest news.

I'll never forget the day Mr. Buchanan's replacement showed up to be interviewed. Doubt that anyone else there will forget it either. All any of us had to do was take one look to realize C.R. Simon was no ordinary person.

3

Centerfold

Seemed half of River Bend ignored the freezing weather to hang around River Bend High School to check out the new teacher. Chemistry students brought their parents. A few of the Upper Crusts, or UCs, as we *common* folks call them, descended from Snob Hill and drove by to get a look at this C.R Simon. Clarence Elrod even left Martha Anderson, the old widow lady who works for him, alone at the store while he drove over to River Bend High.

Me? Front and center. I figured coaching cross country would be part of the deal—Title IX and all—and I wanted to size up my new coach.

At three forty-five, a Porsche—yes, a *Porsche*—wheeled up. A group of guys had just left Van Winkle's Snacks and was walking toward the high school. When they spotted the silver sports car, they stopped dead in their tracks.

The door of the Porsche swung open. I stretched my neck. The driver slid out. *This couldn't be the new chemistry teacher,* I told myself. Then, it hit me. *C.R. Simon is a woman.* Ashamed to say, like the principal, I just assumed someone who calls themselves "C.R." would be a man. But this was no man.

Her black hair caressed shoulders covered by an open leather coat. She looked to be about five nine, and her curvy figure was perched on long, shapely legs exposed by a short dress, accentuated by spiked heels. She probably weighed about a hundred and twenty or twenty-five pounds. As this C.R. Simon approached me, she smiled and said, "Hello."

I didn't answer back. Just nodded. My eyes were locked on her dark—almost black—eyes and on her velvety, olive complexion highlighting features that seemed sculpted by one of those old Italian artists I learned about in art appreciation class. Maybe that Michelangelo guy. As she passed, I got a whiff of perfume. Not that cheap junk, but something that costs real money. Suddenly I had two emotions—disappointment and jealousy. Disappointed because she was a woman. Sure, other schools had women coaches who were great. But *this* woman who just paraded past me couldn't be much of a coach, not all swagged out like that—not with a shape like that.

My jealousy was because of Jake Nader, who had just stepped out a side door of the gym. There he stood, all two hundred ten pounds of stud stretched over six feet five inches, eyeing the driver of the Porsche as she strutted up the sidewalk.

As usual, a basketball was propped under one arm, and a gym bag dangled from his hand. People think Jake will be Mr. Basketball—top player—in Indiana this year. I couldn't care less if he knew a basketball from a pumpkin. Been nuts about him since sixth grade.

I turned and watched as *this woman* swayed toward him.

Jake reached up and smoothed his messed hair away from his face that was always tanned, even in winter.

Obviously he'd been working out. But it wasn't just exercise causing the vapor to drift off of him. Jake has this *It* thing that was radiating serious body heat. I struggled to control my breathing.

This C.R. Simon woman stumbled a little, causing papers she had been carrying to spill onto the cold ground. Jake dropped his gym bag and the ball, which rolled and stopped at my feet. He knelt down, snatching up the papers. The woman knelt beside him, her dress sliding up her thighs, nearly to her hips. The group of boys that walked down from Van Winkle's stood like statues. Hands in his coat pockets, one guy shifted weight from one leg to the other as he gawked—and tried to act cool.

Jake handed her the papers as they rose together. She said, "Thank you." And then my heart crashed. His blue eyes looked into the woman's eyes as he touched her arm and said, "Be careful. It's slick and the cement's hard." She nodded, smiled, and said thank you a second time, touching his arm in return.

Mr. Basketball ogled her as she disappeared into the building. Made me sick. But I could hardly blame him. Gorgeous with a movie star figure poured into that dress, she could pose for one of those dirty magazines I'd peeked at once at this girl's house. Megan Willett's dad has a stash of porn, plus he's bookmarked a bunch of porn sites on a laptop he thinks no one else knows about. *Are these the women I'm competing with?* I'd asked myself. Disgusting—and depressing. There I was with toothpick legs, skinny backside, and flat chest. To make it worse, Jake Nader was drooling all over himself. I hated this C.R. Simon.

He gathered up his bag and then strolled over, bent down and grasped his ball with one hand. "That the new chemistry teacher?"

I was a little tongue-tied, at last managing to spit out, "Yes—I mean—I assume so." He glanced towards the building. "Wow!" Then I watched him walk away.

There I was just too insecure to let him know how I felt, always shoving my feelings deep inside. But those emotions would pop back up and take control of me, and I'd be sure it was love—lonely love. When I wasn't near him, he was on my mind, and when I was near him, he was in my heart. I was so stupid about it. I was afraid to even flirt a little, yet when other girls showed interest in him—which was all the time—I would get all jealous and mad. I was so dumb. But who was a girl like me to even think about having a guy like Jake? He was popular, the best at everything, and so cool. And me? I was convinced I was plain—yes, I hate to say it—*mediocre.*

Being a Saturday, Henry Elrod had come over to school to fire up the boiler to warm up the building. Later, I heard he took one look at this C.R. Simon and stood next to the principal's door pushing his broom over the same spot for a solid hour, listening in—and hoping to catch another look.

Henry couldn't hear everything, but Prissy Butt McGrady took notes for the principal, and she was thrilled to plug the gaps. By the time Henry beat a path to his brother's convenience store, he was about to bust. I knew the latest news would be flying at Elrod's Quick Mart, so I decided to head over there and get a candy bar.

4

Latest Gossip

"From New York City originally," Henry said. "Been living in Indianapolis since she graduated from over in West Lafayette three years ago—from Purdue. None of 'em knew she was a woman, 'cause she just goes by C. R."

"Must not list sex on the application," said Clarence.

"They sure know she's a woman now," replied Henry.

"What's she been doin' in Indianapolis for the past three years?" asked Judd Overstreet, a farmer who lives on the Marion blacktop.

"Been working for a pharmaceutical company over there plus getting more schooling," answered Henry. "To hear the principal tell it, she's got credentials out the wazoo."

"Why would she quit a cushy job at a drug company to teach a bunch of high school kids in River Bend?" asked Clarence.

"Good question. Mrs. McGrady thinks Miss Simon's running away from something."

"Huh," growled Mrs. Anderson as she shoved cans of beer into the cooler. "This Miss Simon oughta be running away from McGrady, that so-called secretary."

Martha Anderson hates Prissy Butt. The short version is twenty years ago Prissy had Mrs. Anderson's youngest son expelled. Something about dirty words on a wall. Anyway, Mrs. Anderson swears Prissy set him up because he turned down her daughter for the Sweetheart Swirl, the annual bash where the girls ask the guys.

"What kind of a name is *C.R.* for a woman?" asked Clarence.

Henry cleared his throat. "Stands for Charna Rothstein— Charna Rothstein Simon. Like I said, she only uses C.R."

"Good God!" Mrs. Anderson snapped. "Who'd name a girl *Rothstein*? Sounds like a breed of cow."

Henry shrugged. "Principal says girls' cross country is included." I perked up my ears. Henry looked puzzled. "Miss Simon says she's never even been to a track meet, let alone to a cross country meet. Told the principal, though, that she's willing and eager to learn."

Oh, great! People who say they're willing to learn are dorks. They're usually the ones who learn the least. I handed Mrs. Anderson the money for a Snickers and stuck it into my coat pocket.

Clarence wiped his greasy hands on a rag. "What's the difference? She's not being hired as the basketball coach. Don't have to know anything about cross country. Just tell 'em to get out there and run."

Henry rubbed his chin. "When I mentioned how attractive Miss Simon is, Betty McGrady puckered up her face like she'd sucked on a lemon and said, 'Well, it's been my experience that the pretty ones aren't too bright.'"

"Huh!" Martha Anderson snorted and set her jaw. "Betty McGrady is neither bright nor pretty."

Henry chuckled.

"What's so funny?" asked Martha Anderson.

"Just thinking about how Mrs. McGrady darts around that office, high heels clicking on the tile floor like a tap dancer. Once I saw her set a ream of paper in four different spots in less than a minute, and it ended up right back where it had started."

Everyone laughed.

Henry Elrod was right. The prissy way McGrady acts is why people call her Prissy Butt. That, plus her not-a-hair-out-of-place, not-a-wrinkle-anywhere grooming.

"She's like a gnat with hemorrhoids," agreed Clarence.

The group roared.

Enough heard. I left and walked home gnawing on my candy bar. I had gotten the information I'd come for, and I didn't want to hear any more about old Prissy Butt McGrady, and I especially didn't want to hear any more about C.R. Simon. She was beautiful, smart—Jake Nader obviously thought she was hot—and she didn't know a lick about cross country.

Poking the last chunk of candy bar into my mouth, I yanked out my phone and put my thumbs to work texting my teammates: "seen new chem teach. new coach ?!?! OMG! feel like hangin' up runnin' shoes!"

5

Dumont Hates Her Too

Guess it was the novelty of her name, because at first I usually referred to the new chemistry teacher as *C.R. Simon* or just *C.R.*—never *Miss Simon*. Anyway, she started teaching at RBHS a week before Valentine's Day, and my feelings toward her were colder than the snow drifting over our driveway. She was all we girls gossiped about hanging out at Van Winkle's or cruising on the weekends. In between times, we about gave ourselves carpal tunnel texting back and forth. C.R. Simon not only didn't know cross country, but she was a magnet for the guys. Every time I walked past the chemistry lab, they were frolicking around her like puppy dogs. Made me gag.

Sherry Dumont hated her too. One day she caught up with me as I strolled down the math/science hall. As usual, C.R., wearing a white lab coat, was with groupies sucking up to her.

"Just look at them," said Sherry. "Mr. Buchanan never carried on like that."

They were laughing as she pointed to a test tube. I felt like a trap door had been sprung when I spotted Jake Nader laughing hardest of all as he scribbled in a notebook.

"I'll bet she's telling them something dirty. My father says she's easy." Now, as much as I disliked C.R. Simon, I couldn't let that pass. "He wishes."

Sherry twisted up her face like a baby with a bellyache. "You listen here, Cassie. My father is a very Godly man!"

Sherry's whine was all it took. Jake stopped taking notes, and the others turned as C.R. walked to the door. I could've died. She asked if something was wrong. We shook our heads, and then stood motionless like a couple of boutique dummies.

The crowd broke up; all the guys stared at Sherry and me. Jake gave me a glance, and then turned to the chemistry teacher. "Great class, Miss Simon."

God! I couldn't decide whether to throw up or kick him where it counts.

"I'm glad you enjoyed it, Jake." She looked at Sherry and me. "Nice day, isn't it?"

"It is for some people," Sherry said.

Simon gave her a "What's-that-supposed-to-mean?" look and went back into the room as students wandered in for her next class.

Against my wishes, Sherry tagged along as I headed for English lit. Her mouth raced like it had a busted switch. "Did you hear what she said to Nader? 'Glad you enjoyed it.' I'll just bet he enjoys *it*. There's more to that relationship than student and teacher."

"Like what?" Of course, I knew what she was driving at.

"Oh, come on, Cassie." Sherry planted herself in the middle

of the hall, and with kids passing on each side whispered, "Sex!"

"Give up on it, Sherry."

"Cassie, Nader grins all the time like he's been getting more than good grades in chemistry."

"That's ridiculous," I said. Yet, the same dirty thought had crept into my head.

"My mother says men are always happy when they get what they want from us."

I looked her square in the eye. "Sherry, no man wants anything from you." I left her standing in the hall looking like the nut job she is. I was bummed, though. Jake seemed goofy over C.R. Simon. Not just hot for her, but like he might feel something deeper, which drove me into a panic.

6

Lady Coyotes' New Coach

A week before summer vacation, a notice on the school website announced a meeting for the cross country team that coming Monday. It was from C.R. Simon. I sat at my computer at home and stared at it for the longest time, debating whether I should go or not. One minute I would think, *Screw it! This woman isn't gonna coach me any better than Buchanan.* Then, the next minute I'd tell myself that running was the one thing I was even halfway good at, and quitting the team wouldn't make me better at it. And down deep, getting better—being the best runner I could be—was what I wanted more than anything. So, at last I decided to go to the meeting and see what was up. "Who knows," I said to myself as I pushed away from my computer, "miracles do happen." Then, I added, "Yeah, right!"

Buchanan never met with us until a week before the first cross country meet in August, so the team was pretty curious why our new coach was having this early meeting. That is, everyone except Sherry Dumont. She didn't care *why* there was a meeting. Sherry was just pissed that there *was* one, and she bitched nonstop. "Simon must be out of her mind to hold a meeting for a sport that's three months off," Sherry spouted the next day in P.E. class. "My father says that she has too much idle time on her hands, and idle time is the Devil's workshop."

"I think someone said that before he did," I informed her. But Sherry's mouth was wound like a cheap wristwatch. On and on she went, until finally I turned to her in the middle of a softball game and told her to put a lid on it, or I was going to peel off my sweat socks and jam them down her throat. She shut up.

We all agreed at lunch to congregate by the gym and go together to the chemistry lab. I got there first, standing alone looking through the glass into the RBHS trophy case that spanned the length of the hall between the twin set of double doors leading into each side of the gym.

Suddenly, I felt a hand on my shoulder and heard a voice say, "Wonder if we'll ever win some hardware to put in there?"

I turned and looked into Taylor Meterburg's smiling face. Just a little shorter than me, Taylor wears her blond hair trimmed in a retro wedge. My mom calls it a "Dorothy Hamill."

"Dream on," I answered, shaking my head slowly as I looked through the glass at the big gold trophy our boys' basketball team captured by winning their regional, and that March making it to semi-state, the tournament right before the state finals.

We stood quietly gazing into the case, and then I looked back and studied Taylor; petite but not scrawny or fragile, she's a year younger—would be a junior—but we click. A "school" friend. And really smart—in all the honors classes and carries a 4.0. But she doesn't show off with her brains like some brainiacs. We eat lunch together almost every day and

20

sometimes hang out at Van Winkle's, although we've never been to each other's homes. Oh, Taylor's invited me; I've always made excuses. She's a UC from up on Snob Hill, and the thought of going into one of those big rich houses makes me uncomfortable. However, Taylor is a really nice girl. Quiet but not stuck up, even though her dad's a big shot at the car plant in Marion.

Destiny Berry, who would also be a junior the coming year, rounded the corner wearing shorts and a midriff showing a lot of cleavage. Her flip-flips were smacking with each step. A scowl was plastered on her face along with heavy lipstick, blush, and eye shadow.

"What's up?" I asked.

Tall and slender, Destiny's muscles were always tensed for action—any kind of action. "Ah, that old A-hole of a principal gave me a detention for the way I was dressed." She spit the words out, ready to take on the world. "I told that old skin-headed dweeb he should quit worrying how other people are dressed and pay a little more attention to his own wardrobe. Looks like he shops at the fu...." Destiny caught herself just as a teacher walked by. She flicked a lock of long brown hair away from her eyes then swept her hair over her shoulder and behind her back with the same hand. "Told him it looks like he buys his clothes at the friggin' Goodwill store."

"What did he say to that?" asked Taylor.

She rolled her eyes. "Told me I was headed for real trouble. Get this." She stopped and planted her feet firmly on the marble floor. "He had the nerve to say that in a couple years he expected to see me around River Bend with a little kid propped on my hip— then he gave me a second detention."

Taylor and I glanced at each other. I didn't know what Taylor was thinking, but I agreed with Destiny : *It did take a lot of nerve. I can't imagine someone who was supposed to be helping students talking to one that way. Destiny's family hardly has two nickels to rub together, and she sometimes walks on the wild side, but she's a stand-up person. She deserves better than that.*

At last, here pranced bubble butt Sherry. She had her head down scrolling through her smart phone. Kayla Thomas trailed behind. Kayla would be a senior, like Dumont and me. She's a mystery. Lives with her grandma on a little farm outside of town. To this day, I don't understand her, only to say that she doesn't know how to fit in.

When we arrived at the chemistry lab, C.R. Simon wasn't anywhere to be seen. But three girls from the junior high were there. Obviously, the new coach had been recruiting. Two of the girls, Samantha Peters and Emily Lutker—another UC girl—didn't surprise me. Emily had won the junior high 3200 meter run a week before, with Samantha nipping at her heels. Like Dumont, both had their eyes buried in their cell phones flipping the screen with their fingers.

Ashamed to say that the third one, Kyesha Hendrix, was a real shock. Kyesha's black. One of only two black kids in the River Bend schools. The other one is her little brother. The Hendrix family moved here from Fort Wayne about three years ago. I'd heard her dad was a janitor over at the auto plant in Marion. A lot of townspeople were pissed when Leopold Cox sold them the new house he'd built and then left the state. Oh, no one burned crosses like the Ku Klux Klan or anything. People just bad mouthed the Hendrixes when they weren't around and ignored them when they were. But grouchy old Mr. Van Winkle let the Hendrixes know right away that he didn't like them being in town. Of course, he didn't like it when the UCs built Snob Hill and moved in either. "Upsettin' our way of doin' things," he'd told my dad. As for me, I'd never spoken a word to any of the Hendrixes—to any black person.

That afternoon last May, Kyesha sat quietly, her eyes fixed on the smart board fastened on the wall at the front of the room. My teammates stared so hard at the black girl, they practically drilled a hole through her. Naturally, Sherry Dumont had to make some crack. Old Mighty Mouth whispered in my ear, "Good Lord. What is she doing here?"

I didn't respond. We all hopped up on those high lab chairs and waited in silence, except for Sherry, whose mouth worked overtime. Finally, C.R. Simon entered and strutted to the front. It was a steamy day, but while the rest of us were wilted wrecks, she didn't have a single strand of her dark hair out of place. "Doubt if she even sweats," I mumbled. No one paid me any attention. They were too busy glancing from the chemistry teacher to Kyesha Hendrix. Heads swiveled like a tennis match was going on.

"Well, ladies," she began, "you comprise the girls' cross country team." Glancing around, I counted eight. If we all stayed out, it would be our biggest team.

"As you probably know, I haven't been here long, and I don't know any of you very well. Although I remember that you young women stopped at my door a few weeks ago." She looked first at Sherry Dumont and then me. I could've died. I felt the blood rush to my face in a blush. "We should introduce ourselves." *Oh, BS. This isn't a social event.* "Let's start with you." She nodded at me.

I cleared my throat and said, "I'm Cassie Garnet." *How dumb. Introducing myself when everyone knows me, except for her—and the Hendrix girl.*

"Nice to meet you, Cassie." C.R. stepped forward, extending her right hand. Her nails were long and beautiful. I placed a limp hand into hers. She squeezed it firmly and went on to Sherry Dumont.

Each of the others said their names and shook hands with her. When C.R. Simon came to the black girl, a cold silence filled up the room. She slid down off of the chair and seemed to catch her breath. "My name is Kyesha Hendrix."

"Kyesha, glad to have you with us." The chemistry teacher pressed her hand into the black girl's.

I don't know why I did it, and it seemed weird at the time, but now I'm proud that I turned to Kyesha and said, "Yeah, we're happy to have you on the team, Kyesha." The other girls stared at me, so I added, "I'm glad all three of the junior high girls came to this meeting."

"Thank you, Cassie," replied the chemistry teacher.

I gave a little nod.

"You're probably wondering why we're having this meeting now instead of in August." C.R. Simon leaned back against a lab table, and a smile crossed her lips. "Don't feel alone. Other people are wondering the same thing. In fact, people keep telling me it's a long time before school starts—and cross country's not basketball."

Yep, that's the attitude, I told myself, exchanging glances with Destiny and Taylor.

"Ladies, the meeting is being held today because August would be too late for us to develop a winning team.

Winning team? We five veterans shot looks at each other, certain that this rookie coach was out of her mind.

"I have to be honest with you," she went on. "I've never coached before. In fact, I have never even done much running." She chuckled. "Only to catch a taxi."

I recognized she'd tried to make a *funny*, only none of us laughed.

"However, I've started working out—running. Also, I've

recently read a great deal about cross country." She stepped away from the lab table and toward us. "Ladies, if we all help each other out, we can do well. I believe that."

None of us made a sound. All eyes were locked on C.R. "I've designed a summer workout schedule, and I want to give it to you now."

"What?"

"Sherry, do you have a concern?"

"I don't run in the summer." Dumont smirked. "Summer is for other things."

"Sherry, if you work out early in the morning, like I've scheduled it, you'll have plenty of free time." Simon walked to her desk and picked up a stack of papers. She thumbed through them on her way back. "Here's yours." She handed a sheet to Sherry, and then passed out the rest. I studied mine. It had different workouts for different days.

"I put these together based on what few records Mr. Buchanan left, on what the P.E. teachers told me, and on what I've read. You'll have to get in mileage and speed over distance on alternating days. Two days rest each week is very important. It's all explained there." She turned back to Sherry. "You can do some of those other things on off days." Then, C.R. Simon scanned the group. "The weight room will be open for basketball and football players each week day. I've arranged with Mr. Railing, boys' basketball coach, to have someone supervise you three days a week. This lifting regimen is specifically for runners."

"Is this really necessary? Summer is our vacation," Sherry huffed.

The new coach stepped forward, smoothed down the front of her dress, and smiled. "Sherry, I can't pry you out of bed and force you to work out. However, you won't be on this team next fall if you don't run this summer."

Should've seen Sherry's face. The rest of us couldn't help but smile—a little short of an all-out laugh. I could tell that Sherry was trying to think of a comeback, but C. R. had yanked the rug out from under her, and the chemistry teacher stood, hands on hips, staring down at Sherry. Then, she scanned the room. "Now, I also need to find out when during the month each of you have your period."

I cleared my throat, shifting my eyes toward the other girls. Destiny smirked and Taylor's face was as red as a spanked butt. Kyesha Hendrix looked down at her hands. Me? I was too dumbfounded to speak. But big mouth Dumont blurted, "What's that got to do with running? That subject is not fit for conversation. It's personal; it's sinful to discuss such a thing."

Boy, what a hypocrite. Dumont, who whined continuously to all of us about her cramps, was reaming out the coach because it was "personal" and "sinful".

"Sherry, I respect your concern," C.R. Simon told her. "This information, cross-referenced with your times, will help me check for a possible iron depletion."

"Iron depletion? Like not enough iron in our blood?" I asked.

"If an athlete doesn't eat right or get her rest, it's a risk, Cassie. When you work out hard—particularly a runner—you use up ferritin, which is an iron-containing protein. Low ferritin can adversely affect your performance." She scanned the room. "It's essential to eat right and get your rest . . ."

Kyesha interrupted. "Miss Simon?"

Every eye was on the black girl.

"Yes, Kyesha?"

"I read that some girl runners train so hard that they stop having their time of the month."

"My God!" declared Sherry. "What are we going to talk about next?"

The new coach ignored her. "That's right. Some do. But studies show that condition is linked more to improper diet combined with over training."

"Is it bad to stop having your period?" asked Taylor.

We were quiet for a nanosecond. Then everyone except Sherry busted out laughing. "I mean because of working out too much, not because . . ." Taylor let out a huge laugh. We roared—even C.R. But not Dumont. "Disgusting," she muttered.

Our new coach got hold of herself. With the palm of her right hand pressed against her chest, she tried to keep from laughing. "I know—what you're—trying—trying to say . . ." More giggling. "To answer you . . ." She caught her breath. "A woman athlete should train in such a way that she's likely to stay on her normal cycle."

No problem here. Regular as basketball season in Indiana.

I sneaked a peek at Dumont as Simon kept talking. Sherry's face looked like a—like a menstrual cramp. I lowered my head and snickered, and then looked back at the coach.

"Every woman is different. We all have to eat healthy and get our rest." She hesitated. "By the way . . ." C.R. walked over and looked down at Sherry. "Studies show that some female athletes do better when menstruating. It's no excuse for lack of effort."

Simon had Dumont's number. *Wish I could read people like that*, I thought. I glanced at the other veterans. Grins all around.

While the rest of us wrote the information down on a chart, Dumont sat there mad as a bull, refusing to press pen to paper.

When the chart was completed, Sherry announced, "I refuse to run on my summer vacation."

"Then you may go," said our new cross country coach. "I'm very sorry I wasted your time."

Dumont got up, dissed C.R. Simon with a dirty look, flung her purse strap over her shoulder, and stormed from the room.

Our new coach's eyes followed her before returning to the team.

7

Captain Cassie

C.R. Simon went on to explain that we'd run in pairs so we'd have someone to push us. She must have thought my comment to Kyesha made me the logical partner for her, so she put us together. I felt uneasy about that. Really, I wanted to partner with Taylor, but Kyesha was part of the team, so as a veteran I decided I should step up. Samantha and Emily, the other incoming freshmen, wanted to run as partners, and Destiny, Taylor, and Kayla would run together.

I asked myself how C.R. would know we were doing our workouts. Let's face it, partners could lie for each other. But, she had it planned.

"We must have verification," she said, sliding up onto a lab chair, the foot of one leg propped on a rung, the other leg extending down straight, sleek and long, so the toe of her high heel touched the floor. "The rules of the state athletic association do allow me to supervise practices during the summer; however, to start with, I want our team captain to supervise. That's how I will monitor progress—and, frankly, your dedication. So we need to elect a captain. Nominations?" Buchanan never worried about a captain, so this was a new wrinkle, and we sat there dumb as stones, afraid to choose the wrong person or something. Out of the blue, Kyesha said, "I nominate Cassie."

I glanced back at her, and then looked away, kinda embarrassed, yet kinda proud. Taylor seconded my nomination. Now I felt really good. As I said before, Taylor might be UC, but she's a friend. I was the only nominee, but it wasn't unanimous. I didn't think it was right to vote for myself, so I wrote down Taylor's name. Not long after Simon read off the results, naming me as the captain, that good feeling was pushed aside by panic. *What have I gotten myself into?*

Our new coach explained that as captain I was responsible for getting the data to her so she could chart our progress. I knew what *data* meant, but I wasn't sure *what* data she was talking about. *Can I handle it? Do I really want this job?*

"Cassie, do you have a stopwatch?" she asked. I pointed to the runner's watch on my left wrist.

"How about the rest of you?" The veterans had them; the new girls didn't. C.R. said that we all needed a runner's watch because our times for each workout would be recorded. The freshmen said they'd get them.

"You'll run with your partners five mornings each week. Plus, I want you to meet as a team Thursday evenings and race over this." She strolled around the room handing out a map of a course she'd laid out. "I won't be there, so Cassie's in charge." Then C.R. Simon stopped and scanned the room, looking each of us squarely in the eye. "I demand integrity. Each of you will report accurate times to our captain." She looked at me. "And, Cassie, you will be honest in reporting those times directly in person to me." Again she looked at each of us. "Any cheating and you're off the team. Is that understood?"

Some of us nodded, others answered with a slow "yes." All of us knew she meant business.

C.R. Simon said our first practice with her would be in August, but if our times didn't keep improving, she would meet with us as a team. Ream us out, I figured.

We went over the course map. She had measured and run it. It was five thousand meters—little over three miles—same as we'd run in competition.

8

Kyesha, The Girl We Ignored

That first morning I rolled out of the sack at six-thirty and dressed in as little as the law would allow: underpants, running shorts, shoes, sports bra, and a T-shirt with *The Indianapolis 500* printed on it.

Kyesha and I agreed to meet in the vacant lot across from Clarence Elrod's Quick Mart. I should have picked her up as I ran by; her house is on the way. But I felt uncomfortable. Like I said a while back, before that day in the chemistry lab I'd never even spoken to a black person. Had no idea how I was going to make conversation with her—afraid I'd wind up saying something that would piss her off.

I jogged around the corner. Elrod's store and garage came into view, and there was Kyesha. She's very thin, thinner even than me, and she wears glasses. She keeps her hair medium short with the curl, not straight like some black girls I see on TV or the internet. Kyesha was dressed in running shorts, tank top, and a fairly worn pair of Nikes, which told me she'd done some running before that day.

"Hi," I said.

"Hi."

"Ready to go?"

She nodded.

We were scheduled to run the five-kilometer course. Our new coach didn't want any pulled muscles, so she insisted we warm up and stretch before running hard. We trotted around the block and went through the stretching routine, not uttering a single word. Kyesha watched me, copying each stretching motion. Mel Dumont, Sherry's weirdo dad, drove by and gave us a psycho stare. For some reason, his seeing us together made me defiant—proud to be seen with Kyesha. I set my jaw and smiled at him.

Then, I spotted Sherry sitting in the passenger seat. She was turned, looking at us. The Cadillac circled the block, rolled past us again, then pulled into Elrod's and circled back, creeping by in the opposite direction. Sherry glared at Kyesha and me, and then said something to her old man. Mel Dumont hit the gas, and they sped away. Neither Kyesha nor I said anything as we watched the Dumont's car disappear. *Forget Sherry and her freak of a dad,* I told myself.

It was muggy. Ah, Indiana in the summer—armpit of America. I hadn't run really hard since the season ended in November, and I worried about going three miles. But I figured that Kyesha wouldn't set much of a pace. Wrong! From the start, she burned up the course.

We headed out of town on the hard road. Some captain I was. I had forgotten to wear my runner's watch, and Kyesha hadn't bought hers yet. But I knew we were doing better than seven minutes a mile. Kyesha's arms worked smoothly; her skinny legs gobbled up ground with every stride. I got the impression she wanted to prove something—beat me.

She won't last, I told myself as we raced by a cornfield then turned onto a gravel road, a shortcut to Marion. We began to run up the big hill outside of town. Simon had labeled it *Monster Hill* on the map. Everyone in River Bend calls it Mount Pisgah. Not sure why. Something to do with the Bible, I've been told. Monster Hill is a better name. I'd run it once last year—avoided it ever since.

Lord, the wet, hot air scalded my lungs and the blood rushed to the surface of my flesh, tingling my skin. I tucked in behind Kyesha, trailing her up the hill as she split the air, both of us straining and leaning forward, digging hard to scale the incline. Drops of sweat fell into my eyes as we reached the top, the one-mile mark. Both of us panted. We headed down the other side, my legs wobbling with each step.

Kyesha surged down the hill ahead of me. *When's she going to poop out?* I relaxed and let gravity pull me along. When Kyesha hit the bottom and started up a second hill—a smaller one—she actually picked it up. I'd learned about stereotypes in school, and she was busting up the stereotype that African Americans are sprinters, not long distance runners. *I can't let her beat me. I'm going to be a senior! The best times on the team! The captain! No way am I going to lose to an incoming freshman! Even if it kills me, I'm not going to fold!*

At the two-mile point, we turned down a grass-covered lane that runs up to an old abandoned farmhouse, and then shuffled down a hill into a grove of trees and began the last three-quarters of a mile along a path beside the Mississinewa River.

We'd both slowed. Our bodies were drenched, and we sucked the air for oxygen. Kyesha's stride had shortened. *This is the time to take her.* Reaching way down for everything I had left, I lengthened my stride and turned it over faster. With every muscle screaming to knock it off, I shot past her.

We turned along the big bend of the Mississinewa. The river was low and meandered in the opposite direction. Out of the grove of trees I came. Up a little hill, then down, repeating this for two more hills: up and down, up and down, like a roller coaster. As I headed back to where we had started, I could tell that Kyesha had not come with me. I was glad; my body couldn't have answered a challenge. I finished about twenty feet ahead of her, and if I hadn't felt so rotten, I would have been impressed with both of us.

Sticking my hand out, I said between gasps, "Nice run—you must have—run on your own—before today." Kyesha grasped my hand loosely and gave a little nod. She caught a big breath, her mouth opened wide, and her face trembled as air rushed in and out. Kyesha removed her glasses and tried to wipe away the moisture that covered the lenses.

An awful feeling suddenly gripped me. I dropped to my knees in front of Clarence Elrod's garage and tried to vomit. Fortunately, I hadn't eaten anything. I'd learned long ago not to eat right before running. Unfortunately, I had the dry heaves. *Oh, gross-out! How nasty! How embarrassing! On my knees retching like a sick dog.*

Kyesha waited until I got up before she spoke. "Are you all right?"

"Yeah," I answered. Adjusting my bra and pushing my brown hair away from my face, I fumbled to reposition the scrunchie that had once held my hair in a ponytail.

"Let me help you," Kyesha said and began fixing my hair.

At that moment, Clarence came out of the side door of the garage rolling a car tire along. He stopped and looked at us. I smiled and weakly said, "Morning, Clarence."

He mumbled, "Mornin'," as he stared.

Kyesha finished with my hair, and then we half-heartedly stretched out and headed home.

Thinking about it now, here on the bus, it's hilarious. Down on my hands and knees trying to barf. Kyesha standing there watching. What a sight. Didn't think it was funny at the time, though. So humiliating!

It would have more humiliating to let a freshman whip me. But I wasn't in shape for that pace. Probably averaged a little under seven minutes a mile. Couldn't be sure with no watch.

Like I said, Mr. Buchanan never got me in top condition. Before this year, I never averaged better than six nineteen a mile. But that workout with Kyesha made me wonder, *If I can run like that when I'm not in shape, what could I do if I am really fit? Maybe C.R. Simon can help me answer that question.*

9

New Friend

Kyesha and I drug ourselves toward the Hendrix's house. I started to tell her I'd meet her the next day, when it hit me that it would be nice to mention something more about her run. "You did a great job. How long have you been working out?"

"About six or seven weeks." Kyesha looked down, thinking, and then at me. "I started right before spring break. Running back and forth on the lane in back of our place, so actually it's been two months."

To tell the truth, Kyesha's performance had me worried about the other two freshmen, Samantha Peters and especially Emily Lutker. If Kyesha could push me like that, what kind of a challenge would the other two give me? I mean, Emily had won the eighth-grade two mile run, with Samantha second.

"You had a good run, too."

"I'm a little out of shape. That's why I got sick." God, it sounded so limp, and I just knew she thought I was Alibi Alice. We were quiet. Then I said, "Kyesha, you're going to be a great runner." She didn't say anything. I couldn't hold it in any longer. "How in the world did Emily Lutker and Samantha Peters manage to beat you in the two mile run—the eighth-grade race?"

"I didn't take part."

That explains it. "Why not? You'd have done great."

Kyesha shrugged. "I don't know. Guess I didn't think I was ready."

I nodded. We were silent for a few more steps, stopping in front of Kyesha's place. "Well, I've got to be going now. See you tomorrow morning at the same time. Only, why don't we meet here? It's dumb to meet across from Elrod's when I jog right by your house."

"Okay—that's cool," she answered.

"Hey, could I have your cell number in case we need to text or talk?"

"Sure, be right back." She disappeared into her house, jogged back out, and handed me her number on a piece of paper. Then, she punched mine into the contacts on her phone.

I started walking home. From a distance, I heard Kyesha chasing after me.

"Cassie, thanks for being my partner."

Jeez, I felt funny—but good. "Glad you came out for the team."

"Me too."

"Catch you later," I said.

"Yeah, later."

10

Connecting With C.R.....Not!

The second day of training, Kyesha and I were supposed to run five miles. This time we didn't take it out so fast. I figure that first day she was jazzed and wanted to prove herself. By day two we were past that. Our new cross country coach definitely had a plan. Each day my stamina and speed increased, and so did my enthusiasm. C.R. Simon mailed us all a little book she'd written up. She didn't miss a trick. It not only had all the team's cell numbers and e-mails, it covered the waterfront: everything from what to eat to going *number two* regularly. She also sent along a note, saying we should read the book carefully. I made sure I did. Her booklet is in my bag beside me right now on the bus.

She'd set up our schedule so that we would run five to eight miles at a good pace on Monday and Friday, sprint up and jog down Monster Hill for forty-five minutes on Tuesday, Wednesday, and Thursday mornings, and then on Thursday evening the whole team would meet across from Elrod's and do what Simon called "speed-over-distance." The team would race over the five-thousand-meter course to check if we were improving. After we cooled down and cleaned up, usually a bunch of us would head over to Van Winkle's Snacks, where some of my teammates would come on to guys and gossip.

Once, Taylor was able to get her mom's SUV. Kyesha and I hopped in, and we picked Destiny up at Van Winkle's, and then drove by Samantha's and got her. Emily's mom wouldn't let her go with us. Kayla said she had things to do.

We five girls had a blast driving to Marion and cruising Baldwin Avenue, stopping to eat, then driving some more, then eating some more. A bunch of Marion guys were at McDonald's, and we flirted with them.

We five talked girl talk and laughed like hyenas.

Taylor, Kyesha and I dumped off our teammates: Samantha at her place and Destiny at Van Winkle's. Destiny hopped in her old beater of a car and headed the opposite direction from where she lived, blue smoke trailing behind.

Destiny's night wasn't over, but her driving would be for a while. Early that Friday morning, she raced through a red light in Marion and the police pulled her over. When the cop saw the age on her license, she not only ticketed her for running the light, but for a curfew violation, too. Destiny's traffic ticket was her third, which gave her too many violation points, so she lost her license for a year. Most coaches would have kicked her off the team, but not C.R. Simon. She talked with her, and then only suspended Destiny for a couple practices. A lot of folks in town thought she got off too easy, but I thought our new coach did the right thing.

As captain, I was responsible for getting the Thursday race times to C.R., who lived in some new apartments next to Van Winkle's Snacks. Old Mr. Van Winkle built the apartments a couple years back—calls them "Van Winkle Estates." Really, some people. Van Winkle Estates consists of three duplexes sitting side-by-side.

Mr. Van Winkle is the richest person in River Bend. But like I said, he's no Upper Crust. His old three-story Victorian house sits in the middle of River Bend almost a mile from Snob Hill, and he wouldn't be caught dead near a golf course or give a sack of mud from the Mississinewa River to belong to a country club. Making money is his recreation. My dad says on any given day old Mr. Van Winkle will have a couple grand in the wallet shoved in his back pocket and chained to his belt. He owns the snack shop, a men's clothing store, the apartments, and a clothespin and clothes hanger factory near Bluffton, a few miles away. He runs his businesses out of a little paneled office— several decades out of style—at the rear of the snack shop, phoning the managers of his businesses multiple times a day and sometimes making surprise visits.

Anyhow, I went over to C.R. Simon's apartment with the *data*. I had the fastest times, and between all the running and weightlifting, I was sore.

At first, the weightlifting was BORING! One of the assistant coaches would sit behind a desk reading the sports section of the newspaper. He or she would glance up every now and then, while some football jock—who I was totally not interested in—spotted me as I struggled to get the weights over my head. I bitched about it; however, C.R. put on the hard sell and convinced me that the strength would help my running, so I gritted my teeth and endured it.

But the day Jake Nader walked into the weight room to give us pointers and spot us, lifting suddenly became my favorite thing in the world. Having that hottie hover above me while I stretched out on the weight bench was worth a torn rotator cuff. However, I was so tender in spots that the first couple weeks of training, I walked around all stiff like that monster of Dr. Frankenstein's I saw on TV in a really old movie. Plus, the weather was sticky. Soaking in a cold bath helped to cool my skin and revive my muscles, but I hated it. Every day, after working out, I shivered in a tub of freezing water. At night Mom rubbed my back and legs with *Icy Hot.* I went to bed reeking like a locker room. Though I made sure that I smelled a whole lot better on days I lifted.

Naturally, my dad was 100 percent in favor of the hard workouts. Once, he took the morning off his job and rode my bike while Kyesha and I ran. About halfway up Monster Hill, he gave out. That was the last time he "worked out" with us.

At first, Mom didn't like all the training. Went on and on about how foolish it was. She changed her tune, though, when I started eating like a pig—especially devouring more meat. I also put on pounds—muscle, not fat. It made me look more developed. Oh, I'm no C.R. Simon, that's for sure, but definitely more womanish.

Before Simon told us that lifting weights wouldn't do any good without protein, I practically had to be force-fed any kind of animal flesh. But more protein meant more meat, so between C.R.'s nutrition program, and Jake Nader spotting me as I did bench presses, I began stuffing myself with roast beef, chicken, burgers, and the Indiana favorite—pork in any form.

C.R. told us carbs would give us energy. I love carbs anyway, so no one had to fight with me to pack in Mom's cookies, cakes, and pies. Veggies and fruit, too. Plenty of water. And in bed no later than ten thirty. Suddenly, Mom thought this summer workout thing was a "wonderful idea." She'd always stewed about my rest and eating habits, but now she was in Mom Heaven.

Anyway, I took the sheet of times over to Simon's. Her Porsche was sitting in its stall behind Van Winkle Estates, so I figured she was home. This particular June evening was warm but not too muggy. I was comfortable in my shorts and top.

I rang the bell. The door opened and there she was, tanned and smiling—as gorgeous as ever. I still felt threatened by her. I mean, her body—her looks—and she had to be a brainiac teaching chemistry. Worst of all, Jake was gaga over her.

"Cassie, how are you?"

"All right," I answered, trying to act coy and cool. Like I was in control.

She held the door wide open for me. Her apartment was air-conditioned, and it felt good. She said something, but I was taking in the surroundings. Jeez, instead of wallpaper, Simon had books covering her walls. She'd fastened bookshelves to the studs, I could tell. River Bend makes everyone take wood shop in eighth grade, and I picked up tons of carpentry skills in that class. Besides, my dad had done the same thing with *a* bookshelf at home. But C.R. Simon's apartment looked like a library. There were more books than I could count, let alone read. A laptop computer sat on a table by a desk, which had books scattered and stacked all over it. I recognized a menorah as it jumped out at me from behind the glass door of a cherry-wood cabinet sitting back of the couch.

Then it hit me that C.R. Simon had said something. Like a dope I answered, "Huh?"

"The times?"

"Oh, yeah." I handed her the paper.

She sat down on the couch in the middle of the room and studied hard, like I wasn't there.

When she realized I was still standing, she looked up from the paper. "I'm sorry, Cassie—have a seat." She motioned toward the couch. I walked over and sat down beside her.

I always have to check out what other females are wearing. Maybe what my mother says is true, that women really dress for other women, not men. Until that evening, I had never seen Simon out of a dress. She had on a loose-fitting top and shorts, and with one long leg crossed over the other, she looked like a job was waiting for her in a fashion magazine modeling casual wear. I looked around, impressed by all of the books.

Finally, she spoke. "Based on what I've read, along with what I've worked out over there," she said, motioning toward the computer, "I think we are making good progress." She glanced at the paper. "Nineteen minutes and three seconds for a little over three miles—good time for right now, Cassie. Are you pleased?"

I sort of looked away and acted, you know, *modest*. "Yeah, well, it's okay, I guess."

"Keep it up. And keep encouraging your teammates. Would you like something cool to drink?"

I wasn't really thirsty, but I didn't want to hurt her feelings. Besides, I wanted to stay a while, but not let her know I wanted to stay—still trying to be cool and in control. So, I said, "Yeah, I guess I'll take something to drink."

"Great." She walked to a little kitchenette off of the living room area—or in her case, the *library*. "What would you like?"

"Pepsi," I said, clearing my throat. "If you have it."

"Pepsi it is." She took a couple glasses from the cupboard and filled them with ice from the fridge. I took up where I had left off surveying the room. C.R. Simon had every imaginable kind of book. Not only chemistry and science books, but novels, poetry, how-to books—everything.

She came back carrying two glasses. Her blouse and shorts were a matching red. And, oh, my God, I hadn't noticed before, but now I saw that she wasn't wearing a bra. My face felt hot—cheeks burned. She was busty—very busty. I caught myself fidgeting with the top button of my blouse.

"Here you are." C.R. handed me a glass and a napkin.

"Thanks."

She walked to the laptop on the desk and studied the screen. "I don't know about you, but I wonder who some of these people are who send e-mails. How they get a person's information."

"Yeah, makes you wonder," I said, not really interested.

C.R. Simon closed the computer and sat down beside me. She took a swig of the soda she'd fixed for herself. "I'm not tech savvy enough to understand how e-mail works," she said. "But sometimes it's a little scary."

"Yeah, it's scary." I didn't really have a clue what she was talking about. I mean, my e-mails weren't scary, but I decided to just drop it.

I sipped slowly on my Pepsi. On the second sip, I missed my mouth so that the soda dribbled onto my chin. *Oh, God!* Another blush. Quickly, I wiped the soda away with the napkin. She smiled. My body relaxed. I smiled back and giggled softly—like a goof.

"You have tons of books," I told her, looking around for about the hundredth time. Practically more books than the River Bend Public Library.

"Are you a big reader, Cassie?"

How do I answer that? I said, "Yes." *Liar.*

"What genre interests you?" she asked, setting her glass on a coffee table in front of us, and then drawing her left leg underneath her right and stretching her left arm across the back of the couch.

"Uh . . ." *What kind of books do I like?* I asked myself, taking another sip of my Pepsi. Back then, I just read pop culture magazines and the tabloids, so it wasn't an easy answer to come up with. "Mystery books and books about horses," I blurted, giving her a dorky nod. "Yep—mysteries and horse books."

She got up and walked to one of the bookshelves. She pulled down a couple of paperbacks and brought them to me. "Here you are, Cassie," said C.R. Simon. "When I was about your age, I also loved horses and mysteries, so I got into reading books by Dick Francis."

I hadn't even heard of Dick Francis, but I took the books from her.

"Dick Francis wrote mysteries set around the horse racing tracks in the UK."

"The UK." I nodded like I knew something.

"The United Kingdom," she said.

Of course—the United Kingdom. Sixth grade—we studied about it in sixth grade. England, Scotland, Wales and—I forget the fourth one.

"You have both of your reading preferences right there." She picked up her glass.

At that moment, I didn't know if I'd ever read them. Like I said, I wasn't a heavy reader. I wasn't remedial or anything. Hey, starting in seventh grade, I'd religiously read *People* magazine and the *National Enquirer* cover to cover. But I didn't read books unless I had to—like for a school assignment. I thumbed through the ones she gave me, though, to make it seem like I was interested. "When do you want these back?" I asked after I finished the Pepsi.

"They're yours," she said.

Gosh, even though I doubt I'll read them, it's really nice of her. "Thanks," I said. But it made me feel a little funny—in her debt—like I owed her something in return.

"You're welcome, Cassie. Enjoy them."

"It's sure nice of you."

"It's nothing. I've given many books away. It's just something I do." There was a long silence. As I thumbed through one of the books, pretending to be interested, C.R. drank some more of her Pepsi. I turned, spotted the menorah, pointing to it. "Where'd you get that?"

She turned and looked at it. "My mother brought that to me from Israel."

"Did she go on one of those Holy Land tours over there?" I laughed. Then, a phrase I'd heard my whole life from my parents and others shot out of my mouth. "Your mom Jew down some Jew merchant and get a good price?" Another chuckle.

C.R. Simon looked at me, hesitating. "No, she lived there. After my father died, she made *aliyah*—moved as a Jew to Israel as the Jewish homeland."

We were quiet—painful silence. *I should tell her how sorry I am, but it might seem phony.*

"I'd better be going. Have to meet Kyesha early in the morning."

"All right, Cassie. I'm really glad you could stay and visit awhile," she said, walking me to the door.

"Yeah. Thanks a lot for the Pepsi and the books." I lifted up the paperbacks.

"You're welcome. Come back anytime."

I hesitated when Miss Simon let me out; a little plaque fastened to the doorjamb caught my eye. *Must be something to do with her religion.* Guilt surged through me, so I quickly stepped out into the night air. "Bye," I said, glancing over my shoulder.

She watched me round the corner, heading home. I went to my room, shut the door, and spent the next hour searching for the right words so the next time I saw Miss Simon I could let her know how genuinely sorry I was for the crack I made about Jews. But nothing I came up with seemed good enough, so I opened one of those Dick Francis books and began reading.

11

Race Relations And An Apology

We have different churches in River Bend—a Dutch Reformed, a United Methodist, a Disciples of Christ, a Presbyterian, a Mennonite, and a Wesleyan church. I've never been in any of them, but people who attend say they're each different. You couldn't tell it, though—except for Sunday. They're all Christian—and Protestant. Even River Bend's few Catholics have to leave town and go to Marion. Jews? Forget about it. Up until C.R. Simon moved in, the only Jews anyone from River Bend had anything to do with were the few who own businesses in Marion. Sure, not all Jews in Marion own stores or sell stuff, but I'd never been around any of those that don't.

I couldn't tell you how many times I've heard someone around here use the expression "Jew down." Plenty. Another stereotype I packed around—that all Jews are good at making money. I never gave it a thought before I said it to Miss Simon.

Now I know it's wrong. As soon as I found out she's Jewish, I felt guilty for saying it. I wrestled with how to apologize or if I should maybe just drop it. Didn't know what to do. I sure wasn't going to talk about it to anyone.

People in town would find out soon enough that she's Jewish, and I worried about how they would react once they did. Maybe some of them knew already. At Van Winkle's Snacks, I'd overheard a couple crusty farmers complain about C.R. Simon's big city ways. I worried that "big city ways" was just code talk for "Jew". Then, the two horn dogs got off on "how good looking" she is. That was bad enough, but I got really pissed when the perverts started discussing certain parts of Miss Simon's body. Before I could rip them a new one, Old man Van Winkle told them, "Knock off that kind of talk. This is a family place." The two did as they were told.

I was starting to like Miss Simon. She was nice and easy to talk with. Most importantly, she was whipping us into shape. *With her, we might actually do better—a whole lot better. Maybe even get out of our sectional. Maybe I'll wind up not being...mediocre...actually being good.*

I'm not a religious person, but I figured I needed to do penance. Do something to make up for the crack I made about Jews. So, that night, after leaving Miss Simon's, I broke training. I stayed up really late and actually finished one of those books by Dick Francis. It's called *Dead Cert*. I liked it. But I won't give a book report.

As for cross country, the team kept to our new coach's workout schedule like it was a high-paying job. Everyone's times kept dropping. I'd never been that far along before the season started. In late July I ran the training course in a little under nineteen minutes, and Ky (that's what we started calling Kyesha) wasn't very far behind. I look at her now sitting in the seat across from me on this old school bus. Headphones on.

Eyes closed. I know, though, she's not asleep. She told me that she imagines the race in her head before she actually runs it. That it helps her. She's already a great runner, and she's going to get better—better than me. Every morning last summer after our workout, she and I would cool down by walking and talking.

She told me her dad is a tool and die maker, not a janitor, at the car plant over in Marion. Her mother is a nurse. She said her little brother would be going into the third grade. I told her that I'm an only child. She asked me if I'd ever wanted brothers and sisters. I told her no, I liked being an only child. "That's a shame," she said, "because I'd like to find a new home for my brother. He's such a brat." We laughed.

At first, my mom didn't like me hanging around with a black girl. One night while we were around the table eating, she said, "You've been spending a lot of time with that colored girl."

"'Colored girl?'" I said. "You mean Kyesha?"

"Yes. Who else would I mean? She's the only one in town."

I noticed Dad shift his eyes towards Mom, then look down at his plate and shake his head as he continued eating.

"Well, Mom, first, Kyesha is not 'colored'; she's African American—or black. Second thing is, I like hanging with her." I pushed away from the table and marched to my room.

I didn't get at all why it was a big deal. She was just a *girl*. I'll say it flat out, Mom's a bigot. It's the way she was raised. My dad didn't care, though, if I hung out with Ky.

They're really opposite. I don't know how they ever got together, but they did, and they seem to get along better than most husbands and wives. At least the ones I know of. But just to show how opposite they are, Dad says he votes straight Democrat and Mom claims she votes Republican. Who really knows? Once they get into the voting booth, they might wind up voting for each other.

I invited Ky to spend the night, and finally I built up my

nerve to tell Mom. It was a Saturday morning. My parents refuse to subscribe for the newspaper online, so both were hiding behind a hard copy of the Marion *Chronicle-Tribune*. Dad the sports page and Mom the community section. The TV was on, so I picked up the remote and muted it. Dad put the sports page down. Mom kept reading. "Ky is coming over for supper—to spend the night," I announced.

Mom dropped the community section into her lap. The paper lay there crumpled as she glared at me. "Supper? Spend the night?"

"Yep."

"Did you ever think about asking?"

"I haven't had to ask to have someone before—since I've been in high school I haven't."

"This is different."

"Different how?"

My dad chimed in. "Yeah, different how?" he said looking at my mom.

"I don't even know what they eat," said Mom. "What do you expect me to fix?"

"*Food*—I'll just bet the Hendrix girl eats *food*," said Dad. He winked at me.

"I smiled."

"My God, my mother would just die if she knew a pair of black feet were going to be under my table tonight." Mom raised the paper, shook out the creases, and took up reading.

Ky showed up at 5:30, exactly when we agreed. She was carrying an overnight bag along with a garment bag. Her mother came to the door with her. Dad invited them both in.

"Hi, I'm Cassie's father." There was tension in the air. Then my dad spoke directly to Ky's mom. "Cassie and Kyesha are both on the cross country team." He grinned.

It was obvious that he was uneasy, even though he had been an ally earlier in the day.

Mrs. Hendrix looked at him kind of funny, and then nodded. "Yes, I know."

Mom came into the room, trying to control nervous breathing, but failing. Fidgeting with her necklace.

Mrs. Hendrix must have sensed it, because she stepped forward, stuck out her hand and said, "I'm Kyesha's mother. You must be Cassie's. Thank you for having her over."

Mom gave Mrs. Hendrix a limp hand. "How are you—today?"

"Fine. And you?"

"Fine," Mom answered and cleared her throat.

Then Mrs. Hendrix shook hands with my dad too. She thanked my parents again for having Ky over and left.

I don't know what Mom was trying to prove, but she went all out for supper: roast, mashed potatoes and gravy, seasoned green beans, corn on the cob, Caesar salad, dinner rolls, and chocolate cake with ice cream for dessert. All on her best china, and eaten with her best silverware. We drank pink lemonade—from her best glasses.

Mom passed each dish to Ky first, but she sat patiently until everyone's plate was filled. She hesitated when we all started eating, and then did something that took all of us by surprise: Ky bowed her head and said some kind of prayer in a whisper.

Dad looked at me, Mom looked at Dad, I looked at Mom, and then we all looked at each other. It wasn't a long prayer, so when she raised her head, we went on and ate.

Ky's polite. Oh, I don't mean fakey polite. She's for real—genuine. More than once during the evening, Ky thanked my parents for having her over. And she's probably smarter than me, too. She told me what her grades were, and she's no *mediocre* student.

We had a great time messing around in my room. Played with our smart phones. Played music. Played crazy games on my computer. Did each other's hair. And about made ourselves sick by devouring a large bag of Doritos and guzzling a liter of pop. Mostly, though, we talked girl stuff. But as much fun as we were having, I couldn't keep the thought of the crappy thing I'd said to C.R. Simon from popping back into my head.

It was a Saturday night, and my mom was impressed when Ky asked if we were going to church the next day. Ky even lugged along some church clothes. That's what was in the garment bag. Actually, we're not churchgoers, so Ky went on to church with her family. But Mom was really impressed. Oh, her prejudice didn't just poof, up and vanish, but at least she stopped being a pain about it.

Funny thing, I think Mom liked having her over as much as I did. A couple of days after Ky had been over, Mom got a note in the mail from Ky thanking her and Dad for "the good time" she'd had. My mother didn't just toss the note in the wastebasket like I'd see her do with others she'd gotten. Instead, she waited until my dad got home and showed it to him too. Then she stuck it away in a drawer, and never complained again about me hanging around with Ky.

Two mornings after I'd rammed my foot into my mouth at C.R. Simon's, Ky and I spotted her running ahead of us on the course. "Let's catch up," Ky said. Then she raced after her, but I lagged behind. When she realized I hadn't come with her, Ky slowed and looked over her shoulder. "Come on, Cassie. We can't let Miss Simon finish the course before us."

I picked up the pace.

We caught her at the bottom of Monster Hill. She had on this stylish Dri-FIT running shirt with shorts, and looked great. But I didn't hold that against her anymore. We each said "Morning"—Ky enthusiastically—me sheepishly. C.R. Simon seemed happy to see us. Both of us. She and Ky made conversation, but I couldn't bring myself to say anything else, couldn't even look at her face. Just stared down the road. For the only time in my life, I was glad to be running up Monster Hill; it gave me a reason to be a mute. Halfway up, I surged. They came with me. We sprinted down together. I was surprised Miss Simon could keep pace.

I was wired, and my heart slamming against my chest and my blood pumping relieved my guilt. As we ran onto the lane by the old abandoned farmhouse, I dashed away from them. Ky tried to keep pace with me, and she left C.R. Simon behind. But I lost Ky beside the Mississinewa, charged past the finish, pressed *stop* on my watch, and raced toward my house. However, at the end of the block, my conscience got the better of me. I stopped. Just stood and thought for a minute. Finally, I turned and headed back to Elrod's.

Ky was stretching and C.R. was just finishing her run. She was bent over, hands on knees, catching some oxygen.

"Where'd you go?" Ky asked.

"Wanted to run a little extra this morning," was all I said as I walked past her.

Miss Simon straightened and gave me a smile. "You ladies are more than I can handle."

"Um . . . can we talk?" I said.

She nodded.

"What I said—the other night—what I said about Jews was wrong. I apologize. It was just plain wrong." I extended my hand, and Coach Simon grasped it firmly. She smiled.

"Thank you, Cassie."

As soon as she uttered those words—had accepted my apology—a light feeling came over me. My mind was clear. Guilt floated away once I'd made it right with Miss Simon.

I said so long to her and told Ky I couldn't walk with her that day. As I sprinted for home, Sherry Dumont passed me going toward the Quick Mart in her dad's car. We exchanged killer looks, and I picked up the pace.

12

A Hunk Spots Cassie

Like I said, weight training ceased being a drag with Jake Nader spotting me. After strengthening my lower body with lunges and thrusts, I'd stretch out on the weight bench ready to press a few pounds and say, "Please, Jake, don't let it crush me."

"Don't worry, Cassie, I've got you spotted," he'd tell me. Yes, a girl's dream can come true. All six feet, five inches of him straddled me, one leg on each side of the bench. My heart thumped. I was about to hyperventilate. I'd clear my throat—once, twice, a third time. *God, don't let me make a fool of myself.* Then, I would remove the weight and pump it toward the ceiling once, twice . . . five times.

Day after day, that's how it went in the weight room. Jake and I would talk sports. He would do something dorky like hide my gym bag and make me hunt all over for it, and then make up for that by spotting me—or wait for me outside the gym to talk more sports. And each day I liked him more than yesterday. Hey, I even forgave him for scraping his tongue on the sidewalk lusting after Miss Simon that Saturday she came for the interview.

But Jake only seemed interested in having a *sports* relationship with me. I wanted more. Really, though, I didn't think I had a chance anyway. It's an unwritten law in Indiana that star basketball players and cheerleaders are meant for each other. Somebody like Marlo LaPorte. Marlo "the Magnificent" is what the guys have called her since seventh grade. She's blond, tall, leggy with a shape that rivals Miss Simon's—drop-dead gorgeous—and a cheerleader. Just the type Jake is *supposed* to go steady with, not someone like me—a skinny cross country runner. But Jake had never shown much interest in Marlo or anyone else, so I kept trying by making sure I looked as hot as possible when I went to lift weights. I mean, I was the only girl ever who spent an hour putting on makeup before she went to pump iron. And charm—Lord, I should have had a snake. Yet all Jake ever did was give me helpful tips about making my muscles bigger. Believe me, there were times when I got discouraged. I mean, who does a girl talk to about that kind of problem? Her mother? Well, I tried that. She just said, "Honey, someday you'll find Mr. Right." Every mother tells her daughter that she'll find Mr. Right. Oh, my God, *Mr. Right's* going to end up with a bunch of women.

Anyway, I was lying in bed one night this past summer fantasizing about Jake and me when suddenly I had an idea—a revelation. *Maybe Miss Simon could help me. Hey, we'd patched things up after my mouth had raced ahead of my brain.* I figured that she'd lend me an ear. If anyone knew about men and how to interest them, it had to be a woman who looked like her. So, I decided that after I built up my nerve, I would ask C.R.

Simon—you know—how a girl gets a guy to chase her until she catches him.

13

Teacher - Student Affair?

June was hot, but July and August were sweltering. Each day the steamy air coated my skin, making me feel like I was swimming, not running cross country.

And then there was the corn. For some reason, it seems more humid near cornfields than anywhere else, especially in midsummer when the stalks are high and the leaves are deep green. Maybe it's all in our skulls, but that's the way Ky and I felt whenever we raced by corn—and corn is everywhere in Indiana.

People say ladies don't sweat, they perspire—but I sweat! In fact, the blistering, soppy air forced me to do the unthinkable: I stopped wearing makeup to pump iron. One day I was sweating so much at weight training that my mascara ran down my face, mixing in with my blush so that I looked like a clown. Jake kept staring at me and smirking. God, I was so embarrassed. After that, I just looked the best I could without all that junk on my face. Only a little lipstick, that's all. It didn't matter anyway. Other than getting an eyeful of my clown act, Jake didn't notice me—really notice me.

Faithful as an old hound, I packed our times over to Miss Simon every Thursday evening after I'd showered, and she always seemed glad to see me. I think she gets lonely. Oh, you'd figure that with her hot looks, men would be lining up outside her door, but they aren't. We girls—the team—were talking after one Thursday evening workout, and Kayla Thomas said our new coach hadn't gone out on a date once since coming to River Bend. *How's Kayla know so much?* I asked myself. In fact, I had a lot of questions about Kayla. Like why she was always staring at me when we stretched. It was creeping me out.

But it turned out Kayla was right. Miss Simon doesn't date. I think men are turned on by her looks, but threatened by her brains. Besides, she's independent, and I figure she doesn't care what men think of her. My mom says some men are afraid of women who don't need a man, so Miss Simon's independence must scare the crap out of them.

Anyway, I went to her apartment a few weeks before the new school year started, conspiring to bring up the subject of Jake and me. She let me in, and I handed her the results as usual. For a week, she'd had us running long, medium-paced distances—eight to ten miles, six-and-a-half to seven minutes a mile—in the morning with our partner. Those long runs in the hot, humid air had emptied my gas tank. My times—all of our Thursday evening race times—either had slowed or leveled off. And Kayla was way slower.

"Uh-huh," Miss Simon said, looking at that Thursday evening's times. "Heat and humidity sap runners. Read it in an article just yesterday. Wow, what's with Kayla?"

I didn't answer but sat beside her on the couch scheming how I would get her to let me in on the secret to a man's heart. After my run, the shower hadn't taken; I was clammy from the walk over, and although Miss Simon had the air blasting to the max, I had to wipe away sweat as it wound its way down my neck.

"The team has a week and a half before the first practice with me. It's time to work solely on speed. The long distances in this heat and humidity are draining all of you."

"Yeah, I've been stuck around eighteen-forty for two weeks straight."

She got up and placed the sheet with the times by her computer then sat down on the sofa with me. She pushed back her black hair, running her fingers through it, and bunching it all over her left shoulder so that it rested on her breasts. Then, she stretched her long legs out onto an ottoman. *Even her feet look great.*

I was about to spring the big question about Jake and me when she said, "Cassie, contact your teammates. Tell them not to do the long runs on the schedule. You girls need a change."

"Sure," I agreed. "I don't mind telling you, I'll be glad to do something different than those ten-mile runs."

She rested against the back of the couch and stared at the ceiling as she thought. A lock of her hair fell over her left eye, and she brushed it back into place. "Starting Friday— tomorrow—sprint up and jog down the hill."

"Monster Hill?"

"Yes, keep that up for just thirty minutes each day, and as usual race the course next Thursday in the early evening. Then, don't run again until I can be at practice the first Monday in August. The time off will recharge your batteries."

"Fine with me." *Hallelujah! I can sleep in three straight days.*

"I'll bet the rest of the team won't complain either," I said, grinning like an idiot.

"I'll bet not." She smiled. "Hey, a coach has to keep her team from getting bored. Sleeping in should be a part of training." We laughed. I was feeling more relaxed, about to bring up my dilemma with Jake.

Miss Simon and I had always spent time gabbing on Thursdays. Usually my mouth ran a lot more than hers, but this evening I wasn't talking as much—still figuring out how to work in the topic of Jake and me. As I was lost in thought, she was rambling on about rest being essential in a training program. Then, smack in the middle of a sentence, I interrupted her. "Should I keep on working with Jake? I mean, *the team* keeps lifting, right?"

"Thanks for reminding me. We're done with weight lifting."

"What?" My stomach felt like it had been punched.

"It's served its purpose."

No more weight lifting—no more Jake.

"Jake Nader has been coming over to update me on the weight training. He told me a week ago that he thought all of you had peaked out."

"Really?"

"Yes, that was the first indication I had that you were being sapped. Strength and energy weren't there. The weights have become counterproductive."

"Is that right?" I stared at her.

C.R. Simon hesitated, and then nodded. "Actually, I'd planned for you to stop weight training before now. It just slipped my mind."

"Uh-huh." I held my stare.

"Cassie, I really appreciate your leadership."

She waited for a response from me, but none came. She drew her legs from the ottoman and tucked them up beside her hind end. I looked away as she continued with her spiel. "I'm going out of town for a few days. I have to pack tonight and catch a flight tomorrow. Would you mind contacting the rest of the team as soon as possible—tonight? Tell them no weight training and no long runs?" She expected me to say something, like *Sure, be glad to!* But I didn't answer—just looked at her. She went on.

"I'm flying to New York City for a few days before school starts. Jake says that after basketball is over, he is going to run track—the 1600 meters to keep in shape. When I get back, Jake and I are going to drive to Indianapolis to watch a big track meet—check out world-class distance runners." She hesitated as she studied me. "Of course, I received approval from his parents for him to accompany me."

Of course. I tried to play it cool by keeping my trap shut and preventing my body from trembling. She stopped talking. The silence was tense. "I'm really getting into this running."

Good for you. My heart was on the floor; I struggled to breathe. *She and Jake are going on a date, and all the years he and I had lived in River Bend and been classmates in school, he's hardly even spoken to me—until weight training.*

All of those old, nasty feelings toward C.R. Simon returned. Her words had undone all the good between us. *Going to Indianapolis together! What else had they been doing together?* Right then, Sherry Dumont didn't seem like such a nut case when she accused Jake and C.R. of—well, you know.

"Jake is a nice young man," C.R. Simon said.

"Uh-huh," I answered. "He's all right if you like that type." She gave me sort of a funny look, like she was constipated. Believe me, I wasn't hiding my feelings very well.

"Is your family going anywhere before school? A vacation this summer?"

I cleared my throat. "Oh, no, we won't be going anywhere."

There was this long silence. C.R. stared at me like she was trying to read my mind. The laugh lines around her eyes had vanished. "Cassie, are you all right?"

"Of course." I stood and walked to the door. "I have to go. You have fun on your vacation—and you and Jake enjoy the track meet over in Indianapolis." Then, I turned and glanced at her still on the couch. The air was thick, and my skin became clammy. It was like a rubber band was about to snap. C.R. Simon's eyes had a hurt look and she pressed her lips tightly as she clinched her jaw. She got off the sofa.

"Cassie?" She reached out and touched my arm.

I flinched and opened the door. "See you." The bushes behind the parking stalls rustled. An animal, I figured. Didn't care.

C.R. Simon called out my name, but I marched around the corner, glancing only to see that she stood by the door, making sure as always that I was safe.

As I rounded the corner, I was startled by footsteps behind me, and I spun around. Kayla Thomas jogged up to me.

What's she in town for? Her grandma usually keeps her down on the farm.

"Hi, Cassie. I'm just working out—keeping in shape."

I didn't buy it. Kayla never had been in shape. She didn't put much more energy into her training than Dumont had.

"Where you comin' from? I mean, where you goin'? How you doin'?" she asked.

I felt like I was under interrogation, so I refused to answer right away. We stood looking at each other under a street light. *What's with all the questions? I am too tired and definitely not up for this.* "Kayla, I'm not feeling so good. I just want to get home—go to bed."

As we stood under the street light, Kayla narrowed her eyes. "Well, okay. If that's the way you feel."

"Yeah, that's exactly how I feel."

She pivoted and took off. I watched her jog away. *I guess she's pissed 'cause I wasn't answering her questions,* I told myself. *Weird. Did she run all the way into town? In the dark?* "Hey, I don't really give a crap," I said as I continued my march toward home.

When I got in the house, I went straight to my room. I buried my face in my pillow, soaking it with tears. I pushed up and sat on the edge of the bed, folding my arms across my chest in a pout. *Damn those two. I'll show Simon. I'll quit the team. Just screw it!* "I'll let the whole town know they're having an affair—tell everyone," I spoke to the empty room. But I wouldn't do that. That was a Sherry Dumont stunt, and her style sure wasn't mine. *God, I hate Jake. I hate C.R. Simon. What do I do?*

14

A Spill Down Monster Hill

No, I didn't quit or do any of that other stuff. After plotting for a while, I gave up on revenge, washed my face to hide that I'd been sniffling, and texted my teammates. "no wghts! no dstncs! mnstr hill 2moro @ 6 -7a.m. L8R!"

Friday morning I drug myself out of bed. *Whatever I think of Romeo and his aging Juliet, it is only fair to myself to keep running.* For once I was actually getting somewhere with cross country. My dream of being really good at something seemed reachable. *Hey, I've done all of this work, why blow it over a guy?* So I jogged off to meet Kyesha.

However, it tore me up that I didn't have a chance with Jake, but I felt even worse about C.R. Simon. Like I'd *lost* her. Please, don't take that the wrong way. I figured romance was about all I could have with Jake. With Miss Simon, even if she was a teacher, I thought we were starting a real friendship. Destroying

71

that friendship hurt more than thinking Jake and I were over before we even got started. Besides, Simon really was helping me become a better runner. That I had to admit. Ky figured out right away that something was bugging me. She squeezed a "Mornin'" out of me, the way a person says "Mornin'" when she'd just as soon be left alone. She asked if something was wrong. I snapped a "No."

We did our warm-ups and stretched in silence like we did the first day two months before. Ky wanted to talk as we jogged, but I only answered in grunts and one-syllable words.

As we approached Elrod's Quick Mart & Vehicle Repair, I finally opened up. "Simon says to do Monster Hill."

"I know. I got your text last night."

"Oh, yeah—forgot." I threw a goofy shrug of the shoulders at her and took off.

We made it to Monster Hill without another word. I started my watch and flew up the hill at hundred-meter-dash speed. Ky followed me. We turned at the top and headed back to the bottom. I sprinted down as fast as up—faster with gravity yanking me.

At the bottom, I pivoted like a basketball player and raced up the steep incline, Ky on my heels. By now, we were huffing and puffing. The idea of the Monster Hill workout is to build speed and stamina by sprinting the tenth of a mile up then recover on the jog down. But I said to myself, *Forget the jog; I'm going to burn this friggin' hill down.*

On the fourth rotation, Kyesha, between gasps, said, "What's wrong—with you—Cassie? You're 'bout—to—kill me."

"Nothing's wrong." I started another sprint. Halfway down, I looked toward River Bend. In the distance I saw a trio of runners—teammates. Destiny and Taylor were racing stride for stride. Kayla was lumbering way behind.

Destiny and Taylor caught up with Ky and me. "Thirty minutes," I gasped, just to remind them. Then, Kayla came plodding along, and I said the same to her.

They started their watches and all of us sprinted toward the top. Pretty soon two more figures appeared in the distance. The other freshmen, Samantha Peters and Emily Lutker, came striding toward us.

When Samantha and Emily reached the bottom of Monster Hill, I sprinted down ahead of Kyesha. "Only thirty," I growled.

So, there we were that July morning this past summer, RBHS's girls' cross country team racing up and down Monster Hill, the gravel flying every which way. And there I was all alone at my pity party, convinced something was going on between Jake and C.R. Simon. Proof? Forget about it. Didn't need any. I *knew* in my gut.

It was only a little before seven. Too early to be really hot. But the air was damp, so all of us were sucking it for oxygen. My God, we sounded like we were having asthma attacks. Sweat dripped and ran from head to toe.

Ky strained to get out the words, "Got—an—au—di—ence."

I glanced right. A couple cows in the pasture beside the road had their heads hanging over the barbed wire fence looking at us like we were nuts. Because I was getting pooped, I didn't feel quite so rotten.

Usually, at that time of the morning the road was deserted, except for us cross country runners. However, the sun reflected off a car that turned from the Marion Blacktop onto Mount Pisgah Road. The dust flew behind it, and I figured it was someone taking the short cut to Marion. "Car!" I yelled, and we all moved to the shoulder. But as it got closer, it slowed and I could see that it was C.R. Simon's silver Porsche. It stopped at the bottom.

The seven of us came down Monster Hill together as a team. C.R. got out. "Good morning, ladies," she yelled, giving a little wave. Everyone except me waved back. She walked away from her Porsche, the key fob dangling in her hand, and she came over to where we made our turn at the bottom. She was dressed to kill—high heels and the whole bit. *Look at her, dressed like she's in a fashion show, watching seven sweaty, tired high school girls running up and down a great big hill. Now, we have two cows and a heifer watching us.* I laughed.

A little breeze slid down the hill, caught hold of her loose-fitting white dress, lifting it above her knees, and all I had to do was take one look at C.R. Simon standing at the bottom of Monster Hill to see that she was no heifer. Then, for the millionth time, I thought of Jake and her—and I boiled.

Everyone picked up the pace, trying to impress her. When I reached the bottom, C.R. Simon asked me, "How much do you have left, Cassie?" I made a quick pivot and started up the hill like I hadn't heard her.

Ky checked her watch, and then worked her words out between heavy breaths. "Three minutes—for Cassie and—me."

Ky and I raced up, then down. Simon was still at the bottom. I turned and started another sprint up Monster Hill. "Time's up, Cassie!" Ky said as she passed me and slowed.

My watch told me the same thing, but I didn't want to face C.R. Streaking past the slower girls, I reached the top of Monster Hill and came to a standstill, bending over, hands on knees, to grab some oxygen. I glanced toward the bottom and saw Simon talking with Kyesha. Then, I noticed the two cows, their heads still hanging over the fence, gawking at the chemistry teacher.

Maybe they're really bulls in drag. I laughed out loud, and then took a deep breath. Emily, Samantha, and Destiny ran around me. I was still bent over with my hands on my knees, breathing wildly, sweat falling off of me like rain and making little mud spots on the gravel road.

I straightened up and started trudging down, my wind gradually coming back as I got closer and closer to Simon. *God, I don't want to face her.* Three of my teammates sprinted by me on their way to the top. Then, as Kayla passed me on her way down, she piped up and said, "Pooped out, are you, Cassie?"

That hit me the wrong way. Pissed, I took off sprinting down Monster Hill, past Kayla and yelled, "No, I'm not pooped!"

I was flying, and almost to the bottom, when my right foot turned on a stone the size of an egg. I lost my balance and lunged like a drunken frog. My arms reached out and I slid in the gravel like a baseball player going head first into third. Actually, my running clothes protected me from most of the damage, but a knee and elbow got a good skinning.

Ky and C.R. Simon rushed over to me as I began to bawl. Oh, sure, the elbow and knee hurt, but I wasn't really crying because of the scrapes. Some sexist male chauvinist pig would say it was because I was about to start my period, but he'd be wrong. I was bawling because of Miss Simon and me.

She bent down and touched me. "I'm all sweaty," I sobbed. But she didn't pay any attention and helped me onto my feet. Ky watched as the others caught up.

Miss Simon helped me hobble over to her Porsche, me blubbering all the way. She kept a tight hold on me, my sweat mixing with her perfume. My hair, which I'd twisted into a ponytail before leaving home, had fallen down so that some of it rested on my shoulder, while big clumps hung in my eyes and near my mouth. Between sniffles I blew upward to get the hair out of my face. Miss Simon gently pushed it away. She opened the door of the silver car. "Sit down, Cassie."

"I'm wet and dirty—and I smell," I whimpered. *God, I am such a baby, acting like this in front of my teammates.*

She gently lowered me. "Sit down and let me look at you."

Gosh, the seats were leather, and she must have had the air conditioner on before parking. They were ice cold against my hot skin. The other girls gathered around as our coach lifted my elbow, examining it carefully, and then she bent down, took a Kleenex from her purse on the floor and gently brushed away the dirt and little pieces of rock. She did the same to my knee.

"Let's take you into town." As I swiveled my butt on the seat she lifted my legs into the car and shut the door. I heard her say something to the others about finishing up and cooling down, and then she got in and started the Porsche. She wheeled the silver sports car around, and peeled out, throwing gravel behind us as we headed off for River Bend. In the rearview mirror, I glimpsed my teammates standing in a group at the foot of Monster Hill watching Miss Simon and me as we left them behind.

15

Do I Really Stand A Chance?

We were silent. I didn't cry anymore, and she didn't ask any questions. We passed Elrod's and turned down the street that runs past Van Winkle Estates. She pulled the silver car into her parking stall and we got out. She helped me into the apartment, seating me on the couch. I noticed her luggage sitting near the front door. I looked at her white dress. It was dirty, and a blotch of my blood was near her waist. I started bawling again.

"Cassie, you're not hurt that badly."

"I know. It's not my knee—or my elbow—that really hurts."

She sat down beside me and slipped her arm over my shoulder.

"I've trashed your dress."

"Forget the dress, Cassie. I can buy another dress, but I can't get another friend like you."

"Oh, Miss Simon," I sobbed, then threw my arms around her neck and buried my face against her shoulder. This was the first time I'd ever addressed her with "Miss Simon." Before, I had just answered her with "Yes, ma'am," and "No, ma'am," and like I said earlier, to everyone else I mostly referred to her as *C.R. Simon* or *C.R.*—sometimes just *Simon*. But at that moment, she was *Miss Simon*—teacher and friend.

With her arms wrapped around me, she stroked my back and said my name over and over. There I was, sweaty and stinky, and there she was, fresh and smelling good, and I liked being near her. Please don't get the wrong idea. People love to dish dirt. Come on, a girl cross country runner and her coach—woman coach—hugging each other like that? Then, I decided I didn't care what people would think about me. It was friendship.

That day in Miss Simon's apartment was when I learned what friendship means. Here I'd been so snotty to her, but she didn't hold it against me. She cared about me—not just my skinned places, but about my skinned feelings. Still, for her sake, I don't want it to get around. Only she and I know about that day. The funny thing was, I didn't feel dumb or weird about us holding each other. It made me feel good.

"I was really mad at you," I told her as we held tight. "I'm sorry, Miss Simon," I sobbed again. "I'm sorry for the snotty way I acted toward you. I didn't mean it. If you and Jake like each other, then that's your business."

Miss Simon let go and looked at me. "Cassie, there's nothing between Jake and me. "We're just teacher and student . . ."

"And friends?"

"Yes, friends," she agreed. "But that's all, just friends." Then she said, "However, Cassie, I know you have feelings for Jake."

"Is it that obvious?"

Miss Simon nodded.

"I've liked Jake since grade school." I took my arms from

around her neck, looked at my hands, and cleared my throat. "He doesn't even know I exist." I looked at Miss Simon. "Not in that way, if you know what I mean."

"Have you told him how you feel?"

"No," I answered with a sniffle. God, I felt like such a wuss.

She sort of gripped my shoulders, but gently. "Cassie," she said, "you need to be direct and honest with him. Let Jake know how you feel."

"Maybe," I answered, looking first at Miss Simon, back at my hands, then at my skinned knee.

"Cassie, perhaps I can help."

I looked at her. "How?"

"Come with Jake and me to the track meet in Indianapolis. That's why I drove over to practice—to invite you. It was thoughtless of me not to have invited you after all you've done as our captain."

My heart started to pound, but I didn't want to look overanxious. "Gee, I don't know—maybe. Would I be butting in?"

"Certainly not. We'll have to check with your parents. Get their permission."

"Yeah, at least let them think their giving me permission. My mom's home."

Miss Simon laughed. "All right, we'll ask her together."

"Together? You would do that for me?"

"Sure," she answered. "You're the captain of the cross country team; we're friends."

Then Miss Simon gently lifted my arm and looked at my elbow. "Now, what we have to do is get you cleaned up before I drive you home." She glanced down at her dress and laughed. "When I get back to the apartment from taking you home, I think I'd better clean up too. I have to be in Chicago late this afternoon to catch a flight to New York City."

God, I felt so stupid. I'd been completely wrong about Miss Simon and Jake. Did I really stand a chance with Jake after all?

16

All Patched Up

Ky is dozing—gently snoring. I giggle. Her mind race must be over. I can't help but chuckle again. Every time the bus rattles over a rough spot, Ky's head bounces like a bobble head.

The butterflies are fluttering against my insides. As my dad would say, my blood is up—the whole team's blood is up. Strange. Right now on the bus, we're nervous but calm.

Oh, yeah, the track meet in Indianapolis. I felt bad about C.R. Simon's dress. Hold it! I'm going to call her *Ms. Simon*—not "C.R. Simon" or "C.R." or "Simon" or even "Miss Simon"—but *Ms. Simon*. After all, that's what she had put on the door of the chemistry lab. Besides, "C.R. Simon" is what I called her that day I did a header on Monster Hill—when I was pissed at her. We're way past that now.

Anyway, I felt bad because I probably ruined Ms. Simon's dress. But it didn't matter to her. As long as I live, I'll always remember what she said to me. "Forget the dress, Cassie. I can

81

buy another dress, but I can't get another friend like you." Jeez, even now it makes me feel good. And after we talked that morning in her apartment, I felt peaceful, like I do after a hard run.

I guess I had that "sense of peace" that Mr. Bouton, the counselor, told me about. Once every school year, Bouton meets with each student. I guess he wants to check and see if we're still neurotic. Anyway, a year ago this September, he told me most people are happy if they can have a sense of well-being—just be at peace with themselves. Ms. Simon did that for me.

Getting back to that day in her apartment, after I'd gone gravel surfing down Monster Hill, she washed off my skinned places and put some medicine and bandages on them. I felt like I was back in grade school having scrapes and scratches tended to. When I was a kid, I was really clumsy, always crashing and tumbling butt over elbows. Fortunately, I'm a little more coordinated now—don't trip over myself quite as much.

Anyway, after Ms. Simon got me fixed up, she drove me home. She didn't even take time to change the dress I'd trashed. She just put me into the Porsche and took me home.

When we got there, she made me wait in the car until she came around and helped me out. I hobbled up toward the house like a gimpy racehorse from a Dick Francis novel.

My feelings were a little mixed up. I wanted Ms. Simon to meet Mom, yet I didn't want Ms. Simon to meet Mom. Word had got out that Ms. Simon is Jewish. Considering how my mom felt at first about Kyesha Hendrix—her being black and all—I was really worried that Mom might not like Ms. Simon because she's a Jew. That would not only be embarrassing, but might screw up my getting to go the track meet. Then I wouldn't get to spend the day with Jake.

Mom came out onto the front porch. She was wearing an apron blotched with red and orange stains. She'd been canning tomatoes. *So not cool!* Ms. Simon was sophisticated, while Mom looked like a hick from the sticks. I sucked in a breath and held it as Ms. Simon walked to the steps and said, "Hello, Mrs. Garnet. Cassie took a little tumble down that steep hill outside of town. I've cleaned off the abrasions, put some antibiotic cream on her, and bandaged them. I hope you don't mind."

Mom came off of the porch to meet us. I couldn't pry my eyes off of the tomato stains. I felt the blood surge into a blush as I rolled my eyes. Anyway, Mom started to get on the other side of me to help Ms. Simon, but I'd made up my mind that this was dumb. I wasn't hurt that badly. "I can make it."

"Are you sure?" Ms. Simon asked me.

"Yes, it's only a skinned knee and elbow, not like I broke a bone or something."

Oh, sure, it was tender, but I was able to get up the steps without much trouble, leaving the two of them standing on the landing below. I turned and watched.

"Mrs. Garnet, I'm C.R. Simon, Cassie's cross country coach." Ms. Simon extended her right hand, and my mother quickly wiped hers on the tomato-stained apron and shook Ms. Simon's hand. I could've died.

"I'm pleased to meet you," Mom said. "Cassie goes on and on about you—all good, of course." Oh, brother, Mom was really shoveling it high. Sure, I'd said some things about Ms. Simon, but not that much. Then Mom noticed Ms. Simon's dress. "Oh, no, Cassie's got your dress all dirty!" Naturally, that meant that Ms. Simon had to go through the whole spiel about how that didn't matter, because my "welfare came ahead of her dress."

For the next few minutes, they forgot all about me standing there as they chatted it up. Mom invited Ms. Simon in; Ms.

Simon said she couldn't come in because she had to head for Chicago; they spent about a minute discussing the weather, then Mom asked Ms. Simon if she would like some tomatoes from our garden. *Just shoot me now.* I mean, I couldn't imagine Ms. Simon eating tomatoes from *our* garden. It seemed hickish for Mom to have asked her such a thing. However, Ms. Simon said yes, but told Mom it should only be a few because she was going to be out of town for a few days.

Mom hustled around the house. I smiled down at Ms. Simon waiting at the foot of the steps. I started to feel dumb standing there, so I told Ms. Simon thanks and went on into the house. Actually, I stood just inside the door so I could eavesdrop.

"Here you are," Mom said to her, returning with a small paper sack full of tomatoes. She must have had them sitting out in the sun on the back porch.

Ms. Simon took the sack. "Thank you very much. It's so kind of you. I'll eat them for lunch today before I leave for Chicago." And just from the tone of her voice, I could tell that she meant it. She was glad Mom had given her the tomatoes from *our* garden, and I believed she actually would eat them. Most importantly, though, I could tell by the way Mom told Ms. Simon that she was "very welcome" that Mom liked her. I mean, my mother didn't drag the words out of herself like it was a chore; instead there was this little spring to her voice that my mother gets when she's really happy with someone.

Then Ms. Simon decided to close the deal. "Mrs. Garnet, when I get back from New York ..." I listened carefully. "I'm going to a track meet in Indianapolis, and I would like Cassie to go with me, if that's all right with you. It's a week from Saturday." *She didn't say anything about Jake.* I sneaked a peek through the screen door. My mom sort of hesitated, and Ms. Simon coaxed her.

"I'd really appreciate it if you'd let her go along. Cassie has worked hard and has been very dependable as our team's captain. I'll pay for everything. She's earned it."

Mom glanced toward the door. I ducked out of sight. Then she said, "I don't see why not."

I smiled and pumped my fist. *Yeah, like I wouldn't have gone anyway.* If Mom had said no, I would have kicked up sand and appealed to Dad. He would have gotten her to cave in. But it's better to let Mom think she's in charge.

"Great," said Ms. Simon. Then, looking up and waving, she said, "Cassie, we've got a date a week from tomorrow."

Some eavesdropper I am. I opened the door and smiled like I'd just got caught raiding the cookie jar. "See you."

Ms. Simon and Mom shook hands again. Mom followed her out to her Porsche. Ms. Simon got in, gave Mom a wave, and sped off. Mom waved back as she watched Ms. Simon's silver Porsche disappear, and then she came up the steps and through the front door.

"Cassie, you'd better clean up."

"Yeah, okay," I answered, limping away to get some clothes from my bedroom. I was about to leave the room when Mom said, "Miss Simon seems like a real nice lady."

I turned. "She is, Mom. *Ms.* Simon is really nice." Then I got clean clothes, went into the bathroom, and washed up.

17

Like Christmas Eve

This past summer, Saturday and Sunday were usually days off running for Ky and me, so I had two days to let my scrapes scab over. By Monday, Ky and I were back at it. And although the scabs were gross, they weren't as tender as they looked. I didn't notice them too much because all I could think about was going to Indianapolis on Saturday with Ms. Simon—and Jake. My God, the time just dragged.

On Wednesday, Ky and I met Taylor at Van Winkle's Snack Shop. Sitting in a corner booth, Ky confided in us that when her family came to town, old Mr. Van Winkle didn't want the Hendrixes to come into his place. The old grump. Oh, he didn't threaten them or call them names. Nothing like that. "He just acted like we didn't exist," Ky said. "First time my little brother and I went in to buy candy, he ignored us—wouldn't wait on us."

It was hard for me to imagine old Mr. Van Winkle turning down money, but it made me boil that he'd treated Ky and her little brother like that. *Jeez, why can't people just treat everyone the same?* "That really pisses me that he treated you that way, Kyesha. What did you do?"

"Went home and told my dad," was all she answered, and I dropped the subject. And Taylor didn't pry either. But I couldn't help but wonder what had brought about the change. Now Mr. Van Winkle seemed happy to see Kyesha, even called her by her first name.

Once I asked Ky why her family had moved to River Bend. She said her mom and dad couldn't find anything that suited them in Marion, and they found this house for sale. It worked out pretty good, because it was only a few miles drive to their jobs in Marion.

Anyway, Jake Nader was at Van Winkle's that Wednesday. God, as soon as I laid eyes on him, my heart started to thump and pump. When he spoke to me, I could barely squeeze out a "hello."

I prayed that he didn't notice the bandages on my knee and elbow. At least the scabs were covered. Like I told you, they looked gross. But he did notice. "What happened to you?"

Before I could answer, Ky said, "She took a little spill down Monster Hill. Hey, that rhymes." I gave her a look. She smiled.

Jake wrinkled up his forehead and scowled. "You're going to be good to run, aren't you?"

"Of course," I said. *The least he could do is ask if I'm okay, regardless of running.*

"That's good." He hesitated, then went back to the counter and sat on a stool.

For a minute, I debated over saying something to him about that coming Saturday, but I decided he might not know I was going. *Maybe he'll stay home if he finds out I'm taggin' along with him and Ms. Simon.* So Ky, Taylor, and I ordered Cokes and fries and just sat in a booth, where I copped glances at Jake as he ate two cheeseburgers and gulped a large malt. Ky and Taylor spoke to me several times, but I always had to ask them to repeat what was said. Finally, Ky took a peek at Jake and said, "I know where *your* mind's at." Good God, I even made her repeat that.

Friday night, while I was watching TV, the land line rang. My dad answered it and called for me.

"It's your new cross country coach, Miss Simon."

I grabbed the receiver and covered it with my palm. "Dad, her name is *Ms.* Simon—*Ms.*, not *Miss.*"

He shrugged. "Whatever her name is, you're keeping her waiting."

"Oh!" I put the phone to my ear. "Hello."

"Cassie, this is Ms. Simon. How are you?"

"Fine. How was your trip to New York?"

"It was good, but I'm really glad to be back. Cassie, the track meet tomorrow starts at eleven o'clock, so I'll be around at seven-thirty to pick you up. Okay?"

"Yeah, sure, that's awesome," I told her. She didn't say anything about Jake, which discouraged me a little. *I hope he's still going.* I looked at my elbow and knee, wishing I didn't have those scabs. *But at least they're not as ugly as they were.*

Ms. Simon said, "See you at your house tomorrow—seven-thirty sharp." I was about to say goodbye and hang up when Ms. Simon said, "Oh, Cassie, remember, you don't have to worry about money. Everything is on me—my way of paying you for being such a good team captain this summer."

What do you say when someone is being so nice? I really appreciated it, but I didn't want to be gushy. "Thanks," was all I said. "See you in the morning."

As I hung up, I knew waiting for tomorrow was going to be

a lot like Christmas Eve had been when I was a kid: Time would crawl, and I wouldn't get much sleep.

18

Great Day In Indy And
A Weird E-mail

I was up by four-thirty—couldn't stay in bed any longer. I *had* to have time to get myself ready. It was essential.

After I'd showered, I tried to eat something. Motorcycles were racing in my gut, so everything I shoved into my mouth had to be forced down. After wallowing a bite of banana around, I gave up on eating and brushed and flossed my teeth, checked my breath with the cupped-hand test, then tossed in an Altoid.

It took me two hours to dry my hair and get myself just right. Spent forty-five minutes alone putting on my makeup so I had that perfect look—attractive but not slutty. Anyway, at 7:09 (I glanced at the clock on my dresser), I slipped into my bikinis, lacy bra, best shorts and top, tied up my shoes, and made an inspection of myself in the mirror, fluffed up my hair and pulled it back into a ponytail with a scrunchie. One last check. I looked at my reflection nod back at me from the mirror. *Can't do any better than that.* Then, I slipped my smart phone along with the Altoids into a shorts pocket and sank into an easy chair in the living room and waited as patiently as I was able. At 7:30—just like she'd promised—Ms. Simon pulled up— and Jake was with her.

Mom and Dad were still in bed, so I didn't tell them bye, just crept outside, stopping for a second, though, to pull myself together. Then, as cool as I could, I walked to the Porsche. Jake got out. He towered above me, and I could make out his ripped abs and big chest about to bust his tight T-shirt. He wore blue knee-length shorts revealing muscular, tanned calves. I tried to control my breath as I looked up at him and gave a smile and then took it back. His sandy hair was just a little messed by the wind, and his tanned face had about a day's beard. Then I looked into his deep blue eyes and held my breath. *Girl, you've got to get a grip.*

"Hi, Cassie," he said, and my heart did a couple back flips. I managed to say "hi" back to him—that was all, just "hi". Neither of us were wordsmiths. Besides, I didn't have the nerve to begin a real conversation, not yet.

Jake started to climb into the backseat, but Ms. Simon said, "I don't think you're going to fit back there." Then she leaned over and asked, "How are you this morning, Cassie?"

"Fine."

"I think you're going to have to ride in the back. It's too cramped for Jake," she said. I glanced at the back seat. *It is tiny.* So Jake pulled back the front passenger seat and I got in. Funny, a week ago, after my Monster Hill accident, I was so bummed I hadn't noticed how small the Porsche's rear seat was. I could barely squeeze in. Good thing the scabs were mostly healed, because I would have scraped them up for sure.

With Jake and Ms. Simon in the front and me jammed in the back, we buckled up and headed for Indianapolis.

At first I was so nervous that except for clearing my throat occasionally, I kept quiet. So did Jake. Ms. Simon did all the talking. But ten miles down the road we started to loosen up, and we had a great conversation. I found out things about Jake that I would never have dreamed. He told us that he became so shaky before a big basketball game that sometimes he had to barf. I don't know what other people would think; but to me, he was brave to admit that. Jeez, I'd have never guessed he got that upset. Not Jake Nader, the great basketball star.

To make him feel better, I told him I got pretty scared before a big cross country meet too. Of course, I didn't mention that I never threw up. Ms. Simon told us that learning to relax is a big part of succeeding, but that it was also good to be a little nervous. "It puts a competitive edge on people, helps them to perform at their best," she told us.

The traffic around Indy was very heavy, worse even than today on the bus, but it didn't seem to take any time to get to the stadium. I know it sounds crazy, but I was so caught up in the conversation I was kind of disappointed when we pulled into the parking lot.

Our seats were great, right near the finish line, and I felt really good sitting there in the sun with Jake on one side and Ms. Simon on the other. I think Ms. Simon worked it out so I ended up between them. Jake and I were so close together that our legs were rubbing against each other. *Oh, my God!* My breath came hard and fast. I adjusted myself so that we weren't touching. But eventually he and I got so into the meet that our thighs were practically pasted together. He didn't seem to care, and I know I didn't.

Ms. Simon is such an awesome person. She must have paid a lot for those tickets, because it was a big meet—some really world-class track stars. We could follow everything that was going on, because she got us great programs with all of the information in them. And they also had a gigantic Jumbotron we could watch.

Anyway, right after the finals of the men's one hundred-meter dash, Ms. Simon bought Jake and me brats and soft drinks. She said we could order anything, and that's what both of us wanted. Ms. Simon had a Diet Coke and a burger.

"You don't want a brat?" I asked her.

"No, I stay away from pork," she answered.

"You mean, no bacon or sausage or ham?"

"Nope. I don't keep all the dietary restrictions like some Jews, but I don't eat pork or shell fish, and I try not to mix dairy and meat."

"You mean, no shrimp or cheese burgers?"

Ms. Simon shook her head. "Afraid not."

I thought I might be offending her. "Hey, I'm sorry. I didn't mean to ask so many questions."

"No problem." She patted my leg and smiled. "Cassie, that's all right. Ask anything you like."

"Okay—but tell me if I get too annoying."

"Don't worry, you aren't going to annoy me," she said, sending me another smile.

You should have seen Jake eat that brat. He vaporized it. So she bought him another one and me too. Just like that, Ms. Simon bought us two more brats—with everything on them. Except I made sure I didn't have onions on mine, although I would have loved them. But I absolutely didn't want stinko breath, so to be extra safe I popped in a breath mint. The brat was good even without the onions.

Jake had a little spot of mustard at the corner of his mouth. It sort of turned me on. *Should I reach up with a napkin and wipe it away?* I decided against it. Instead, I tapped him on the leg, and then pointed to my mouth and handed him a napkin. His tanned cheeks turned red. He smiled, took the napkin, reached up, and gave it a swipe.

"Thanks."

"Glad to help." I smiled back.

Ms. Simon asked me if I wanted anything else, and although I wouldn't have minded another brat, I said, "No thanks." I figured she'd spent a lot on me, and I was starting to feel uneasy about it. Mom and Dad had lectured me forever about not taking advantage of people's generosity, and their lectures had stuck.

Part of the time, we were sitting out in the sun. My whole body was baking—but I didn't mind. We kept hydrating ourselves and coating ourselves with sun screen, as Ms. Simon insisted. Really, this was the biggest thing that I'd ever been to. Oh, I'd been to a bunch of River Bend High track meets, but like I said in the beginning, they were all for the guys. This meet was women and men. I guess you might call it a festival. With all of the vendors and food booths, it sort of reminded me of the 4-H fair they hold every summer in River Bend. Of course, Michael A. Carroll Stadium holds way more people than the grandstands in River Bend, and what with the runners needing to hear the starter's pistol, the vendors didn't yell out for people to buy things.

The fair was only a few weeks off, but I knew right then that I wouldn't be going to it. When I was a little girl—even up until a couple of years ago—I always looked forward to it. But I'd lost interest. I don't know why, just had. When I was younger, I'd enter some project in the fair, and I'd always wind up with a *participation* ribbon. Now, after spending that day with Jake and Ms. Simon at that big world-class track and field meet, the River Bend 4-H fair just wouldn't cut it.

Naturally, the distance events for women—anything fifteen hundred meters and up—were what Ms. Simon and I were mostly interested in. In Indiana, high school cross country courses are laid out in meters, not miles. Like I said before, girls run five kilometers, which equals five thousand meters—little over three miles.

At the Indy track meet, the ten thousand meters, a little over six miles, wasn't that great of a race. A woman from an African country—Kenya, I think—was a whole lot better than everyone else. Pulled away with three laps to go, and no one went with her.

But the five-thousand-meter run was another story altogether. Runners were all bunched up. They'd been trading off the lead throughout the race like none of them really wanted it. Then, as the bell rang for the last lap, this woman from a European country and an American runner broke away from everyone and started dueling it out down the backstretch. Everyone in the stadium stood and yelled for the American woman. And when the two runners came off of the last curve on a dead sprint for the finish, thousands of people made one gigantic roar, like that Godzilla monster I saw once on TV in a really old Japanese movie. The kind where all the actors move their mouths in Japanese but English words come out. Anyway, what a commotion.

Like everyone else, I shot up from my seat ripping out my lungs for the American runner to reach down and grab a little extra, but at the last instant, the European leaned into the tape and won. Brother, did it get quiet. Godzilla died.

As I started to sit down, I lost my balance and heaved forward. Suddenly, I felt two strong hands gripping each of my shoulders and I was pulled back. When I got my balance, I realized Jake was holding on to me. He slid his hands down my arms as he helped me seat myself. My heart pounded and goose bumps popped out on the surface of my skin. "Thanks," was all I could force out of my mouth.

"No problem," Jake said. "Hey, we wouldn't want you to break something you might need for cross country."

I shook my head. "No, we wouldn't want that." I swallowed, and then cleared my throat. He took his hands away, and I calmed myself down. I glanced over at Ms. Simon. She was jotting some notes into a little notebook, then she put it back into her handbag—designer, maybe a knockoff—and said, "The runner from the US would have won if she had relaxed more."

"It wouldn't have hurt for her to run faster either," I said. Ms. Simon and Jake both laughed.

I don't mind telling you, between the excitement of it all and the long day in the hot sun, I was wiped out by the time it was all over. But, God, did I feel great—very mellow, if you know what I mean. Sure, I never got to be off with Jake—like where we were all alone or anything, but I didn't care because I had a super time.

"Do either of you have your driver's license?" Ms. Simon asked when we got to the car. I'd gotten mine a couple years ago, but I didn't have it with me. Jake didn't have his with him either.

"I thought if you did, maybe one of you would want to drive a little—give me a break." I had mixed feelings. On one hand, I felt bad because Ms. Simon had to be bushed. But on the other hand, I was really glad that I didn't have my license because the only car I'd ever driven was my folks' four-year-old Chevy, and I wasn't too crazy about climbing behind the wheel of Ms. Simon's silver Porsche. I didn't feel that secure about driving, especially operating the floor shift and clutch on that sports car. To be totally honest, I can't even drive a stick transmission, so Ms. Simon had to get back behind the wheel and do all the driving. She didn't seem to mind, though.

It's gonna be Christmas before we work our way through all the traffic and onto the Interstate, I thought.

Ms. Simon told us to call our folks to give them an idea when we'd be home. Both Jake and I just wanted to send a text, but Ms. Simon insisted we call. Jake left a message on his parents' voice mail, but Mom picked right up. Of course, she expected all the details on the spot. "Can't talk now, Mom. See you in a while."

The three of us were tired but excited enough about the day that we gabbed about it for a few miles. Ms. Simon mentioned she'd checked her e-mails on her phone when she'd ducked into a ladies room back at the stadium, and then she was quiet for a while before she said, "I've been getting some strange messages."

Jake leaned his head back against the seat listening to her.

"Like what?" I asked.

"Oh, I don't know. Just weird stuff. The other day I had one from someone called 'Righteousness.'"

"What did it say?" asked Jake.

"'We're watching you and know what you're doing.'"

"Yeah, I think we all get watched when we go online," he answered.

"Probably some consumer testing company spying on me. Next I'll be asked to buy something," said Ms. Simon.

"Yeah," I said. *Probably it's nothing, like Ms. Simon said,* I told myself. Still, I felt uneasy for some reason. Maybe it was because she'd mentioned the e-mails that first night I was in her apartment.

After a while, though, all three of us just ran out of words. Ms. Simon switched on the radio. Light rock music drifted around the sports car. Funny, I figured Ms. Simon for classical or jazz or something sophisticated, but she hung with the light rock station. And while the music played and she drove, Jake and I snoozed.

19

A Weed Pops Up

Living in Indiana, I've weeded my share of gardens, and about the time you think you've gotten rid of a weed, it pops right back up. Monday, we all met across from Elrod's station for the first practice with Ms. Simon, and there was Sherry Dumont—*that weed*—waiting to work out—or not work out—however a person looks at it. She'd parked herself next to Kayla, who was looking sheepish.

What's up with Kayla?

"Kayla told me about the practice. Isn't that right, Kayla?" Sherry said.

We all stared at Kayla, who started doing windmills. "I guess," she replied, head down, bent over, right hand to left foot, left hand to right foot.

Anyway, there was Sherry with her pudgy self busting out of her shorts. I don't know whether it was because the rest of us were in such good shape or just that Sherry had been gobbling extra helpings of mashed potatoes, but it seemed like she'd put on a pound or ten, especially on her butt.

Actually, I had only seen Sherry two times all summer. Either she had been out of River Bend, or she'd spent three months hibernating in her air-conditioned house, gossiping on social media and grazing on junk food.

Anyway, the rest of us just groaned, "hi." But Sherry stuck her nose in the air, ignoring us. Hey, it was no skin off any of us. We all warmed up with a jog around the block, then started stretching.

Ms. Simon showed up. She parked and got out. She wore a skin-tight Under Armour outfit that showed off her figure. Clarence Elrod was changing the receipt tape in one of his gas pumps, and after taking one look, he gawked frog-eyed.

Ms. Simon walked over. She looked straight at Dumont. "Sherry, this was settled last May. I told you . . ."

Sherry tried to interrupt, but the coach held up her right hand like a traffic cop and said, "I told you if you weren't willing to work out this summer, then you weren't a part of this team. You made your choice."

"But, Miss Simon," she whined.

However, the coach didn't let her finish. "That's all, Sherry. It's settled. You made your decision when you opted not to train. Now, live with it. These young women—the team"—she pointed at the seven of us—"have worked extremely hard. And for me to allow you to join this team when you likely haven't broken a sweat all summer would be disrespectful to my runners."

We all glanced at each other, except Kayla, who hung her head, eyes on the ground. Ms. Simon walked past Sherry and began talking with us about the workout for that day.

Whoa, horsey! Talk about setting someone straight. Ms. Simon knows how to do it. As for Sherry, if dirty looks could kill, she'd have been a mass murderer. Her hands were on her hips. She narrowed her eyes, and her lips curled into a snarl. "My dad says your kind oughta. . ."

Ms. Simon turned and stepped toward her. "What?"

Sherry glared, and our coach turned her back on her. Sherry's voice stabbed the early morning air. "You think this is settled! You just wait!"

Sherry's screech startled the team and we flinched, but Ms. Simon didn't even turn around. She kept her back to Sherry and said, "Do whatever you have to do, Sherry. Just do it somewhere else."

I'm ashamed to admit it—but I loved it.

Sherry backed away, and then she took off running faster than I ever thought she could run. Amazing!

All of us stood with our mouths hanging open. But her sprint didn't last long. About fifty yards down the road, Sherry started walking. Every once in a while, she'd glance back to sling a poison look. I could only imagine what she was mumbling about us, especially Ms. Simon.

But, ah heck, we didn't care what she thought or said about us, so we all went back to our stretching. Besides, it wasn't long before Ms. Simon made us forget all about Sherry Dumont.

Coach gave us a pep talk about keeping ourselves in good shape. Brother, of all the things I like about Ms. Simon, the one I like most is what she calls "speaking with candor." She doesn't dodge any issue. Not only did she tell us we'd have to keep up our grades, she also said, "I want every one of you to eat right and get your rest. No soda pop." We all groaned. "I mean it," she went on. "Dr. Roger Bannister is convinced soda keeps you from using oxygen efficiently."

"Where does this *Dr. Roger Bannister* practice medicine? In Judd Overstreet's barn?" I cracked.

Everyone laughed.

"In the United Kingdom."

Again with the United Kingdom, I thought. *First, Dick Francis, now this Bannister dude.*

Ms. Simon went on. "Roger Bannister was the first person to run a mile under four minutes. I don't know if he's right or not about carbonated drinks, but we're not taking any chances." I glanced at my teammates. "Also, as it says in the booklet I sent you, be sure to eat food with iron to offset any depletion when you menstruate. Foods with high iron content are listed in the booklets."

Then, Ms. Simon lobbed a grenade. "I certainly would prefer that you didn't engage in sexual activity." I could feel my face turn red. I looked down, and then peeked at Kyesha. She was staring at the ground. "However, if you are sexually active, demand that a male partner use a condom."

Wow! Blunt as a ball bat.

"If you can't talk to your parents about this, then see me and I'll gladly advise you how to obtain and use protection—if that's what you want." She minced no words, and you knew you could trust her. I glanced at the others. At first, they were stone-faced and silent. I looked at Destiny and shrugged. She smiled, and the rest of the team—except Kayla—smiled, too.

Then we began our first practice with Ms. Simon, and she worked us 'til we about dropped.

20

Pick You Up At Six

If we hadn't been in great shape, that first practice with Ms. Simon would have killed us all. Her plan was to have us stay together as a team, but still bring in our best times. That was the plan.

"It's obvious," Ms. Simon said, flicking through data she'd put into her phone, "that Cassie's the runner the rest of you want to stay with."

I held back a grin.

Then she said, "If any of you beat Cassie, you get to take this away from her and keep it as long as you're not beaten by a teammate." She stepped over to me and pinned a little pink piece of cloth about an inch square to my shirt. It's weird, that patch of cloth wasn't worth any money, but because it stood for something important to us, it was valuable.

After she'd finished her pep talk, Ms. Simon lined us up in

front of Clarence Elrod's Quick Mart, just like we were running in a meet, and then set us off.

Believe me, I wanted to keep that pink patch, so I set a fast pace, figuring the rest of the team would either get pulled along or get burned out. Ms. Simon sped past in her Porsche, heading for the sixteen-hundred-meter—about one mile—mark on top of Monster Hill. Ky was on my left elbow. Hard breathing and footsteps mixed; teammates weren't far behind. As we turned onto the gravel road, I glanced back toward the corner. Sure enough, the other freshmen—Emily and Samantha—were just behind Kyesha, while Taylor and Destiny were about five yards further back. Kayla hadn't even reached the corner.

At the top of Monster Hill stood Ms. Simon, her Porsche parked at the side. She called off our times as we passed the sixteen-hundred-meter mark. Gosh, I was shocked when I heard her yell "five fifty-eight" as Ky and I shot past. We were really jazzed. Ky wanted to take the pink cloth; I wanted to keep it. Mostly, though, we all wanted to impress Ms. Simon. The amazing thing was, in spite of the pace, I didn't feel tired.

By the time Ky and I passed two thousand meters, we had put more distance between us and the other girls. At the grassy lane that leads to the abandoned farmhouse—the two-mile mark—I was pulling away from Kyesha. By the time we went into the grove of trees beside the Mississinewa, the team was pretty spread out.

I charged out of the shade into the morning sun and shot over the roller coaster hills, driving for the finish line where Ms. Simon was waiting beside her car. I shot past the five-thousand-meter mark as she called out "eighteen twenty-three," my best time ever. Ky finished second, Emily third, and Destiny and Taylor sprinted in together, Samantha right behind. Finally, here came Kayla.

Each of us, except Kayla, had a personal best. I figured the way we tore up the course, Ms. Simon would call it a practice and send us home. But after we caught our wind and guzzled water and Gatorade, she scolded us about being too spread out, lecturing us that we needed to practice running together as a team. That's when she introduced us to what she called the "Native American Relay" or "Indian Run."

We stretched, then all got in a single-file line. Kayla was first, Ms. Simon was behind her, I was last, and the others were in between according to their times. Kayla set the pace, and after a few yards, I sprinted to the front, and then came Kyesha, followed by Emily and so on.

We kept repeating that over the three-mile course. Everyone stayed together for a while, and Ms. Simon surprised me by setting one of the fastest paces. Then Kayla fell back, leaving the rest of us to finish the course together.

What a workout! Over six miles total—hard, fast miles. We were wiped out. But, know what? It felt really good. I think that's because being tired stood for something. We were becoming a team. That first practice with Ms. Simon was when I knew this season could be better—and not just ordinary, but better than ordinary.

"Let's take a slow lap around the block," said Ms. Simon. So all eight of us—Ms. Simon included—jogged together laughing, jabbering, and feeling good. As we jogged, Kayla reminded me that she almost had a personal record. I told her she'd done great—we'd all done great.

When we got back, there was Jake waiting for us. He'd ridden a bike. God, I could have just died because there I was dirty, sweaty—stinky. My teammates were self-conscious, too. They clammed up and looked at each other. Ms. Simon was the only one who wasn't all shook up.

"Hard workout," she said to Jake as she handed us each a

new practice schedule. "Lots of personal records."

"Cool," said Jake, acting interested, but wasn't. Then I was about knocked over when he said, "Cassie, how you doin'?" His voice seemed to crack slightly. My teammates glanced at each other, smirking.

My heart pounded. I cleared my throat. "Fine." I cleared it again. "I'm fine." *Wow! What a way with words.*

He nodded. "Good—that's good." There was a pause, and then Jake said, "Yeah, that's good."

Ms. Simon had us stretch again. Jake kept hanging around, watching. When I was leaning over touching my toes, I sniffed my pits to get a whiff of how bad it was. I caught my breath and mumbled, "Oh, boy."

Every now and then, I sneaked a peek at Jake. Each time he was looking right at me. That only made me sweat more and breathe harder. God, I felt my cheeks burn into a blush, and I hoped he'd think it was from all the running.

When we were done, I played it coy by just sauntering toward home with Kyesha. I swigged on a bottle of Gatorade, hoping, of course, that Jake would say something. Jeez, I could not have walked any slower. Finally, Jake called after me. "Cassie, could I talk to you a minute?" He said it like he was about to tell me I had a terminal disease, but with no crack in his voice, now more determined. My heart raced, and my stomach felt yanked up and down by a bungee.

Ky is nobody's fool. When she looked back and saw him walking his bike toward us, she said, "I think I'd better run along. Call you later, Cass."

"Okay." I turned, still trying to play it cool. Ms. Simon pulled away in her Porsche. The rest of the team walked past me, grinning like idiots.

"Catch you at Van Winkle's for all the latest," chimed Taylor. I gave her a look. Then Kayla said she would see me later.

"Yeah, see you later." Now, Jake was next to me. I glanced at him. God, I felt funny. I mean, here's the person I'd hoped would pay me some attention, but now that he had, I was scared it might turn out bad. Besides, I wanted Jake's attention when I looked my best—and believe me, I didn't. My hair hung in sweaty clumps, and my drenched shorts and jersey gripped my flesh like they were glued on. My face dripped sweat.

"Pretty tough workout, huh?" Jake said as we strolled along, him walking his bike and me keeping my armpits pressed to my sides so he wouldn't pass out. Jeez, I felt awkward. Besides that, I thought of the dumbest stuff. I gazed up at Jake and thought, *Boy, is he tall.* Then I noticed his nose. *He sure has big nostrils.* I prayed he couldn't read my mind.

I cleared my throat. "Yeah—I mean yes, it was tough." I cleared my throat again. *What an annoying habit. Stop it!* "Excuse my appearance."

Jake sputtered a laugh. He sounded like an old car turning over on a winter's morning. "Hey, Cassie, you look fine—I mean considering the workout and everything—you look just fine."

What does he mean by "everything"? But I let that go. "I do?" *Did he really mean I look FINE, or does "fine" just mean okay?* "Thanks," I told him. "It really was a rough workout, and it's sort of hot." I pushed the hair away from my face. "Hot." I smiled.

He smiled. "Yeah," he said. Then he got really quiet. *Oh God, I musta screwed up.* Yeah, I know it was dumb to think that, but remember I was nervous and sort of paranoid.

"Rode your bike, huh?"

Jake nodded. "Yeah, well, Dad has the truck—Mom the car."

I could've kicked myself. *Jeez, why did I mention the bike? He'll think I'm poking fun at him.* I was about to explain that I wasn't putting him down when Jake said, "Cassie . . ." Again, there was just a hint of a crack in his voice. It was sort of sexy. Sounded kind of like Cary Grant, an old-time movie star I saw on cable.

I encouraged him. "Yes, Jake." I could tell he was trying to be cool.

"Well, Cassie, I was wondering if you would like to go out—maybe tomorrow—or tonight—any time—whenever you want—maybe go to a show or something—or not?"

At first, I figured I'd play hard-to-get. You know, pretend I wasn't sure if I wanted to go out with him. But I gave that up. It seemed like such a cheap trick, so I said, "I'd love to go."

The biggest smile I ever saw spread across Jake's face. "Great!" he said. Then he got a grip on himself. "Oh, good. That's really good. How 'bout tonight? Pick you up at six?"

"I'll be ready." I was about to bust.

"Good—that's good."

We walked on for a ways making chitchat—weather, sports, music—probable size of the pending harvest. We stopped at the corner a few yards from my house, and Jake said, "You've got a great place."

He was just being nice; it's not that great. Not a dump, just not that great. But I thanked him. Then there was this awkward silence. You know the feeling: You don't want to go, but you do want to go—everything is all uncoordinated and confused. Finally, I said, "I have to clean up. See you tonight."

"Yeah, I'll see you tonight, Cassie." Then Jake reached over and touched my shoulder. I nearly melted. He jerked his hand away, gave me a goofy grin, hopped on his bike, and pedaled away, his long legs pumping the pedals awkwardly. Kind of like a giraffe on wheels.

I watched him until he was out of sight, then I let out a big shriek and raced for home.

21

Stag Applebee
Almost....Terrifying!

Until last summer, my experiences with the opposite sex hadn't been too great. Let's see, there was Noah Shepherd, who asked me to go steady with him in sixth grade. God, that was dumb. To begin with, I didn't even like the kid. Like I said earlier, I was crazy about Jake even way back then. But you know how it is, everybody else was going steady, so I figured it was the thing to do.

The other dorky thing was that we called it going steady, but we never went anywhere. We traded these stupid little rings that we bought over at Halpern's Jewelry Store in Marion, made a big deal out of going steady, and then hardly spoke to each other after that.

High school didn't improve my love life. Jeez, a girl begins to wonder if something's wrong with her. I would just die if this got out. But back in my lovelorn days, when there was a big dance and I hadn't been asked, I'd go to my room and put on my earphones and play old people's music—*really old* people's music—from the 1950's and 1960's that I put onto my iPod. Sometimes it cheered me up; usually it depressed me more.

Oh, don't get me wrong, before this past summer I did have dates—two. Caleb Dykes, who was a junior, took me to Homecoming when I was a freshman. What a dweeb!

Caleb's a nice enough guy; he's just dull. We danced a couple of fast dances, and then we sat around saying nothing. Caleb has such a way with words—two, *yes* and *no*. I tried to strike up a conversation, but every time I asked him a question he would just say *yes* or *no*. And if he couldn't use one of those words, he shrugged his shoulders and grinned.

Really, I don't know how Caleb ever managed to ask me out. The kid must have practiced for weeks to learn his lines.

That was my first big date before this summer. The second was when I was a sophomore, and the thought of it literally sends a cold chill through me. It was with Stag Applebee, a UC from Snob Hill. His real name is Terrance, but everyone calls him Stag. I have no idea why.

Stag used to be a halfback on the football team. He's a year older than me, but started this school year as a "super-senior." He failed so many courses that he was going to have to go an extra year in order to graduate.

Anyway, Sherman Applebee is Stag's dad. He owns the bank in River Bend. Stag is the only kid the Applebees have, and they give him anything he wants. Stag drives the best and newest car, wears the best clothes, always has a wad of cash, and used to talk to people in town any way he pleased. I should have known better than to go out with a guy called Stag. But he was UC and I wanted to be popular—and I was naive.

I'm not sure what he'd heard about me, or whether he'd

thought it up on his own, but we didn't go anywhere—not any place where he'd have to spend money. Stag just drove down by the Mississinewa, parked his car, and began pawing me in the light of a full moon. I didn't even like the guy, and there he was breathing his boozy breath in my face, trying to ram his tongue down my throat and expecting me to like it. I clenched my teeth.

"Come on, baby, you know you want it," the moron kept growling. I kept my mouth clamped. Stag's about as graceful as a baby hippo. He tried to shove his paw up under my dress and into my underpants. It was all I could do to force it away. Then the creep says, "Come on, baby, don't you want to do it?"

Believe me, guys like Stag don't just lose their appeal, they're downright scary.

"As a matter of fact, no I don't want to *do it!*" I told him, trying to straighten my dress. And would you believe the big thug had the nerve to lean over and stick his hand down my front into my bra. I'd had enough. At first Stag was just annoying, but now he was terrifying. I was all scrunched up against the door with him lying all over me, so I reached back and searched for the door handle. But before I could find it, he wrapped his arms around my waist. I kicked and struggled, but he flipped me over onto my stomach and hiked up my dress from behind. I pushed up and was able to prop myself onto my hands and knees, then smashed an elbow into the side of his neck. Stag released me long enough so I could grab the door latch and yank it. The door sprang open and I tumbled out onto the sandy ground, leaving his face buried in the front seat.

He rose up and said, "What's wrong with you anyway?"

"What do you think is wrong?" I screamed into the night. "Nothing's wrong with me!" I got to my feet and brushed myself off. "And I'm going to keep it that way—jerk." I was about to freak out and run, but got a grip, afraid if I turned my back on him, he'd chase after me and drag me to the ground.

"Hey, don't you ever get horny?" he snarled.

God, what a stupid question. Of course, I *get horny*. And I have desires and get urges and fantasies and dreams and—well, anyway, it wasn't any of that creep's business, so I didn't answer.

He sat up and gripped the wheel with both hands. In the bright moonlight I could see the white of his knuckles. The only sounds out by the Mississinewa that night were frogs croaking, crickets chirping, and the river splashing against the rocks. There were no other humans, just Stag and me. If you dare call him human. I tried not to let him see me tremble.

Then he said, "You're frigid."

Now I boiled. The nerve of that creep saying a thing like that to me. No way I'm frigid. I'm just not going to lie down spread-eagle and let some Neanderthal jockey me to the finish line. What gives that creep the right to turn me into one of those plastic blow-up dolls I've heard about?

Of course I think about sex and have urges. But I think about other things too—like love and—well, I can't exactly explain it, except to say that Stag Applebee wasn't going to be the one I *did it* with. Besides, Stag wasn't going to get pregnant. Maybe the best way to explain it is to say it in plain words. Candor. Let's face it, the guy doesn't get knocked up—the one who has to decide to get an abortion or not. And if the girl doesn't get one, it's not the guy whose belly swells, and he's not the one everybody in town whispers about. And most importantly, I just *did not* want to do it with Stag Applebee. Some people might think I was square, but at that moment, I figured I'd wait until I was married. Remember, I said I *thought* I'd wait.

Anyway, Stag Applebee scared me, and then he made me so mad. Believe me, I wasn't about to get back in that car with him. I backed slowly away, like I would do a rabid dog. He reached over and slammed the passenger door shut, and peeled out onto the hard road and disappeared. Then I raced for home, never breathing a word of it to my mom and dad.

Now, I was going out with Jake. I was excited and scared all at the same time.

22

Greatest Player Since Larry Bird

Our bus is stuck in traffic on I-465, heading around Indianapolis. I see our exit ahead, but we still have to travel quite a ways on I-70.

Anyway, Jake had just asked me out after that first practice with Ms. Simon, and I was about to burst. But I didn't want my mom to think I was a psycho, so before going into the house, I settled down. Believe me, though, the closer it got to six o'clock, the more nervous I became.

It was about four o'clock that afternoon when I told Mom that I wouldn't be eating supper with her and Dad because I had a date. She'd been rolling out pie dough, her back to me, and she stopped and turned slowly. "Who with, Cass?" And when I told her Jake Nader, a little smile crept across her lips, and she went back to her pies without saying anything. Mom's known for a long time how I feel about Jake.

When Dad pulled into the driveway, Mom went outside to meet him. They stood there for a minute. I watched from the window in the living room. She did all the talking. Her hand touched his shoulder as he kept his eyes locked on her. Then, Dad's body straightened and a grin spread across his face like he'd just won the lottery.

It was five o'clock, and I was nervous. I'd already started getting ready but couldn't decide on what to wear; I changed outfits three times. I expected Dad to tease me, but he didn't. In fact, he didn't say anything about me going out with the *great* Jake Nader. As usual, he asked about my workout. He was particularly interested because he knew it was our first practice with Ms. Simon. I told him it had been a great practice, and then we talked a little bit about other things. Mom and Dad are both pretty good about talking with me. Oh, they let me know that they're the parents, but they also cut me a lot of slack, especially considering I'm a senior.

By five-thirty I was as ready as I would ever be and waiting on the sofa, tapping my right foot, about to wear a hole in the carpet. It did make me feel better, though, when I recalled how nervous Jake had been earlier that morning. *Maybe we're both up the same tree. Amazing, Jake Nader nervous about asking me out—me.*

It was six o'clock on the dot when from the window I saw him round the corner in a new Chevy truck. Mom and Dad were finishing supper. Mothers must have a special instinct when it comes to their children's romances. Even before Jake pulled into the drive, my mom rose from the dining room table and started into the living room. But I could hear Dad whisper, then there was silence. I looked out of the corner of my eye, seeing her sit back down.

Jake was out of the car now and heading slowly up to the porch. God, he looked so fine—tall and tanned. I darted away from the window. People would think I'm a goof, but my knees went a little weak, and when I noticed that my palms were all icky with sweat, I began to have a panic attack. "God," I spoke softly, "I hope he doesn't try to hold my hand." *Wait a minute! Am I nuts? I want Jake to hold my hand. Oh, God, not if it's all soppy.*

Now, he was on the porch knocking. I pulled myself together. "Be calm. Be cool," I said on the way to the door. I popped a Tic Tac into my mouth and crunched it.

Mom had put the central air on, so the door was closed. However, I could peek through a little rectangular plate of glass at the top and see Jake staring down.

I tried to dry my hands by rubbing them together really fast, being careful not to touch my white shorts. Then, I grabbed hold of the doorknob, took a deep breath, and pulled the door open.

Jake jerked his head up and we stood there for a moment staring at each other like a couple zombies. "Hi, Jake. Come on in out of the heat."

"Hi, Cassie." He stepped into the chilled air. "Boy, it sure feels good in here."

"Yeah."

Mom and Dad couldn't restrain themselves any longer; into the living room they came. I rolled my eyes and sighed. In a town like River Bend, everyone knows everyone. Besides, Dad saw Jake every week or so at Swen's Barber Shop in the middle of our downtown, and he greeted him enthusiastically. "Hi, Jake. Great to see you." They shook hands. Mom also said, "hi," and shook hands with Jake.

We all made small talk. They offered him a seat. He sat on the couch. I sat beside him—not too close, though—and played with the back of one of my earrings, while Dad and Jake replayed last year's basketball season. Dad said things like "sensational," "fantastic," "shoe-in for Mr. Basketball," and the

117

best of all, "a living legend." Mom agreed with everything Dad said.

Jake acted a little shy, but he thanked them. Jake told me he averaged twenty-seven points a game as a junior. One game he scored fifty-seven points, a school record. I heard all about it, but I missed that game. My dad says that Jake is the greatest all-around Indiana high school player since Larry Bird, and Bird is like a god in Indiana.

Finally, I said we'd better be going. I held my breath, afraid my mom would ask when Jake was bringing me home. But she didn't.

Then, with the AC easing cool air around the cab, Jake and I were driving off in his parents' Chevy truck. He admitted later that it belonged to them. That was one of the many things that I'd find out we had in common; I always have to use my parents' vehicle, too.

23

First Date...Wow!

I'd stewed all afternoon about whether or not I should scoot next to Jake or stay on the passenger side. Sure, wearing a seat belt is the law in Indiana, even in trucks. But all is fair in love, so I thought about disobeying the law and not wearing the seat belt. *If I use my seat belt, I'll have a good excuse not to scoot next to him. But, Cassie, are you some kind of whack job? You've been crazy about this guy for years. Of course, you want to get close to him—as close as possible!* But I snapped the belt anyway.

I settled into my seat. We rounded the corner and went a couple blocks without either of us saying a word. *Ms. Simon is right. I am going to have to be the aggressive one. What do I have to lose? Either he'll like me or he won't. Sitting here like a crash test dummy isn't getting me anywhere, and Jake seems to be having trouble making the first move.* So I slid toward him—the only thing between us was the cup tray and the seat belt—and said, "Jake, I really liked going to the track meet with you—and with Ms. Simon."

"Yeah, that was fun." He nodded. "Fun." His body was tense.

I was starting to relax. Jake may have had his hands on the wheel, but I was in the driver's seat.

"You know, I really enjoyed that more than anything I've done all summer. My family didn't take any vacation, so that trip to Indianapolis was like a vacation to me."

"We didn't either—go on a vacation," he said.

Silence.

Even though he was quiet, he was more comfortable. His body had gone slack, and his hands were no longer clutching the steering wheel like he was hanging off the edge of a cliff.

We didn't seem to be driving anywhere in particular. Now, we were on the hard road passing Elrod's Quick Mart & Vehicle Repair. Next, we turned onto the gravel road, which is a shortcut to Marion and part of our training course.

"My mom and dad both had to work," Jake said. "Dad was late getting into the fields this year 'cause of the wet spring, and the bank in Marion wouldn't let my mom off. We had to stay home, so it was a vacation for me, too—Indianapolis was."

We were starting up Monster Hill. Jake shifted to low. He switched on the radio—a country station. I'd forgive him for that. *Go figure. I thought he liked light rock.*

The volume was down; music was playing softly. A couple of times, Taylor Meterburg and I had driven around on a weekend—to Marion then back to River Bend—but Jake and I weren't cruising around just for kicks. We talked. We talked about everything. The driving was just a way to do the talking. Being such a big basketball star, a girl would think Jake would try to impress me, but he didn't. Oh, at first I think he figured he was going to have to, but he was too nervous even to try. Besides, I don't think he's good at putting on an act. So when I took charge, he actually seemed relieved. Before the evening was over, he was just Jake Nader, the kid who used to sit across from me in sixth grade at James Whitcomb Riley Grade School in River Bend.

Jake asked me several times if I wanted to go to the amusement park in Marion or see a movie or do anything at all. I told him not unless he did, that I was enjoying the drive. He said he was too, but he didn't want me to think he was cheap. I laughed. "How could I possibly think you're cheap when you're burning up all of this gas?" I touched his arm—to emphasize my point. God, his muscles were like steel.

"Never thought of that," he said. Jake was silent. Then he said, "I don't care about the gas. It's worth it." I drew in a deep breath and sort of held it. My heart raced. God, I felt so light I thought I might float away.

We stopped at Van Winkle's. Now that we'd loosened up, we were hungry. He hadn't had supper either. Jake ran in to get us something. I stayed in the truck, but through the window I saw that the whole Hendrix family was sitting in a booth eating. Jake spoke to them for a second, and then old Mr. Van Winkle waited on him. Jake returned with fries, Pepsis, and burgers. Jeez, I felt awful. I'd given up soda, and here he'd spent money on a large. I explained I couldn't drink it. Jake apologized all over himself, and then he ran in and brought out an apple juice, even though I told him not to. He drank both Pepsis while I sipped the apple juice.

"What did the Hendrixes have to say?" I asked.

"Oh, just 'hi.' That's all. They said Kyesha's little brother had done his chores all week without being told to, so they were celebrating."

"That's nice," I answered, wanting to get the discussion back to Jake and me—to *us*.

It's amazing the things you learn about a person—a person you've known for years—when you really talk with them. I knew Jake was the youngest of four boys, but I hadn't known that his brothers are so much older. One's nearly forty. Jake's parents don't seem like old people, but they have to be over sixty. That's a pretty advanced age—and his dad still farms.

"Sounds like you were a slip-up." As soon as the words left my trap I wished I could have snatched hold of them and stuffed them back in. Jake got quiet, then suddenly laughed and said, "Yeah, I guess Mom and Dad forgot to make a trip to the drugstore." I eased out a sigh of relief and laughed, too.

We drove back into River Bend and circled the town a few times. Believe me, that doesn't take long. Then, Jake headed down by the Mississinewa. I thought of Stag Applebee and got a little panicky. But then I calmed down. I mean, with a guy other than Jake I'd have figured that this was when the big move was going to be put on me—he'd try to get into my pants. But Jake didn't even park the truck. Instead, he headed back up onto the hard road and we drove toward Marion.

Thunder rumbled overhead. It started drizzling, and after the rain had built up on the windshield, Jake switched on the wipers. He leaned forward and looked through the glass at the rain falling. "It's been so dry, the corn and beans can sure stand it."

"Yeah." I discovered myself as close to him as I could get without pressing up against him, the cup tray between us; the seat belt stretched taut. I wanted to get Jake to talk more about himself. Mom once told me the way to a man's heart isn't really through his stomach—like the old saying goes—but through his ego. I guess that's another stereotype.

Jake wouldn't talk about how great he is, not anything about his basketball performances anyway. "It gets to be a drag. I

122

mean, that's all most people who know me—everyone around River Bend—ever want to talk about."

"I'm sorry. Let's change the subject," I said, regretting that I'd brought it up.

"It's all right, Cassie." He paused then said, "Only one other person knows how I feel. You'll be the second." He paused again, and I didn't nag him to continue, but I had an idea who the other person was.

After a little silence, Jake said, "People around River Bend don't even know that there's a Jake Nader who spends most of his time off the basketball court. They don't seem to know—or care—that I made the honor roll every quarter last year or that I got a thirty-two on my ACT test. Only Ms. Simon congratulates me on that stuff. Another thing, I draw pretty well, but around River Bend people don't think that's worth much."

The wipers kept saying *swoosh-chunk, swoosh-chunk.*

"Everyone comes up to me, slappin' me on the back, tellin' me what a great player I am. They say things like, 'Boy, Jake, you've got a great future as a college player.'" He drew in a deep breath and let it escape slowly. "I wonder if they'd be so friendly if I missed the winning shot in a big game or went into a scoring slump, or decided to pass up college and just hang around River Bend and help Dad on the farm."

"You can bet they wouldn't," I said. I wished my dad hadn't gone on so, tossing compliments at Jake like they were artificial roses. But I wasn't going to apologize for Dad. He didn't mean anything, and he was no worse than the rest of the town.

"Cassie, I really get sick of all the basketball praise. Really, I do. It just brings more pressure, and, God, how I hate the pressure."

"Do you ever feel pressure about school or your art?"

"Not the kind I feel for basketball. With art—and school

too—it's more a feeling of satisfaction. Anyway, that's the way it is now."

"Now?"

"You know, until Ms. Simon came along, no one ever said, 'Jake, you've got a good head on your shoulders. I bet you'd be a good engineer.' Or 'that was a great drawing you entered in the art contest. You'd make a good architect.'" Everything got quiet again. "Hey, I'd rather talk about you—about your running and what you like."

Boy, the things you learn in this life. Who'd have thought Jake Nader considered being a basketball star a burden? Or who'd have guessed he'd rather talk about cross country and me? Oh, I know—people would think it was all a big line he was laying on me. But it wasn't. I knew right off that it wasn't, because he'd said it from his heart—truthfully. I felt kind of sorry for Jake. Oh, I don't mean I pitied him, but I hurt for him.

A car came toward us, and when its lights shined up onto our windshield, I saw Jake's face for an instant. Either he meant what he said, or he was the greatest actor in the world. He meant it. I could tell.

I reached across the seat and stroked the back of Jake's neck. I didn't even have to think about doing it. I just did it. Then, ignoring the cup tray, I inched toward him, putting my arm around Jake as we drove into Marion, staying like that all the way down Baldwin Avenue, the busiest street in town.

We talked about my running, about the outlook for the cross country team, about school, music, about how much we both liked Ms. Simon. He told me that she was easy to talk to.

I told him that I knew that firsthand. "When I take our times over to her, I always hang around and we talk." I looked out the windshield. "I don't think I feel the pressure in cross country the way you do in basketball. But I've always wanted to be the best runner I could be—be good. I just never had anyone to train me right, until Ms. Simon showed up. Nothing against Mr. Buchanan."

"Yeah, I know. For someone who never coached before, she seems to know how to work you girls—get the most out of you."

The cab of the truck filled with silence. *Maybe we can have a season to be proud of for once. Maybe I can drop my times down in meets. Maybe . . . maybe.*

We pulled into McDonald's. I was still kind of full from Van Winkle's, but Jake bought me another burger and a shake anyway. He said I needed to eat. He had a large Coke, and then both of us used the restroom where I gave myself a quick inspection in the mirror and tossed in another breath mint. Next, we left McDonald's and went back to driving around for a while. Finally, with the gas gauge laying on *E,* we ended up in my driveway.

Except for the porch light, the house was dark. Mom and Dad were in bed. The digital clock on the dash said 1:30 a.m. Jeez, I hadn't stayed up this late for a long time. *Breaking training—but got a great reason. Ms. Simon would understand.*

Jake shut off the engine, and we sat there with the rain tapping rhythmically on the roof of the truck. The drops wound their way down the windows, merging into a sheet that sealed us off from the rest of the world, giving me the feeling that there were no other people on earth except Jake and me.

Other than the rain falling around us, the only sound was our breathing. I turned my head toward the passenger window, suddenly fogged over. *It's now or never.* I unbuckled my seatbelt, the click loud in the silent car. He was so close, so close. I scooted, and then scooted once more. I reached down, fumbling in the dark to unsnap his seat belt. My hands trembled. He helped me, and the shoulder harness slid away, freeing him. I wrapped my arms around him; finally, our lips pressed together. A raw feeling surged over me. I don't know how our kiss rated on the kissing scale, but it was plenty good for starters.

The cup tray stabbed my hipbone, but I hardly noticed as we kissed again. "You've—got to get to bed—so you can run—tomorrow," Jake stammered.

"I know." We released each other. He came around to my side and opened the door for me. He took my hand as I slid out. A mist settled on us. But neither of us worried about getting wet as we strolled to the porch. Jake leaned down and we kissed good night. Then, he left and I went in, standing by the window until the taillights on his parents' truck disappeared.

God, I was so stirred up. I went to bed and tried to sleep, but my feelings pestered me. So I grabbed my iPod—with the songs I spoke about a few miles back—music my grandparents listened to when they were my age. Not *cool* music, but relaxing. When Mr. Sandman doesn't show up right away, I slip on my earphones and let one of the old singers sing me a lullaby.

That night when Sam Cooke sang "You Send Me," I worried about whether I'd been a good enough kisser or if my breath smelled bad. By the time Ricky Nelson was halfway through "Young Love," my mind was on Jake and me. We were lying together on a beach, just us. He had me in his arms. Our lips were locked in a kiss and we were caressing each other.

That was the last thing I remember. The next thing I knew, my mom was shaking me awake, telling me that Ky was waiting for me, that I was late for practice.

24

Called On The Carpet

I don't know where the expression "called on the carpet" originated, but it's not just a saying at River Bend High School. When you're called into Principal Broadneck's office, you stand on his fancy rug in front of his fancy desk while he reams you out with his fancy words.

News got around that Ms. Simon got called on the carpet. Do I need to say about what? No, not her sex talk. Good guess, though. It was the period talk at that first meeting in May. Henry Elrod saw Ms. Simon go into the principal's office with Prissy Butt McGrady strutting behind, notepad in hand, and then Broadneck closed the door. Later, McGrady told Henry all of the details—fact and fiction. Henry told Clarence. Clarence told Mrs. Anderson. Mrs. Anderson told my mom. And Mom delivered the news to Dad and me.

"From what I hear, Betty McGrady got a big thrill out of seeing Ms. Simon get scolded like a child," Mom said to Dad as I came in from a rare Saturday morning run.

"What's this about Ms. Simon being scolded?" Mom went on to tell us that the principal had advised Ms. Simon that she was "a chemistry teacher and cross country coach, not a feminine hygiene teacher, and had no business talking to any students about personal things."

"Oh, my God, she was just giving us advice on how to keep healthy." I clinched my teeth and folded my arms hard against my chest.

"Seems to me that the girls ought to learn about life's ways from any reliable adult—hygiene teacher or chemistry teacher," said Dad.

Mom agreed. "What really galls me is how pleased Betty McGrady was that Ms. Simon got into trouble."

"Mean-spirited old bi. . ." Dad muttered under his breath.

"God, some people. Ms. Simon was just trying to make sure we weren't going to get anemic and lose strength."

I told Jake about Ms. Simon getting reamed out by the principal, but we decided we wouldn't bring it up with her. We didn't want to embarrass her. Besides, we figured it would blow over.

A few days after learning about Ms. Simon getting *scolded* by the principal, I sat down at my computer to watch some old track films from the Olympics on YouTube. I typed *Olympic running events* into the search bar. One of the choices that came up was the women's marathon at the Los Angeles Olympics back in 1984. So I clicked on it. I propped my right elbow on my desk and rested my chin on my palm, getting lost in that race held back in the day. I'd never heard of Joan Benoit before, but when I saw her run that marathon—gosh, she was the greatest long-distance runner ever. She just destroyed those other runners.

The next day, I was in a sports memorabilia store in Marion, and I spotted this big vintage poster of Joan Benoit Samuelson—*Samuelson* 'cause she got married—standing by the track in her Olympic uniform holding an American flag. I bought it and I hung it in my room.

One evening I was lounging on my bed, just looking up at that poster, thinking about running a marathon. I hadn't thought anymore about Ms. Simon getting in trouble—shoved it to the back of my mind. Then, it hit me. *When it comes to grudges, Sherry Dumont is like a marathon runner; she never quits until she really hurts someone. Known her since kindergarten. Always stirring up trouble. Had to be Sherry who tattled on Ms. Simon. Who else? I'm surprised she waited so long.* "If that dirty little snot tries. . ." My words vanished into a snort. *What would the team do without Ms. Simon coaching us? What would I do?*

I wanted to throw up, but I got a hold of myself, thinking, *Ah, Sherry can't get Ms. Simon fired. Chemistry teachers are too hard to find.*

25

A Notebook Full Of Poems

Ms. Simon kept working us hard. I mean hard! And no one took the pink patch away from me. Jake and I started going steady—and we actually *went* places.

I look at him now as our bus rattles down I-70. He's studying a map of the course. Basketball season starts in a week. Jake was the leading scorer in a league with top players in Indiana this summer. He's been practicing with the basketball team for over a month and helping our cross country team in his spare time, which isn't much with basketball soaking up so many hours. This year I won't miss a single game.

Actually, our relationship caused trouble for "Mad" Max Jarvis, the football coach who always has a scowl plastered on his face. It's like this: Although Jake's a basketball star, River Bend is a small town and they've needed him to play football, too. But he told me one night after we first started dating in August that he didn't really like football, so he was quitting.

"Besides, I'm afraid of getting hurt," he said, "so that it screws up my basketball. Even though I get tired of all the pressure, I still want to play." He was quiet, and then said, "Besides, I want to follow the girls' cross country team this season—go to your meets and help out. I'm skippin' out on football and spendin' the fall keeping stats for Ms. Simon."

When Mad Max found out Jake wasn't going to play football anymore, the you-know-what hit the fan. He tried to send Jake on a guilt trip. "You'll be letting your school and all of River Bend down," Jarvis told him. But Jake didn't owe anything to Jarvis or the people of River Bend.

He told Mad Max, "I'm not a great football player anyway. It won't be any great loss."

Truth is, Jake was a good tight end. But most folks in town were glad he wasn't playing football. And no one was happier than Jimmy Railing, the basketball coach. He and Jarvis had fought about this before. Heck, no one wants Jake banged up so he can't play basketball.

But Mad Max went ballistic. Jake told him that he didn't care how loud he yelled, he was spending the fall keeping stats for the girls' cross country team. That made Mad Max about have a stroke. Of course, when Coach Railing heard that Jake was quitting football to keep cross country stats, suddenly he thought cross country was the greatest thing since the jockstrap. Shoot, Mad Max had to give up; he couldn't match Jimmy Railing's clout around River Bend.

Mad Max really pissed me off, though. Henry Elrod told Clarence that he overheard Jarvis and Prissy Butt talking in the office. They were blaming Ms. Simon for Jake not playing football. Clarence said, "Jarvis accused Ms. Simon of being a bad influence on the kids, and McGrady said, "'Her kind shouldn't be allowed around our young people. No doubt she's got a past.'"

I boiled. *The gall of Mad Max dissing Ms. Simon with Prissy Butt. And the nerve of McGrady saying that about my cross country coach. I could strangle them both.* But I calmed down when I heard Clarence tell a group of farmers standing around the Quick Mart, "Hell's bells, don't seem like she's a bad influence to me. Way she's got those girls out running and gettin' ready." He looked over at me. "Just ask Cassie there."

"Couldn't find a better coach anywhere," I said as I took an orange juice from the cooler.

"Told you. I've watched them almost every morning this summer run by here like a herd of deer."

I handed Mrs. Anderson money for the juice.

Mrs. Anderson rang it up and tossed the money in the cash drawer. "All I have to say is, if Betty McGrady doesn't like this Miss Simon, then Miss Simon is my very best friend. Period—and case closed!"

One of the farmers spoke up. "If this Miss Simon had somethin' to do with getting Jake to stay away from football—which is bound to get him busted up—I say give her a medal."

Clarence set his jaw. "Amen to that. Basketball is what counts." To a man—and Mrs. Anderson—they agreed.

Of course, Ms. Simon didn't have a thing to do with Jake quitting football, but if Clarence wanted to give her credit, I'd let him, especially when Jarvis and that you-know-what McGrady were ganging up on her.

We were all listening to Mrs. Anderson rip on Prissy Butt when Jake pulled up in the truck.

"Got to go."

Everyone had a wisecrack to make about Jake and me. I put my hands on my hips, sending them playful glare, and then laughed, gave a wave, and hurried to the truck, hopping in and giving Jake a kiss. I snapped my seat belt, and guzzled my orange juice, as we began driving around, winding up over at Ms. Simon's. She let us in.

When she went to get us something to drink, I noticed that she'd been working on the computer.

"What are you doing?" I asked her, walking over to her desk, Jake following me. "Thinking up more torture to put us through?"

Ms. Simon came back from the kitchenette without any drinks. "I should have saved and closed."

I got a peek and read really fast, seeing it was a poem about two lovers on a picnic. About them eating, laughing, then talking and finally making love on the blanket. My breath came in quick bursts and my heart pounded. I felt like such a jerk for reading it.

"I think we better go sit down," Jake said.

We started to walk away.

I looked at Ms. Simon. She hadn't meant for it to be read—at least not by a couple high school kids. The expression on her face told a story.

Jake gently pulled my arm, guiding me away from the computer as he said, "Cassie, let's sit down." We went to the couch, and Ms. Simon saved and closed.

She stood at the computer with her back to us for just a moment, then turned and smiled. "How are you two tonight?"

It was just something she said to clear away the awkwardness. Jake and I said we were fine.

Jake reached down and cradled my hand in his. His hands are big and they're calloused from all the farm work. I liked the feel of his hand against mine, so I didn't mind if he displayed that kind of affection in front of Ms. Simon.

"How are you doin'?" asked Jake. I turned and looked at him, then at Ms. Simon.

"All right," she answered. She was quiet for a second. "Just puttering around."

"I didn't know you wrote poems."

"Cassie," Jake said, probably embarrassed for intruding into Ms. Simon's personal life. My faced suddenly felt flushed. Again, my mouth had raced ahead of my brain.

Ms. Simon hesitated. "As a matter of fact, I do."

I swallowed hard, working to think of something to say. "I could never do anything like that. You know, write poems."

Jake piped up. "How do you know you can't, Cass?"

"Why don't you give it a try, Cassie?" asked Ms. Simon.

"Don't know—never thought about it." I felt cross-examined, so I turned to Jake and said, "How many poems have you written?"

"None."

"Why don't you give it a try?" I poked him in the ribs. This was a weird conversation.

Jake let go of my hand and looked at Ms. Simon, who was sitting in a chair across from us. "No, thanks."

I laughed. "Yeah, me either—no thanks. I'll please pass on the poetry."

"See there," Ms. Simon said. "Your alliteration is very poetic without even trying." Then, without another word, she got up and took a thin book from the shelf. Ms. Simon sat back down, opened the book, and began to read. Good Lord, the way she read it and the words of the poem. It was beautiful.

Jake slid his arm around me as Ms. Simon read about how a woman loved her mother, but her mother died, leaving the daughter with emptiness. Then, Ms. Simon ended the poem:

"I chant the Mourner's Kaddish and weep, for She is
gone—has left me alone, and I barely knew Her.
She held me and rocked me and sang to me
and stroked my hair,
But I barely knew Her.
She's gone—has left me alone.
But there was a time She led me by the hand;
Worked for my coming-of-age,
But I barely knew Her.
She's gone—has left me alone.
She pushed me into who I am,
But I barely knew Her. The blame is not Hers;
I always said ". . . too busy."
Now She is gone—has left me alone; I chant the
Mourner's Kaddish and weep, for She is
gone—has left me
Alone . . . and I barely knew Her."

I glanced at Jake. His face was red, and he looked away. Without thinking, I slipped my arm over his shoulders, strong and broad. I turned my face from Jake to Ms. Simon. "That's beautiful. Who wrote it?"

"Yeah, who's the author?" asked Jake, looking back at Ms. Simon.

"I am," she said. Her eyes were wet. She rose and replaced the book.

That night I took two more books home with me—a book of Emily Dickinson's poems—and another book of poems by *C. R. Simon.* I tried reading them out loud like I thought Ms. Simon would. It didn't sound the same. Then I tried writing one. Now, I have a notebook full of poems. They're either about cross country or Jake. Mostly about cross country.

26

The Hoosier Classic

It was a steamy Indiana Saturday morning in late August. School had started, and even though fall was just down the road, summer refused to be chased away.

Our first meet was a big one. Mr. Buchanan had made up the schedule before he died, and once again we were running in the Hoosier Classic in Muncie. The best we'd ever finished was thirty-first out of thirty-two teams. The other two years we were dead last. Pretty depressing, huh? I don't know why Mr. Buchanan ever bothered to enter us in the Classic. We were always in over our heads.

Muncie isn't all that far from River Bend, but we were scheduled to run at nine o'clock, so Jake picked me up at 6:45 a.m. Ms. Simon wanted us on the bus ready to go by seven o'clock.

Mr. Borgman didn't want to leave that early, but Ms. Simon insisted. Borgman is a math teacher who drives the bus to games and meets to earn extra money. No, forget about it; he's not Ms. Simon's type, and he's taken. Mr. Borgman is at least forty, bald, and married with twelve kids. That's right—twelve. I don't know whether it's religion or what, but he and Mrs. Borgman obviously don't use any contraceptives.

On the way, Ms. Simon, Jake, and I went over the course. A girl can be the greatest runner in the world, but if she doesn't know the course, it can screw her up.

"When I studied past times, the ones available, this meet was one of your slowest races, Cassie."

"Yeah, it's a tough meet—on a hilly golf course, Ms. Simon."

"Let's see." She thumbed through computer printouts. "Here it is. Twenty minutes and thirty-four seconds. You placed..."

"Eighty-fourth out of about two hundred and twenty girls." I remember all of my times and places in the big meets.

"Why's this course so hard?" Jake asked.

"It's not just the course. There are tougher ones," I said. "What really slows you down is all the people in this meet. Besides, halfway into the race there is this narrow path in the woods. Runners will block the path. Gets to be a traffic jam."

"How can we prevent getting hung up?" asked Ms. Simon.

I grabbed a piece of paper, and with me scrunched between her and Jake, I began sketching a diagram, doing the best I could with the old school bus thumping and bumping just like it is at this very minute.

"This thing needs new shocks," remarked Jake as the three of us bounced up off of our seats.

"We start here on this fairway at the first hole." I scribbled what I thought a fairway should look like. "It's not so important that we race out in front right off the bat, because after we run to the end of the fairway we circle back one time." I drew a line. "But our team has to keep moving up, picking people off. After we make one trip around the fairway, right here will be sixteen

138

hundred meters." I made an X three quarters of the way down the fairway.

"I want at least three of you to be together at that point."

I glanced around at my six teammates. Some stared out the window, others had ear buds in, all as quiet as rocks. My gut was turning flip-flops, and here I was a veteran. "Yeah, I hope we can stick together at least this far." I circled the X. "Hopefully further." I glanced at Ms. Simon. "And it's really important that we work our way toward the front by the mile and a half mark, because right here. . ." I doodled what were supposed to be trees just east of the fairway.

Jake snickered.

"Hey, Leonardo." I elbowed him. "I'm doing my best here."

"Sorry," was all he said. But he snickered again.

"Anyway, right here is the woods—pine trees—with a narrow path winding its way through the trees. This is the place where we have to really move. We've got to get to this path before the slower runners, or they'll block us out. At the same time, we have to be careful. There are branches hanging down. Two years ago, I was moving up and another runner sprang one back, and it slapped me in the face. I think she did it on purpose."

Ms. Simon winced. "Ouch!"

"We're in these woods for about a mile, and then all of a sudden you run out of them and across a bridge." I sketched the bridge. "This is another place runners can lose time. When you come off the bridge, there's this hill. Actually it doesn't amount to much—nothing like Monster Hill. But it's all of a sudden right there. Runners have to adjust their stride going up, and when you come down, it's steep and you're back on the fairway. From there on it's a straight shot to the finish—over a kilometer, maybe even as much as three quarters of a mile."

Ms. Simon took my diagram and put a check just past where I'd put the X. "I'll be here calling out times as you run past. Jake?"

"Yes?"

"Go back into the woods before the girls' race onto this bridge and encourage them to maintain form—drive their arms, lift those knees, to run tall. Let them know that they don't have far. I'll run back to the finish."

"My dad will be out there yelling. That's for sure."

"Good. We're going to do better than thirty-first this year."

I hoped she was right, but I had to keep pushing doubts out of my mind.

Mr. Borgman wheeled into the parking lot. It was already filled with buses, cars, and trucks. Teams from all over Indiana were arriving, others already warming up. I loved all the school colors. Ours are blue and yellow. We're called the Lady Coyotes.

Our team found a spot under a big tree near the finish chute and spread down a couple blankets. Ms. Simon had us warm up by jogging the course in our sweats.

Four of us had run this meet before. But our freshmen were inexperienced, and we needed them to run their best, so I was careful to show them every twist and turn.

When we finished winding around the course, Ms. Simon told us to strip off our sweats. Then we stretched out really good. She handed out our bib numbers, and we pinned them on. Then, she gave each of us an electronic chip that we attached to one of our shoes. I don't know exactly how it works. Somehow a signal goes to a computer when a runner starts and finishes. Electronic timing is used in all the big meets, but the smaller meets are hand-timed with a stop watch.

Cross country is simple. The course is marked with flags and chalk lines. A blue flag means run straight ahead. A yellow flag means turn right, while a red one means left. The lines are either parallel—creating a path—or just one solid line, or sometimes a series of arrows pointing directions. In the big meets like the Hoosier Classic, there's usually a plastic mesh fence that has been strung along the course to keep the spectators back. The scoring is easy. They just add up the places a team's top five runners finish in. The team with the lowest total wins.

There was a good crowd of spectators. Mostly friends and families of runners. My mom and dad were just getting out of the car. They came over and Dad gave me a playful smack on the backside. Mrs. Hendrix struck up a conversation with Mom. Ky's dad had just let her little brother and Mrs. Hendrix off, and he was trying to squeeze their ten-passenger van into a compact space. Ky says they need the big van to haul church people around. Most of the parents of my other teammates showed up, too. The only ones I didn't see were Emily Lutker's and Destiny's mothers and Kayla's grandma. Jake, Ms. Simon, and our parents—that would be our cheering section. No one else from River Bend would show up. After all, cross country isn't basketball. Ha! Ha!

Really, though, I didn't care—I was too nervous to care. A couple girls dressed in Muncie Central colors jogged by. I heard one tell the other that there were thirty-seven teams. In past years, they would have all been better than us, but this season I was clinging to hope. I fidgeted with my bra. My right leg was jiggling back and forth like it had a mind of its own. I kept clearing my throat, and then I caught myself biting my thumbnail. *Stop it! Jeez, Cassie, get a hold of yourself!* I told Ms. Simon that the teams from Anderson, Muncie, Fort Wayne, and especially Marion would be tough. I wasn't sure about any of the others.

The announcer gave a call for all girls to be at the line in ten minutes. "Let's get up there now," I told the others.

"I've got to pee really bad," announced Kyesha, dancing in one place.

It was contagious. Suddenly, all the rest of us had to pee. Just the mention of it and I felt like I'd burst. Jeez, what a time for this. I mean, for guys it's easy to go outdoors what with that handy gadget nature stuck on them. Not for girls.

There weren't any restrooms or portapotties anywhere to be seen. Then, I spotted a clump of bushes up a hill about fifty yards away. "Come on!"

Kayla stopped us. "Listen, I really don't have to go; I'll stand lookout while the rest of you do your business."

I knew she probably had to go, too. Looking back, I guess she figured that after a while she'd be far behind and was willing to help the team this way. It had to be tough on Kayla. Good thing she did stand lookout, because no sooner had the rest of us got situated than a whole team of boys started into the bushes. Brother, did Kayla ever do her job. We could hear her telling them that they couldn't go in there. "You'll just have to take your business somewhere else."

"Like where?"

"I don't know. Look for another bush, try a fire hydrant, just not here!"

"I don't care!" yelled one kid. "I'm going in anyway!"

"Oh, no, you're not!"

"I'm done." Ky pulled up her undies and shorts.

I finished, too, and pulled up mine. Out Ky and I trotted. A kid was trying to get past Kayla, and she was straight-arming him, both hands against his chest.

"Let me by!"

"No!" Kayla grabbed him around the waist, wrestling him to the ground.

"Let me up!"

Kayla got up with him, mud and leaves caked to her knees.

The kid's friends were laughing, and Ky and I were trying not to.

He stomped away cussing like crazy, his friends teasing him. He looked over his shoulder. "You're a psycho!"

"Same to you!" yelled Kayla.

The other girls appeared from the bushes and wanted to know what was going on.

"It's…let's just say it was *wild*," Ky said, laughing.

Ms. Simon told us to get a move on as we trotted for the starting line. I made sure we had a good spot, nudging and jockeying around until I led my team near the front. The starter arranged us to satisfy herself. A mob was on the line. Kyesha, Emily, and myself were just back of the front line, with the other four right behind us. The starter gave us some more instructions, like what the flag colors stand for. *Duh!* I looked down at the number forty-two pinned to my jersey.

"Stay together," I said to the others. Silence. The gun was up. I glanced at the people lining the course. I spotted my dad pacing back and forth, arms folded, and keeping his eyes glued to me. Mom would stay near the finish line the whole race. Dad would practically run the entire course, racing to available spots along the fence as he cheered me on.

Bang!

Feet stampeded over the ground. The team from Marion dashed out in front. Sarah Rothman, Marion's best runner—one of the best in the state—was pulling the rest of her team along. A golf cart with a digital timer bumped over the ground in front of us.

I made sure I didn't tangle my feet with anyone, and then I started my move, picking it up as we followed the chalk line around a red flag at the end of the fairway. All my teammates, except Kayla, were with me as we started up the long, gradual incline of the fairway. It was hot and the air was heavy, but I felt good and picked it up more, passing several clusters of runners.

As we circled the fairway and headed for the mile marker, I could see the teams were spreading out. A jolt of energy shot through me. Only the teams from Muncie, Marion, and Anderson, along with isolated runners, were ahead of me—twenty or twenty-five runners all together. The leader—Marion's Rothman—was twenty or thirty meters in front of me. *Lord! Never before have I been this close to the lead in the Classic—not by 1500 meters. Can't tell if any of my teammates are with me—don't dare look back.* With runners blocking me, I couldn't see the timer on the golf cart. I was flying, though, and didn't want to do anything to slow myself down. I would listen for Ms. Simon to call off the times. If I heard only mine, I'd know I was alone, but if she called off more times, I'd figure teammates were close behind me.

I was catching runners and zipping by them. Coaches and spectators were packed around the mile marker, kept back by the fence. I spotted my dad and Ky's father and glanced at them as I raced by. Dad clapped his hands. "Drive those arms, Cassie! Keep it up! You're doin' great!"

Ky's dad screamed, "Pick it up a little!" As I passed them, Dad and Mr. Hendrix raced down course stride for stride. I searched for Ms. Simon. Passed one, two, three, four, five more girls. *Where's coach?* Then I spotted her fifty meters or so beyond the mile marker. *She's no fool. Even though it won't be a mile split, I'll be able to hear her call out my time.* At the mile marker, coaches were screaming and shouting. I might have missed her call in that racket. I found another gear, passing three more runners.

"Sustain it, Cass!" Ms. Simon yelled as I approached her. "Five fifty-five!"

I passed the mile in way under six minutes! Keep it up! A pause, then I heard Coach Simon yell, "Five fifty-nine! Six one! Six two!" Another pause and Coach Simon yelled, "Six five!"

We're together!

Ahead, about twenty yards, Sarah Rothman was dashing into the woods. There were six other girls bunched a few strides back of her. Another two girls ran side by side just in front of me. My breathing was coming easily, so I knew I could take the two in front of me. Increasing my stride and turning it over faster, I shot past them right before the woods, racing for the pack of six now within reach.

Someone pulled alongside me. I glanced right. Ky was matching my every stride, both of us closing in on the six who stood between us and the leader. The path shrank. I tromped onto a bed of pine needles, and then sprinted back onto the path. Three of the six wore the purple and gold of Marion Senior High—big girls—tall and broad, running shoulder to shoulder, blocking us out. Our shoes crunched the twigs and pine needles. Rothman was gone—out of sight. The golf cart was gone too. We wove in and out of trees, passing blue flags, and then wound around a red one.

Suddenly the path widened, and I flew past two runners. Ky came with me. Together we picked off another, putting us right behind the Marion trio. Beyond the shadowy cover of the trees I saw light—and a glimpse of the leader. She disappeared. I knew she was on the little bridge. Each plank made a *clunk* as her feet landed on them. The sounds came quickly; she was moving fast.

I had to get past this barrier now or get caught behind them on the bridge. Swinging to the outside, I shot between a tree and a Marion runner, scraping my left arm on the bark of the trunk. I found another gear, racing in front of the last two. They seemed surprised and done in.

I listened for Ky to follow. Heard a groan. I knew it was Kyesha. *She's been elbowed by one of those Amazons from*

Marion. Pissed, I found another gear, churning my legs as fast as they would let me.

Jake was at a blue flag leaning over the fence as I approached, exactly where Coach told him to be. "Drive those arms straight ahead!"

As I came to the bridge, there were Dad and Ky's father. They'd found an open spot in the fence and raced across the course along with maybe a couple dozen people. Now, all of them shouted advice to their runners. But I heard Dad and Mr. Hendrix above the others.

"Come on, Cassie! Come on!" screamed my dad.

"Not far to go!" yelled Ky's dad as he ran along the fence and hopped over a little stream.

I flew onto the bridge. My feet spanked the wood. I heard yells for Kyesha. *Good, she's still not far behind.*

I shot up the steep hill at the foot of the bridge. My legs felt like they were filling up with concrete as I searched for a second wind. It wasn't Monster Hill, but it might as well have been. I dug deep, attacking it like my worst enemy. Up and over, letting the incline pull me down.

Rothman was maybe fifteen yards ahead, kicking it out for the finish. I started my sprint for her. I was gaining. Ms. Simon screamed at the top of her lungs and so did my mom. Dad sprinted along the orange mesh fence. "Cass, you can catch her—dig for a little extra!"

Believe me, I was exhausted, but seeing them excited enough to wet their pants gave me a boost. However, the finish line got to Rothman before I could get to her. I came into the chute as the electronic timer flashed, "18.13." Second place. My best time ever—and by far my best finish ever.

As an official took me by the arm and walked me around, I checked the scrape; it was nothing. My breath came in bursts as my open mouth sucked in air and shot it back out. Sweat soaked my jersey and shorts. I glanced back at the finish. Ky was chasing two of the Marion blockers into the chute. She'd whipped a third Marion runner for fifth place. *She must be under nineteen minutes.* She moved through the chute and bent over, hands on knees. I walked to her and touched her back. She looked up and gave a weak handshake.

An official checked our numbers and told us our place along with a word of praise. Ms. Simon was waiting for our teammates to finish the stretch to the chute. My mother came over and hugged Ky and me. Normally, that would have embarrassed me, but I was too pooped. Ky straightened up. Her mother came over. "Kyesha, you did so well. River Bend's girls did wonderfully." Mrs. Hendrix removed Ky's glasses and started to wipe them off on her shirt.

My mom handed her a Kleenex. She told my mom thanks, then wiped the lenses and placed them back on her daughter's face.

Ky's dad came sprinting up, perspiration gushing off of him, his shirt and shorts soaked.

Ky took a step and staggered. She looked at her father. "Daddy, I'm 'bout to fall out."

"You'd better walk around a little to cool down, and then sit in the shade," said Mr. Hendrix to Kyesha.

"Yes, you'd better," agreed her mother.

Kyesha staggered again, and we all helped her walk a little, and then seated her under a big maple tree where she could cool in its shade. "I got elbowed—hurt my ribs," she said, her hand on her side.

Mrs. Hendrix raised Ky's jersey and gently pressed on her rib cage.

"Ow!" Ky flinched.

"Someone find me some ice," said Mrs. Hendrix.

I fanned Ky with a towel. Mom returned with ice and a bottle of water for Ky and me, each of us gulping.

"I think you just have some bruised ribs," said Mrs. Hendrix as she took the towel from me, wrapped it around the ice, and placed it against Kyesha's ribs.

Emily Lutker ran past and into the chute, for twenty-seventh. She was followed by Taylor and Destiny running side by side, places thirty and thirty-one. Samantha Peters finished in the forties, and it would be a wait for Kayla.

My dad and Jake ran up the incline and over to where we were. Both of them were drenched with sweat. My dad was about to burst. Grinning like an idiot, he ran up and hugged me. "Great job, Cass—just great! I am so proud of you!" His voice was raspy from yelling.

All right, Dad, enough already.

Jake was more reserved. I'd get my reward from him later.

Mom was on her knees beside Kyesha, taking turns with her mother as they held ice on her ribs. Ky's dad started fanning her with a towel.

Sucking on a bottle of water, I turned and peeked over my shoulder at Ms. Simon. Girls by the dozens kept running past us and into the chute. She had our score tallied. Believe me, when we met in her room last May, I never dreamed that we'd wind up scoring ninety-five in the Hoosier Classic. Now, we'd have to see what place we got. It looked good. I figured in my head. The Marion team probably had a better score with places one, three, four, and nine. It all depended on their fifth girl. Not even Ms. Simon knew when Marion's fifth runner came in. Girls jogged past us into the chute. Kayla straggled in—186th. A bunch of girls had dropped out along the way. Now, everyone waited as the officials added up and double-checked the numbers on the computer.

27

Second Isn't Good Enough

Weird. When you're always on the bottom, like we had been in cross country, you figure if you ever get near the top, you'd ride cloud nine. Then, you work your tail off and get so good that you can hang with the best, suddenly anything except first place is a letdown. That's how it was for me when they announced our team had gotten fourth. Sure, I figured that Marion had whipped us, but all five of Muncie's runners had finished in the teens, racking up a seventy-eight, while a high school from Anderson beat us by two lousy points. It was a heartache.

It didn't even make me feel any better when they called off my name for second place. Oh, the River Bend fans clapped and cheered, especially Dad and Jake, and that made me feel good, but I figured I could have whipped that top gun from Marion, Sarah Rothman. She hasn't lost a single race this year, but I really do believe I can beat her. For a brief moment, I felt I wasn't ordinary—wasn't *mediocre*. Then, it evaporated.

My teammates high-fived and talked trash as we got on the bus. Sitting with Jake, I gazed at the green-brown blur of beans and corn streaking past the window. Harvest was a month or so off. But my thoughts were not on Indiana fields; I was back on that golf course in Muncie.

I played the race over and over in my mind. *If I had gone after Rothman—dueled with her from the get-go—I could have burned her off my back in the stretch. 'Course, as Dad says, if the dog hadn't stopped to take a pee, she'd have caught the rabbit. Besides, if I had raced with Rothman from the start, my team might not have done so well. Not to brag, but they wouldn't have had me to pace them, and maybe they'd have slowed down.* Anyway, that's what I told myself. I wondered for a second, though, if I shouldn't be selfish and look out for me.

Jake slid his arm around me, and I turned my eyes away from staring out the bus window to look at him. I made up my mind that I should run for the team, not for just myself. Sounds corny, but looking at him made me decide that. *I've watched you give up a shot and pass the ball to someone closer to the basket—to a teammate with a better shot. I want to be like that as a cross country runner.* Then, I looked at Ms. Simon and caught her looking back at me. She smiled, as if to say, "I know—I know."

With my teammates yelling "We're mighty, mighty River Bend—R—B—H—S—High School Lady Coyotes!" over and over, I smiled back at Ms. Simon, and then turned back to watch the corn and beans as the bus passed the fields. *Jeez, Cassie, your team got fourth in the Hoosier Classic. You got second out of over two hundred runners. Let yourself enjoy it. You couldn't have imagined doing this well before.*

Still, I wanted to do better.

28

"I'll Just Say 'Coach'"

School seemed a little more interesting than usual—not quite as boring as other years. I think it was because of Ms. Simon—got me interested in Dick Francis's books, and then I started writing poetry and all.

Hey, know what? From now on, I'll just say *Coach* when referring to Ms. Simon. That's what I randomly called her one day, and everyone else started calling her that, too. I think she likes it. It just came naturally and seemed to be the right thing to call her.

Anyway, I guess Coach's influence just carried over into school. I mean, I studied pretty hard for my first test in English literature and made an A-. I'd call that a better than ordinary grade. My other subjects—biology, world history, trigonometry, Spanish II—were also going just fine. Oh, yeah, the principal announced on the P.A. system that we got fourth out of thirty-seven teams at the Classic. There was like total shock in the whole school.

Sherry Dumont is in my first-hour biology class, and when she heard the news, her jaw dropped open like a trap door. Then, she pulled herself together and made a face like an old farmer's fist. I loved it. We sure didn't need her on the team giving off negative vibes—and dragging tracks in the dirt with her big butt.

Jake and I kept right on dating. But with school, cross country, and harvest starting, there wasn't much time for us to be alone. Then, basketball started up, and it was like we were living on different planets. Before basketball practice started—and before he had to spend weekends helping his dad bring in the crops—Jake took me out either Friday or Saturday night. Sometimes both. We did a lot of talking, and a lot of other things, too. Now, don't get me wrong, I'm not saying that we had sex—like *all the way*. I'm also not saying we didn't; I'm just not saying. Truthfully, he's got more sense about this relationship than me. Anyway, he always seems to know when to yank me down out of the ozone. Enough said.

Our team was rolling right along, too. We ran against some nearby schools in three different triangular meets. That's where just three different teams run against each other. Jeez, did we ever surprise everyone. Guess they hadn't heard about our fourth place at the Classic. We won all three meets. Wasn't even close, which the other teams couldn't believe. And I kept the pink patch, but Ky was really pushing me, even with her sore ribs.

The team improved with every meet. Ky's mother said we were blessed. "The Lord has blessed these girls with His hand," she told my mom after we finished the last triangular meet, winning all five spots, first through fifth. Coach said the Lord had nothing to do with it. She chalked it up to training properly. But she didn't tell Mrs. Hendrix that.

Except for Marion High School, most of the schools around

us are small, and heck, we proved we could run with the big dogs, so we knew we could handle the schools River Bend's size. And the meets with small schools also gave us a good chance to practice running together like a team. Ky and I held up our pace just enough to let the other four keep with us, yet fast enough to pull them along to better times. But Kayla was always way back—out of it.

Actually, holding up was tougher for Ky than me. Sometimes she wanted to set a blistering pace for the others. I'd be forced to match her stride for stride so she wouldn't take away my pink patch. Sometimes we had to run away from the others after two thousand meters or so; I was bound and determined she wasn't going to beat me.

Coach kept right on working us. She added this workout she called "Up and Down the Ladder." Every once in a while, she'd have us sprint fifty meters, followed by a hundred meters, two hundred, four hundred, eight hundred, a mile, then repeat the whole process starting with the mile and ending with another fifty meters. The tough part was, she made us do all that running in the tall grass in Judd Overstreet's hilly south pasture, and gave us only a few seconds rest between each race. We ragged at her about it some, but it was making us even better.

Later in the season, Coach would give us our only break from practice when she took a day off school for her religion. "You've heard of 'Christmas and Easter Christians'?" she asked me one night in her apartment late last summer.

"Yeah, I've heard of them."

"Well, I'm a 'High Holidays Jew.' I don't go regularly but always show up for at least Yom Kippur, the Day of Atonement. I feel compelled to atone for my sins—ask forgiveness."

"Can't imagine what your sins are."

"Oh, I've got them." Then, she looked at me and said, "And I'm always there for my mother's *yarzheit*." She saw that I was puzzled. "The date commemorating my mother's death," she explained. I responded only with a nod, but I felt sad for Coach. *Now I know what Ms. Simon's poem was about,*" I told myself.

The night Coach got back from her Yom Kippur religious service, I would wind up over at her house. We'd have another one of our talks—an important talk.

As far as our studies, Coach also checked our grades twice a week. Each teacher is supposed to keep our current grade posted on the school's computer system. "Cross country is one thing," she lectured us, "but you're not here for that. You're here for academics." I wish I had a nickel for every time she preached that sermon. Once a week we all met over at her house to do our homework and generally goof around. While we were there, she'd meet with each of us individually, get into the grade system, and check how we were doing. Kayla was the only one who didn't show up regularly.

The week before the sectionals for the Indiana High School Cross Country Tournament, Coach worked us really hard—and we were thrilled to work hard. But our team was a little disappointed that Marion wasn't in our sectional; we wanted to prove we could whip Sarah Rothman and her teammates. But as my dad would say, our blood was up, and after getting our butts kicked for so long, we weren't letting this one get away, regardless of who was or wasn't in our sectional.

The top five teams would move on to the regional. Mississinewa High School is upriver from us and they hosted the sectional. It's a hilly course, but nothing was going to stop us. The adrenaline was rushing through every one of us Lady Coyotes—even Kayla—and from the get-go, it was a blowout.

Ky and I slowed it down for the first fifteen hundred meters so we could all run as a team. When she and I picked it up, Emily came with us, but Taylor and Destiny fell behind about five yards or so and paced each other. For the first half of the race only two runners from other schools separated Taylor and Destiny from us three Coyote front-runners, and then other runners caught and passed them.

Ky and Emily kept at the front with me through the first three quarters of the race as runners from other teams caught up and tried to stay with us. Ky, Emily, and I rounded a yellow flag together and kicked it out for the finish—four hundred meters away. We were side by side. Then Emily fell back and was caught by a couple other runners. Ky pulled ahead of me for an instant, and then I caught her, sprinted past and into the chute. She was right behind. Emily raced in a split second after three runners from other teams, putting her in sixth place. Taylor and Destiny overtook the two girls in front of them, but couldn't quite catch four others, coming in eleventh and twelfth with Samantha on their heels in thirteenth. Although Kayla tried, she fell way back. But the Lady Coyotes totally rocked. Champs in our sectional! And with our top five scoring a thirty-two!

Not only did the *River Bend Bugle*, our weekly town paper, run a spread on us but the Marion *Chronicle-Tribune* even sent over a reporter and photographer. The photographer took the team's picture with the trophy, and the reporter wrote a huge spread—page one and page two of the sports section—on how we dominated our sectional. My dad said that it was uncommon for the *Chronicle-Tribune* to give that much space to a little school like us, especially for cross country.

Of course, the Marion High's girls' cross country team also won their sectional. Experts say they're the best team in Indiana, but for once we pushed them off the sports page. For a while, Marion's Lady Giants had been getting huge coverage for a cross country team. Two or three times a week for a month the *C-T* ran a big story on the Lady Giants, giving a bunch of space to Sarah Rothman and how she has been going "great guns"—"is unbeaten"—"has best times in the state"—"sets

155

course records"—blah, blah, blah. Point being, I guess all the interest in cross country spilled over onto us. Of course, basketball season is rolling around, so lately the newspapers have been giving a lot less coverage to cross country and more to basketball.

Anyway, getting back to the *C-T*, that reporter wrote about my pink patch and what it stood for. He even asked us what made this season so much different from our other seasons. I told him that was easy—Coach Simon.

Then, he turned to Coach and said, "Ms. Simon, I understand that this is only your first year of coaching."

"That's correct."

"Have you taught long?"

"No," she answered, "this is just my second semester."

"Late bloomer, huh?"

"Late to teaching. I was a chemist for the pharmaceutical industry for three years."

The reporter wrinkled up his forehead. "Why would you leave a job like that to teach chemistry—in River Bend?"

The entire team looked at Coach and waited for her answer. She hesitated. "Let's just say, I felt like I needed to do something different."

"Well, this sure is different," said the reporter.

Coach smiled. "Yes, it is."

We were celebrities. Even a few basketball fans read about us. They stopped me downtown on the street and complimented me. I mean, everything was so cool, and we expected it to stay that way—but it didn't.

The next morning, I rushed out to get the Marion *Chronicle-Tribune* off of the porch. When I unfolded the paper, an envelope with my name on it fell out. Inside was a note. I stood on the porch in my pajamas and read, "Your team won't last and neither will that bitch you call a coach."

I looked around. No one was in sight. I hurried to my room. My mom and dad were still asleep. I closed the door quietly and sat on my bed breathing hard as I stared at the message.

At last I got up and shoved it into a desk drawer. *Should I tell someone?* I decided not to. I didn't want to upset Coach.

29

Love Trouble

Love? What is it? Mr. Bouton says it's like quicksilver. You can't pin it down. Basketball practice had started the first week of October, and Jake cut back on keeping stats for Coach Simon. Anyway, I was getting ready for the regional meet, and he was always practicing or harvesting, so we didn't get to see each other all that much, except when he picked me up early in the morning for school.

After basketball started, Jake's body was on earth but his mind was somewhere out in space. Like the morning I asked him how his mother was when he came to drive me to school. She'd had her wisdom teeth yanked out the day before and had a bad reaction to some pain medicine.

"Is your mom feeling better?" I asked as I slammed the door on the truck and clicked the seat belt. But he just stared straight ahead like he was all by his lonesome. He stepped on the accelerator and we headed for RBHS. Again I asked, "How's your mom?" And again he just stared onto the road. So I poked him in the ribs.

"Hey!" he yelled as the truck swerved. "Why are you doing that?"

"Sorry," I said, "But I've asked you twice about your mom."

"What about her?"

"Is she feeling better?"

"Yeah, she's okay," he answered.

"Well, you could've answered me the first time," I snapped.

"Whatever," he mumbled, and then continued staring straight ahead in silence. It had been like that for a few days. Jake would bark at me, and I'd be locked and loaded to fire right back.

It wasn't just Jake. I was obsessed with cross country just like he was with basketball, and truthfully my brain and body weren't always connected either. All our energies were being poured into our sports. He was by himself in his world, and I was off in mine. The two of us would be riding along in his truck, or he'd be walking me down the hall, when I'd find myself looking at him and thinking, *Who is this person with me?* Jeez, it about drove me nuts. The excitement we'd once had seemed to be gone, which left a big hole—like finding out there's no Santa Claus when you're a kid.

Anyway, one day after practice, I dragged my carcass over to the gym and sagged into a spot on the bleachers. The cross country team had just finished a hard workout to get ready for the regional, and I was pooped. I rested an elbow on a knee, then propped my chin on my fist, like that statue *The Thinker*. Jake scrimmaged with the team, tossing in shots from all over. Every practice before, the sight of him dominating everyone on the court had sort of turned me on, but today—nothing. Sitting there, I battled with doubt. I tried to convince myself that it was just a phase. That it would soon pass like a bad meal. But the harder I fought the emptiness, the less feeling I seemed to have for Jake. Mr. Bouton is right: Denying your feelings makes things worse—gets your negative juices surging.

That evening after supper, Mom and Dad had gone into Marion. I had finished my homework and was just loafing. Honestly, I was enjoying doing nothing—with no one. I was still pretty bushed, and besides, my periods had never stopped like some women runners' periods do, and I was flowing heavy and feeling crampy. All I wanted was for everyone to just leave me the hell alone. But about seven o'clock, here comes Jake knocking at my door. I could tell by the rhythm of his *ratta-tatta-tat. God, that annoys me!*

I pried myself off the couch and let him in. We kissed. Nothing. We sat on the couch, and he put his arm around me. Nada. We started making out. Zero. Then, just like that, we stopped. For a minute there was stone cold silence, then out of the blue, Jake turned to me and uttered the four little words no one in a relationship—even a dead end relationship—wants to hear: "We have to talk."

I glanced down, and then at him. He rested his folded hands in his lap and sat there staring at them. He was like a stranger to me, just some random guy.

"Talk about what?" I finally asked. But I knew.

"Oh, I don't know."

Come on, spit it out, I thought.

"We never spend any time together anymore."

"We're together now," I said.

"Yeah, but you're always running. Sometimes even on the weekends after you've already run in meets."

"Well, the regional is a week from this Saturday. I think it's pretty important." I started a slow boil. "Really, whose fault is it that we're never together? You're always practicing basketball."

He glared at me. "That's different."

"Oh, I get it. Cross country isn't basketball—especially girls' cross country."

"Hey, I never said that." He pointed his finger in my face. "Don't you put words in my mouth!"

"I wouldn't dare try; my words would just get lost in that big hole of yours!" I shoved his finger aside. "Get that outta my face."

He jumped up, holding his glare. "If you're going to act childish, then I'm leaving."

Now, I was really pissed and shot to my feet. "You're jealous! Can't stand it that I'm getting a little attention."

"That's ridiculous," he said. "That's just not true."

"Yes, it is."

"No, it's not."

"Well, I think it is. My mother told me all about the *male ego*."

"Your mother," he snorted.

"Hey, don't you say anything rotten about my mom. Leave her out of this." I gave him a shove.

"What? You're the one who dragged her into this." Silence. "This isn't going to work out. I can't be involved with someone who's married to . . ."

"What? What were you going to say?"

". . . married to cross country," he said.

"Well, at least cross country makes me feel good."

"Fine! We're through!" he shouted. "I feel better already! Goodbye!" He stomped out, slamming the door behind him.

Crazy. This awful feeling suddenly came over me, and I wished I could roll time back to when Jake had walked into the house. I ran to my room, and like a wimp, buried my face in my hands and bawled until my mother and father came home from shopping. Mom and I talked for the next two hours.

30

"This Creep Could Be Dangerous"

That night I concluded that Jake Nader wasn't the only guy in River Bend. Hey, kinda like the old song goes, "Got along without him before I met him, I can get along without him now." Right? You betcha. Sure.

Come Wednesday I was making every effort at being a *free* and *independent* woman. Word flew over the River Bend telegraph. Everyone buzzed. But I didn't care. Anyway, that's what I told myself.

At school, Ky and Samantha Peters ran right up to me. "Jeez, what a bummer," Samantha said. "Jake dumping you like that. I'm so sorry."

Ky scolded her for her lack of tact.

"Save your sympathy," I snapped. "*I* dumped *him*."

"Right," answered Samantha. Neither one of them believed that.

"Besides, he's not the only fish in the pond," I said.

"But, Good Lord, he's one big, gorgeous catch. That's for sure. What a hunk," Samantha sighed. *What a dork*, I thought.

Ky nudged Samantha back to earth with an elbow in the ribs.

"Oh, yeah," said Samantha. "Hey, you'll get over him—eventually."

"I'm over him now," I answered, then walked away.

"See you at practice," Ky hollered.

I gave her a nod over my shoulder. *Let 'em talk*, I told myself. But I could have just died when Jake came strolling down the hall with Marlo LaPorte. "Marlo the Magnificent"—and as I mentioned several miles back, she is *magnificent*—and a cheerleader. *Damn!*

Everyone had a comment about us splitting up. Megan Willett—the girl whose dad has the stash of porn—was waiting at the door of English literature class and said, "Oh, God, Cassie, you must be devastated about Jake dumping you."

I stuck my finger in her face. "Hey, I dumped him! Got it?"

"Yeah, all right. Fine. Whatever makes you feel better," she said before beating a path to her seat.

That Megan about made me puke. *Hope her old man goes blind lookin' at those raunchy pictures and videos.*

No matter where I went, Jake and Marlo turned up. Each time I set my jaw, pointed my nose toward the ceiling, and walked past them like they didn't exist. But I boiled. *The nerve of that guy, flaunting Marlo. The dirty . . . Never mind.*

What hurt the most was the biggest dance of the year was coming up. The Hooptown Hoedown was that very Friday. I know, it's corny; only a place like River Bend, Indiana, would have a dance called the "Hooptown Hoedown," but it's a really big deal celebrating the opening of basketball season. It's like a cotillion—fancy dresses, tuxedos, and everything. Mom and I had already picked out and bought my dress over in Marion. But, as always, it looked like Cassie Garnet would be staying home without a date, while Jake and Marlo danced it up, made out, and God knows what else.

Maybe some other guy will ask me. Let's face it, Nader's better looking than any other guy in town—and popular. Going with him has definitely raised my stock with River Bend's guys. Down deep, though, I didn't want to go with another guy.

The news spread so fast that Mr. Bouton stopped me in the hall. "Cassie, how's everything going?" he asked in this pitying tone of voice. He just stood there waiting for me to pour my heart out or something. But he wasn't fooling me. What I thought he was really asking was, *How is everything with a mediocre girl like you, who was unbelievably lucky to have gone with Jake Nader—the best looking guy in River Bend—but who's finally come to his senses and dumped you for the magnificently beautiful cheerleader, Marlo LaPorte, who should have had him in the first place? Huh, how are you, Dear?*

I was so paranoid. But I answered him with one of my father's expressions, "Oh, I'm just peachy keen." Truthfully, I didn't feel anything like I had Monday when our relationship had its blowout. Now, I missed Jake.

That Wednesday night in October, two days after the breakup, I went over to Coach's. She'd canceled practice and hadn't been at school. I wanted to check if she was okay. It was dark, but I spotted Coach getting out of the Porsche as I walked up. She greeted me with a "hi" and shut the car door. "Let's go inside. I can finally eat," she said, then hurried past me. I hustled to keep pace.

Once inside, she asked if I wanted something to eat. I said, "No." She flung open the refrigerator and started setting dishes onto the counter, then filled a plate and stuck it in the microwave, taking time only to look up and ask again if I was hungry. I shook my head. Coach sat down. Her plate was loaded like a buffet, and she began gobbling.

She swallowed, and then explained, "Cassie, you'll have to excuse me. Took a personal day—Yom Kippur."

"I've heard of it. Don't know anything about it."

She took another big bite, and then swallowed hard. "Holiest day of the year for Jews. Fast and pray. . ." Another gigantic bite. "Ask forgiveness for sins. You know, I told you about it."

Like I said a while back, I couldn't imagine what sins she had committed; figured it was none of my business anyway.

"As I've said, I'm just a Rosh Hashanah and Yom Kippur Jew, but I do observe *those* holidays—especially Yom Kippur."

"So you haven't eaten all day?"

She shook her head, "No—fasted." She gobbled up the rest of the food and washed it down with a glass of water, then got up and set the plate and glass in the sink. Coach sat back down in a chair across from me. She leaned back and stretched her arms full-length over its sides. "I spent all day at the synagogue in Marion. They were going to have a *break-fast*." A puzzled look crossed my face. She explained. "A meal that breaks our twenty-four-hour long fast." I nodded.

"But I couldn't stay. Papers to grade." She motioned to a stack sitting on her desk beside the computer.

"Starved, huh?" I asked. *Wow! Not eating all day! Coach sure has the will power. I couldn't do that.*

"Let's just say I had a healthy appetite." She smiled. There was a pause as she studied me.

"Just dropped by to talk a little cross country, but if you have work. . ."

"No, I have time to talk." Coach knew I wasn't there about cross country; she'd heard the news. So, we made a little chitchat, and then I spilled my guts. She sat and listened. When

I wound down, she told me, "Cassie, we learn a lot when we take detours in our lives. Maybe this is just a detour that you and Jake are on. Maybe you'll get back together. Maybe not. If you don't, you'll adjust. Trust me, Cassie, I've taken my share of detours, and I've always found my way back."

"I've learned my lesson," I told her. "I'm done with men because they're dorks."

She laughed. Not a mean laugh, but an understanding laugh. "So you're not going to have any more to do with men, huh?"

"That's the plan."

She laughed again. "Well, Cassie, to paraphrase a famous poet, 'The best laid plans of mice and *women* go awry.'" She explained that a guy named Robert Burns I learned about in lit class wrote something like that a long time ago, but she didn't have to tell me what it meant. I knew that *my plan* was BS. As my dad says, I was just blowing smoke. Ms. Simon knew it, too.

"When it comes to the person you love—the person you want to . . ." Her voice trailed off into silence. I looked at her, a little embarrassed. Then she picked up her comment. "Loving someone—really loving another person—can fuzzy a person's thinking."

I nodded like I understood. And I did understand her point that love—or at least infatuation—can mess with your head—screw up how you think about things.

Like, how I was crazy about Jake, and then got all worn out and felt no passion, then regretted it when we broke up. My emotions all tangled.

I got the feeling, though, that Coach wasn't talking about people in general, but was speaking of herself—about her own relationship with someone or something in her life. I didn't pry, but I could not help but wonder.

The conversation had slowed, and we sat in silence. "Excuse me a minute, Cassie." Coach got up and went over to the laptop and sat down. "I want to check my e-mails, if you don't mind."

"No, go ahead."

She opened the computer, logged in, and locked her eyes on the screen, and then leaned back and drew in a deep breath.

"Is something wrong?" I asked.

"I'm not sure."

I got up and looked over her shoulder. There, a message from the person calling themselves "Righteousness," that Ms. Simon had told Jake and me about coming back from the track meet shouted, "BE SURE YOUR SINS WILL FIND YOU OUT!—NUMBERS 32:23."

"What's Numbers 32:23?" I asked.

Holding her eyes firmly on the screen, Ms. Simon said, "It's a verse from the Bible. She motioned over her shoulder with her right thumb. "That figure attached to the doorframe—a mezuzah—has a different verse from the Torah—the Bible—inside."

"Oh." Then I spotted another message written in much smaller font at the bottom of the email: "Evil people like you should either repent or get out of River Bend."

"Coach, how many of these have you gotten?"

She turned and looked at me. "Almost one a week since summer vacation started."

"What! Coach, you need to go to the cops about this right away!"

She shook her head. "It wouldn't do any good. I have already had a friend of mine—a regular computer genius—check this out. The IP is not traceable. He calls it a spoof IP. The police wouldn't be able to do anything. Besides, it would only give this person attention and make him or her think it's getting to me. I refuse to cave in—give them the satisfaction."

"But, this creep could be dangerous!"

"I don't think so. Just some crank. Every town has at least

one, and River Bend is no exception." She closed down the computer and walked back to the chair. "I would ask, though, that you not say anything about this to anyone."

"Okay, if that's what you want."

Then she changed the subject, acting all cheery like it didn't bother her. But it sure did bother me. Someone was trying to run Coach out of town, and every time I thought about that, panic overcame me. *Should I tell her about the note stuck in the newspaper or not?* I debated with myself, finally deciding that Coach was probably right: just a crank who wanted attention.

Eventually, though, our conversation returned to Jake and me—and men in general. Yet, the thought of those e-mails kept popping up and gnawing at me. What could I do, though? Nothing. She'd sworn me to secrecy.

31

Making Out In The Mississinewa

It was during breakfast three days after the breakup, and one day before the big dance, that I decided if Jake could strut all over school with his arm around Marlo LaPorte, then I wouldn't wait for someone else—I would find another guy. When Jake and I had been together, primping had become an obsession with me, but since we'd gone our separate ways, I had sort of let myself go. Hey, but no more moping. Two could play this game. So I set the bowl of unfinished Cheerios in the sink and headed to my room for a makeover. Less than an hour later—and running late for my first class—hair, nails, and makeup were perfect. As for my figure—well, a girl can only do so much.

Off to school I rushed. I even stooped to being a tease. God, now I look back and hate myself for that. But so what? Flirting is natural. Right? Found out I'm pretty good at it, too. In the meantime, Jake and Marlo kept putting on their public displays of affection. Holding hands, walking by my locker with their

171

arms around each other, sucking face in the parking lot. And wouldn't you know it, the first—and only—guy to show me any attention was that pervert Stag Applebee.

He slithered up to me and said, "Hey, Cassie baby, heard you and Nader ain't a *thing* anymore. Want to go out? I'll show you a good time." Stag not only gives me the creeps, he scares me. But I refused to show it.

"No thanks," I said. "I'm interested in a date, not a wrestling match."

He shrugged and walked away.

Finally, after I had practically thrown myself at him, Zach Hatfield, a lineman on the football team, phoned me Thursday night and asked me if I'd go to the Hooptown Hoedown with him. I told him yes. I'd show *Mr. Basketball* a thing or two.

So the dress I'd paid all that money for, expecting to wear when Jake took me to River Bend's biggest dance of the year, I wore with Zach Hatfield as my date. But there was no excitement, only revenge. Please don't get me wrong; Zach's a nice guy. But you know. I couldn't let Jake strut around with Marlo on his arm and not do something about it.

I started off dancing with Zach; after all, he brought me. But I spent most of the time spying on Jake and Marlo. Twice I caught Jake looking over at us. I really put on a show, dancing it up with Zach. Then, near the end of a slow number, Jake cut in on Zach. My heart raced and I struggled to breathe. Zach stepped aside.

"I see you've lowered your standards, going out with football players."

"No, Jake," I said, trying to be calm. "I've moved up several notches, thank you very much." Then I added, "Zach's very nice."

"Nice?"

"Yes, very nice."

"Yeah, so is my prize Holstein, but I wouldn't go out with her."

"Could have fooled me," I said, glancing over at Marlo as she danced with Josh Nitram, the Coyotes' point guard. "Seems that your prize Holstein might be an improvement."

I suddenly felt his hand press hard against my bare back, moving me closer to him as we slow danced. *Good God in Heaven.* My heart was going to bust through my chest as we stared into each other's eyes; him looking down and me up. I smiled, and in a breathy voice I kept up the charade. "Really, Jake, don't you think you could do better than her?"

The band had stopped playing. We had stopped dancing, but kept holding each other. Zach came up to us. "If you don't mind, Nader, I'd like my date back now."

My breath came in little bursts. Jake and I were pressed so closely I thought they'd have to use the jaws of life.

"Yeah, sure, she's all yours, Hatfield."

We peeled apart but held a lingering stare. Good God, my engine was revved and ready.

The Hooptown Hoedown went on. I didn't say another word to Zach until the last dance was over. Then, I suddenly suggested to Zach that we go down by the Mississinewa and park. He didn't argue.

There was a big, bright harvest moon. I studied it. *Jeez, the moon looks like it did the night Stag Applebee brought me out here.* That scared me, so I pushed it out of my mind.

Cars and trucks were parked up and down the riverbank. The full moon helped me find Jake's truck. "Park over there," I ordered. Zach did as he was told and pulled in close enough to the red Chevy pickup that we could have reached out and keyed it.

I stole a peek. My heart sank. Jake and Marlo had the seats back, and Marlo wasn't letting the cup holder stand in her way.

With my eyes on the pickup, I yanked Zach to me and laid a sloppy one right on his mouth. Startled, Zach hesitated, but he shook off the shock and kissed me back. We made out like a couple of dogs in heat. At first, I was getting nothing much out of it, but then I glimpsed Jake sitting up, jacket and tie off and shirt unbuttoned. He was glaring at us as Marlo strained to get him to lie back down with her. Now, I was so heated up, my horns nearly shot through the roof of Zach's car, and I went back to work kissing and caressing Zach.

Knuckles rapped against glass on the driver's side. "What the. . ." Zach jerked his head away from my neck. I looked up and smiled. It was Jake. He threw open the door. "Hey, what's the idea, Hatfield, parkin' here and spying on Marlo and me?"

"What's it to ya? Think you're a detective or something?" I said.

"We're not spying on anyone, Nader. Got as much right parkin' here as anyone, including you—hot shot." Zach turned back toward me, and I kissed him with my eyes wide open on Jake.

"Come back in the car, Jake," begged Marlo, her head hanging out the window. "Forget about them."

"Just wait a minute!" Jake barked at her. "Hatfield's going to get out of here with Cassie before I get back into the truck."

"We're not going anywhere," I said.

"That's right," agreed Zach. "You get the hell outta here." He jumped out of the open door.

A head shorter, but thick and muscular, Zach clenched his fists and stood looking up in Jake's face. "What's it matter to you? It's over with you and Cassie—she dumped ya!"

"She dumped me? Like hell she did!"

"Yeah, I dumped you."

Jake pushed past Zach and stuck his head in the car. "What a lie!"

Now, Marlo was out of the truck. Hair messed up and dress cockeyed. "Yeah, what's it matter to you, Jake?"

Jake started to pull his head out of the car but cracked it against the inside of the door frame.

"Ouch! Damn!" He rubbed it, and then yelled for Marlo to get back into the truck.

A chorus of honking came from the other cars—lovers interrupted by the uproar.

"Well, Jake, what does it matter? We're through, aren't we? What's it to ya?" I asked. Tormenting him was just plain fun.

He looked back into the car. "You shut up in there! It's plenty to me!"

God, I was so excited. I scrambled over to the driver's side.

Zach grabbed Jake and spun him around. "Hey, Nader, don't tell her to shut up!"

"Screw you!" Jake shoved Zach.

More honking. Car doors slamming. Couples scurrying toward us.

Zach tore into Jake. The two swung wildly, mostly hitting nothing but autumn air, but every now and then landing a blow. Then Zach tackled Jake. The two tumbled to the edge of the bank and rolled around like a couple of groundhogs trapped in a drain pipe. A huge crowd gathered around them, yelling first for one, then the other. I rushed from the car and pushed my way to the front along with Marlo.

Now, the two gladiators were on their feet circling each other, fists up and ready. Jake swung and missed. Zach smacked him in the right eye. Jake grabbed the right side of his face—his cheek and eye socket. Then Zach drove a right-handed fist into Jake's nose. Blood shot out, and down tumbled Jake, butt over elbows into the chilled water of the Mississinewa.

Oh, God, I thought, *I hope he's not seriously hurt.*

Fortunately, the river was down and running slowly. Jake

rose and stood knee deep in the water flowing past him. His white shirt was spotted with red polka dots as drops of blood dripped onto his chest. Jake blotted his bloody nose with his shirt sleeve, and then started up out of the Mississinewa, slipping on the bank and back into the river.

I rushed to him. "Jake, are you all right?" I said, wading into the river, then wrapping my arms around him and his soaked collar. Ignoring the blood, I pulled him down to me and we kissed.

"Hey, what the. . . you're my date," said Zach.

Jake and I kissed even harder. Actually, I felt kind of bad for Zach. He'd been a good sport, and I'd used him. But an apology would have to wait. Right then, I was busy. I mean, like my dad says: All's fair in love and war.

Marlo came down the bank and splashed her way into the river. "Jake, do you mean to tell me that you still care about her?" Some in the crowd were laughing, others were clapping and cheering. Jake and I continued to kiss. "You do, don't you? You haven't really dumped her. You still like her!"

Duh.

Marlo turned and struggled to get up the bank. "I've never been so disrespected in my life!" Zach came down and helped her. She charged into the crowd, and then turned to Zach. "Will you take me home? I can see that *lover boy* will have a new passenger."

"Ooh!" went some in the crowd. Others—the guys—snarled and hissed. "Cat fight!" someone yelled. Still others made *dirty* comments.

"Be careful, Nader, she's a hot one," said a drunk Stag Applebee, staggering to the water's edge.

Jake and I barely noticed.

32

"We Did Some Talking, Too"

The water was cold, but at first we didn't really care. Eventually, though, we caught a chill, let go of each other, sloshed out of the Mississinewa, and struggled up the bank. The crowd parted like the Red Sea for Moses, kids cheering as Jake and I scampered to his truck, my soppy dress dripping all the way.

"Let's get out of here," Jake said, wiping the blood from his face with a wad of napkins he grabbed from the glove compartment. His nose had stopped bleeding, so he tossed the clump of bloody napkins out the window. He jerked up the seats, turned the ignition key, revved the engine, and then switched on the heater. But even with the hot air blasting into the cab, I couldn't stop shivering.

Jake looked around. "Here." He reached into the back seat and pulled a huge parka to the front. "Let's wrap this around you. Dad keeps it handy in case the weather turns on him while he's out mending fence."

I hesitated.

"Don't worry, it's clean. Mom washed it, and Dad hasn't worn it yet this fall."

"Won't mind, will he?

"Heck no." Jake wrapped the parka around me.

But the parka wasn't helping either, as my high-priced dress clung to me like an icy sheet. "I—am—free—zing." My teeth chattered on every syllable. Suddenly, I threw back the parka. "Un—zip—me!"

"What?

"Quick—un—zip—me!"

Jake did as ordered. I grabbed the hem of the dress with both hands, raised my butt off the seat, and pulled the dress over one shoulder, but got the other shoulder and my head wedged between each side of the waist band. "Help me!" Jake made a feeble attempt to assist as I tugged with all my might. "Harder!" He put a little muscle into it, and together we got it to slip past my shoulder and over my head. I heaved the fancy dress into the back. Then, in only my bra and bikinis, I buried myself in the parka and leaned into the heater to trap the warmth. I sat that way for maybe a minute when it hit me that we weren't going anywhere—still idling in park.

The moonlight struck Jake's face; he was gawking at me wide-eyed. "Hey, good-lookin', there's room in here for both of us." I grinned and quickly opened then closed the parka. He was breathing in heavy bursts. So I let the parka slide down. Now, I wasn't cold anymore.

The other couples had either meandered back to their cars

and trucks, or pulled up onto the hard road, heading for other places.

Jake leaned down to kiss me. I flung my arms around him, stroking the back of his neck as our lips melted together. He caressed my bare back, fumbling to unsnap my bra.

"Wait!" Jake jerked away as I reached behind me with both arms, fingers ready to release myself from the bra. It fell down. Then, he whispered, "I can't."

"What?" I stopped with my arms still behind me. I brought my arms around, crossing them over my bare breasts.

"I gotta get out of these wet clothes," he said.

"That's what I've been trying to do—get you out of your clothes." I chuckled, and then cleared my throat.

"I can't do this. Let's get out of here—ride around," he said.

I sat staring at the moonlight shimmering on the lazy Mississinewa. "I have to know something."

"What?"

"Is it me? Is there something wrong with me?"

Jake faced me. "No! Of course not. God knows I want to do it."

"Then, why don't we—do it? I'm ready, willing, and able—for sure."

"Do you have protection with you?" he asked. "I don't."

Damn, wouldn't you know it? I've been packing a condom around ever since Coach's talk, and now that I need it, I don't have it. "No, I don't."

"Cass, I don't want to take a chance. Don't want to get you pregnant. Don't want the responsibility."

"Hey, I don't want that either," I said, pulling the parka around me. "Okay, let's just drive around and talk."

"I want to get into some dry clothes first," he said. "And you can't ride around like that." He slid his arm around me, drawing me toward him.

"No, I can't ride around like this." I laughed.

Before shifting into reverse, Jake switched on the dome light and checked his banged-up eye and nose in the mirror.

"I'm really sorry Zach slugged you," I said, reaching up and gently touching the red area, causing him to flinch a little.

"Forget about it. It's nothin.'" Jake turned off the light, backed the truck around, and headed for my house. When he saw the lights on at my house, he freaked out. "Jeez, what are we going to tell your folks?"

"Just calm down. Stay in the truck. I'll do the explaining."

When I pranced into the house wrapped in a parka, wearing nothing but my underwear and toting the soaked, blood-speckled dress along with my bra and shoes, Dad demanded to know, "What the hell is goin' on?"

But Mom told him to just simmer down. She tagged along as I headed for my room. Suddenly, I turned, dropped the dress, shoes and bra, and then threw my arms around her. She returned the embrace. "Honey, what happened?"

"Had a little mishap down by the Mississinewa. Jake brought me home."

She held me tighter. "Not hurt? No trouble?"

"No, Mom, I'm fine; there was no trouble. Just accidentally ended up in the river. It's runnin' low. Jake and I are going to ride around. Talk and ride around."

We let go of each other. My mother picked up the dress, fixing her eyes on the blood. She looked at me. "You sure everything's all right? Are you hurt?"

"Good, Mom. Everything is good. Promise."

"Be safe, Honey."

"I will, Mom." I kissed her cheek. She kissed me back.

As I started toward my room, Mom whispered, "Be careful." I sent her a little smile. "I will."

She quietly opened the door for me and walked away

carrying the wet clothes. I pressed it shut and stood for a moment studying the closed door, and then I took a quick shower, hopped into some dry things, fixed my hair and makeup, and headed out of my room. But before leaving, I took the condom out of my other purse and slipped it into my jacket pocket.

When I left, Mom and Dad were in the bedroom, but they were still up. A sliver of light peeked underneath the crack of the door, and I heard their voices.

I hopped into the truck, and we sped away.

Jake's folks were in bed. "Farmers and their wives are dead to the world by this hour," he explained. He sneaked in through his bedroom window and changed.

The two of us stayed out until 1:00 a.m., forcing me to shove away the guilt of breaking training, but it was worth it. I won't bore you with all that went on, but we did some talking, too.

33

Dim Outlook For The Lady Coyotes

By Monday, Jake's eye had gotten black where Zach slugged him and his nose was swollen a little. Actually, he was proud of it—gave him a tough look. I apologized to Zach for using him. He said that it was okay, that he'd driven Marlo home and they'd hit it off pretty well. He said they were going out on a "real date" that coming weekend. I'm not sure what he meant by a "real date," but no offense taken.

That coming Saturday was important to me, too. It was the regional meet, and Coach wanted us ready. But after lunch on Tuesday, I left the cafeteria feeling kind of weird. At practice that afternoon, Ky and I battled most of the way on the course, and I nearly got whipped by her. In fact, if she hadn't stumbled at the finish line, Ky would have wound up wearing *my* pink patch.

I collapsed and lay on the ground breathing like a race horse. Coach ran over to me and felt my head. "Cassie, you go over to my car right now. I'm taking you home."

I didn't disagree.

On the way over, Coach used her cell to call Mom. Mom met me on the porch, and I hadn't anymore than stepped inside than it hit me like a tsunami—gagging, puking, and other unpleasant bodily eruptions.

Mom took my temperature—102. It was after hours, and the River Bend Clinic was closed, so Mom called the physicians' answering service and asked for Doctor Randall to call her. A few minutes later the phone rang. "Sounds like the flu. It's been goin' around," Doctor Randall said. "Other than plenty of water and Motrin every four hours, we just have to let it run its course."

I prayed that no one else on the team would come down with it before the regional. Doctor Randall said that would depend. "If Cassie hasn't shared food or breathed directly on any of her teammates, maybe they'll escape this—maybe not."

Jeez, medicine is so *not* a science.

Then, what was his parting comment? Good guess. "Anyway, cross country is not basketball."

What's a girl to do?

Jake called later in the evening, but I didn't feel like making chitchat. Mom told him I was really sick with the flu. He wanted to rush right over. "Don't you dare," I heard Mom tell him. "We don't want you sick with this junk." It wouldn't have mattered if he had come over. By the next day he had it too. We lucked out, though—no one else on the cross country team came down with it. Mom smiled and cracked, "Shows who you've been *close* to." That night she and Dad both came in to check on me.

What bothered me most was whether or not I'd be on my feet and ready for the regional on Saturday. Coach called to see how

I was. Mom talked quite a while with her. Of course, I only heard Mom's side of the conversation, but cross country didn't seem to come up. By supper time on Wednesday I was feeling better, but mom insisted I stay home another day.

Late Thursday afternoon, Ky called and dropped a bombshell. "Destiny's off the team." Her tone was panicky.

I hesitated. "Off the team! For good?"

"Yes—for good."

My heart sank. Destiny had consistently run fourth or fifth. It would be next to impossible getting to state without her.

"What'd she do now?"

"She was driving." Ky breathed hard into the receiver, and I could hear her swallow.

"Driving?" I interrupted. "The law took her license away."

"I know," said Ky, "and she got picked up by the cops last night. Coach kicked her off the team. Cassie, are you going to be back for regional? We won't make it without you."

"I'll be back."

"Thank God."

What a bummer. After such a great season, here we might get knocked out of our first regional—wouldn't move on in the tournament—because of a few random germs and some lousy judgment. I didn't care if they had to lug me to the starting line, I was going to run.

On Saturday, the only one who wasn't a nervous wreck was Coach. I stewed about how the layoff would affect me. She encouraged us to relax and just run our race—stick close together as long as possible. Her pep talk made me feel more confident as we toed the starting line.

The gun went off, and I labored from the very first stride. I forced myself, turning it over extra fast, while at the same time battling fatigue. At the sixteen-hundred-meter mark, I was running just behind Ky trying to match her stride for stride, but she inched ahead with every step.

Then, with three hundred meters to go, she sprinted away like I was a statue. Ky raced into the chute third. I staggered in at eleventh, and then flopped down under a big tree. Emily raced in thirteenth, and Taylor came across in the low twenties. Kayla was nowhere to be seen. *But where's Samantha Peters?* I watched for her, but didn't see her come into the chute—didn't see her anywhere.

Ky sat down beside me as I looked all around. I didn't see Coach either. I leaned back against the trunk of the big tree. Now it was a waiting game. The top five teams would move on to the semi-state meet. God, I was so nervous as they added up the scores. At last they announced the results.

34

Down By The River Side

Samantha didn't come through the chute; she'd lunged and fallen just past the finish line, and Coach had helped her to the first-aid tent. As I struggled to pull on my sweats, Coach told me Samantha ran the race of her life—seventeenth! Good thing—we'd just squeaked through in fifth, enough to qualify us. Beat out the sixth place team by three points. We'd move on to semi-state. We hooted and hollered, chanted cheers, and high-fived coming home on the bus. I took off my pink patch and pinned it on Kyesha. But I vowed to win it back.

About halfway down the highway, my euphoria wore off, replaced by a slow boil that simmered inside of me all day. That night I tossed and turned in bed; couldn't get to sleep for the anger. Finally I dozed off, then jolted awake to dawn breaking through my bedroom window—and I was still thoroughly pissed. Throwing back the covers I scrambled out of bed, tossed on my clothes, and ran my toothbrush over my teeth.

As I headed for the car, I checked Mom and Dad's room. They were still asleep. So I slipped quietly into the crisp fall air then drove toward Destiny Berry's place, all set to rip her a new one.

She about wrecked our season. Probably did wreck it, considering she is off the team for good.

The car rocked and swayed as it bounced over grooves in the dirt lane leading up to the Berry place, a shack no more than fifty yards from the Mississinewa. In fact, the Berrys had to evacuate two times in the past decade because of flooding. Never fazed them, though. No sooner had the waters receded into the banks of the river than they traipsed home, cleaned up, and moved back in. Both times they'd made repairs with money from the government, and according to the latest news, the government people told Mrs. Berry that the next time the river got out of its banks they'd be on their own—no more taxpayer help. So, if they didn't want to lose everything in another flood, then they should head to high ground and stay there. But once a river rat, always a river rat. Mrs. Berry said the government could go "f" itself. This was a free country and she'd live where she wanted. So there they were, close enough to the Mississinewa that it lulled them to sleep each night.

I slammed the car door and mounted the steps, a series of wooden planks nailed to notched posts graduating toward the dilapidated building. The Berrys' car was sitting at the side of the house. I rapped on the screen door—once, twice, three times.

"All right—I'm coming!" a woman's voice yelled from inside.

The door opened and there stood Bridget Berry, Destiny's mother. A cigarette was propped between the fingers of her right hand. Her housecoat hung open over her thin body so that I could see that she wore only a matching blue bra and underpants underneath.

"What do you want?" she asked, almost snarled. She held the screen door open with her shoulder and ran the fingers of her left hand through blond hair—hair that had been pretty at some point in the past.

"I came to see Destiny."

"She ain't here."

"Hey, Bridget, get your carcass back in here. I ain't got all day," a man's voice came from the back of the house. It couldn't possibly be Destiny's father. He'd packed up and left Destiny, her two brothers, and Mrs. Berry way back when we were in grade school. Bridget works nights at a bar in Marion. I figured it was one of the guys she picked up over there.

Bridget turned and yelled, "Keep your shirt on! I'll be there in a minute!" She turned back and stared at me with glassy eyes.

"Where is she?" I asked.

"What do I look like, her social secretary? I don't know. She ain't been around much since she got in trouble driving with a suspended license. Try old man Van Winkle's place. She likes bird-doggin' the boys over there."

"All right, thanks." I headed down the steps.

"You tell her..." Bridget began but was interrupted by the man's voice coming from the rear.

"Get back here," he yelled.

"Ah, put a lid on it!" she screamed, then turned back to me. "Tell her she owes me for keeping the law from taking her to juvie the other night."

I nodded and left. *Poor Destiny, putting up with that mess.*

As I pulled out of the drive and headed toward town, I spied the broad spot by the banks of the Mississinewa where lovers go to park, make out—and do other things. I smiled when I thought about Jake and me standing in the river wrapped in each other's arms, soaked to the bone. But then I thought about Stag Applebee and stepped on the gas.

35

Destiny

Sunday is no different to Mr. Van Winkle than the other six days. He was already open and doing business by the time I got there. But Destiny wasn't there. Old man Van Winkle said he hadn't seen her for a couple of days. A few people were in the place having Sunday breakfast. They'd read in the Sunday *Chronicle-Tribune* about our team qualifying for semi-state. Everyone had to give his or her congratulations, but I didn't have time to bask in the praise. I thanked them and hopped back into the car.

I didn't have the foggiest where I would look next. Elrod's Quick Mart? She wasn't there. However, on the third trip through town, I spotted a lone figure huddled on the bleachers at the RBHS football field. It was Destiny. I just knew it.

I parked and walked over to where she was sitting, gazing off toward the horizon, her back to the morning sun. She was nursing a bottle of iced tea, and she took a swig as I sat down beside her. My anger had faded after seeing life back at the Berry place, so there wouldn't be any lecture coming out of my mouth. Neither of us said a word, and we sat there like that for probably five minutes. Then I spoke. "Destiny, why?"

She looked at me. "'Why' what? Come on, Cassie, it ain't really all that hard to figure out. I drove with a suspended license and got caught." She took a gulp of the tea and seemed to be searching for something to appear out of the horizon. But I guess she was looking out there just to look out there.

"I know *what* you did, Destiny. But *why* did you do it when you knew you'd be hurting the team?"

She turned away from her gaze and looked at me. "Cassie, sometimes stuff just happens." Then she looked straight ahead. We were quiet for another spell, and then without warning, the bottle slipped from her hands, dropping between the bleacher seats, glass shattering against a cement pillar, iced tea splashing the dirt. She buried her face in her hands and sobbed. I put my arm around her.

"Cassie, I didn't mean for anything bad to happen. Didn't mean to hurt the team. Cross country was the one thing keeping me in school. But sometimes you have to do things."

"What do you mean 'sometimes you have to do things'?"

"I can't say any more about it." She sniffed. "I just got caught driving when I wasn't supposed to be driving. Let's leave it at that."

"What really happened?"

"Cassie, I told you I can't say." Then, she wiped her eyes on her sleeve and drew her coat around herself. "Good luck to you girls. I know you'll do great at semi-state without me. I just need some alone time."

I'd started down out of the bleachers when Destiny said, "Cassie?"

I turned. "Yes?"

"I'm sorry."

I nodded, and then left her sitting there.

36

Snatched From Stag's Grasp

The only cure for a guilty conscience is making it right. That's what my dad always says, and I believe him.

I wasn't angry anymore, just bummed. Mom was fixing breakfast for her and Dad when I got back from talking with Destiny. She remarked about how I was up early, but didn't ask why. I volunteered that I couldn't sleep, then went and crawled back into bed, but still couldn't sleep.

About two o'clock Sunday afternoon, I was doing homework when Mom called me to the phone. It was Emily Lutker. I thought, *That's weird. A UC girl calling a commoner on a Sunday? I figured they all went to the country club in Marion in their leisure time.* But of all things, she wanted me to go running with her. *Maybe I can leave some of this funk out on the course.* So I said, "Yeah, okay. I'll call Kyesha—see if she's back from church and wants to go."

"No!"

Wait a minute. If Emily thinks she is too good to work out with Ky then she can shove it.

"It's not that I don't want to run with Kyesha. I just thought maybe you and I could run—run and talk." Her voice had an anxious tone.

I hesitated.

"It would mean a lot, Cassie—mean a lot for us to work out—together."

"Okay," I answered, "meet you at Elrod's in half an hour."

Emily was waiting across from the Quick Mart. I jogged up to her. She hugged me. *What's up with this?* "Thank you for taking the time to come out and run with me," she said, still holding me tightly.

"Yeah, that's okay. Glad to run with you." I pulled myself away. "We better get going."

A tiny smile crossed her lips, and then disappeared. She nodded. "Yeah, let's go."

As we trotted around the block, then stretched out, Emily went on and on about how she admired me so much—looked up to me. "Role model" and all that. *She's shoveling it pretty high. Why all this flattery?*

We started running the course. Not a fast clip; not a slow clip—maybe a little under seven-minute miles. Emily's chatter had stopped by the time we turned off the Marion Blacktop onto the gravel road leading to Monster Hill. She is tall with a long stride, and she picked up the pace, forcing me to lengthen my stride. We kicked gravel behind us as we shot up the Monster. By now, Emily was really pickin' 'em up and layin' 'em down, as my dad says. But when she got to the top of the Monster, she stopped and stood there panting with her head hanging.

"You all right?" I asked.

She looked at me, then walked off the road over to the fence and sank her back against a fence post. Tears started streaming down her cheeks.

What the . . .? "Emily, you sick—hurt?"

She shook her head.

"What is it?"

"I've done something really bad—wrong."

Jeez, all kinds of things hopped into my head. *Bank robbery? Mug an old lady? Kill someone?* "What is it?" I repeated, and then she spilled her guts.

Sobbing, Emily told me how she had gone out with Stag Applebee. A shiver ran through me. "Stag Applebee! He's a pervert!"

"I know," she said between sobs.

"What did he do to you?" I demanded as I took her by the shoulders, bringing her face to face with me.

Emily went on to tell me how he had taken her out a couple of times, got her a little buzzed, but didn't try anything.

"My mom and dad thought it would be okay for me to date him, his father being on the board of the club. I thought it would be a good thing. He was okay at first, but last Wednesday, he asked me to go for a ride with him. What's the harm? I thought." She swiped at her nose. "Dad was against it, school night and all, but Mom thought it was just dandy, 'cause . . ." She gave her nose another swipe. "'Cause Mom's always lecturing me about getting ahead with *'our kind of people.'*" Emily mocked her mother's words.

"What did Stag Applebee do to you?" I insisted.

"Nothing—thanks to Destiny, he didn't get a chance." Then, the rest of the story came out.

Stag had driven Emily down to the Mississinewa. When she realized what his plan was, Emily hopped out of the car and tried to run. But he caught her, forcing her to the ground, where

197

he tried to yank down her underpants and tried to have his way, except Destiny had heard the commotion. She came out of her house with a ball bat, smacked Stag across his head.

"Destiny kept yelling and swinging that bat until Stag raced for his car and peeled out, then she hurried back to me," Emily sobbed. "I was a mess—hair and skin all matted with mud, clothes dirty." But, as you can imagine, Emily was even worse off emotionally. She was afraid to move, afraid Stag was out there waiting for her.

"Finally, Destiny convinced me he was long gone. She took me up to her place. She tried to get me to go to the police. I refused." Emily turned and folded her forearms over each other, bracing them on the top fence wire. She buried her face in her folded arms. "I'm so embarrassed—humiliated," she whimpered.

"You're leveling with me? He didn't . . ." But before I could complete the question, Emily turned and shook her head, reassuring me. "He would have, though, if Destiny hadn't . . ." Another sob. "Now, she's jammed up because of me. The whole team is in a jam 'cause of me. Poor Destiny . . . ." Her voice trailed off into another whimper.

Emily pushed away from the fence and faced me. She told about Destiny continuing to argue with her about going to the police and showing them how she looked; Emily refused and said that her mother wouldn't understand, that she couldn't let her mother know. I was sure Emily was dead wrong about that. What mother would want a guy to get away with hurting her daughter? I couldn't think of any mother like that.

Emily told me how Destiny gave in. Let her shower. How Destiny washed and dried Emily's clothes, put her in an old jalopy, and drove her home. Then on the way back, Destiny got busted by one of the nine River Bend cops.

"Cassie, I just had to tell someone, and you're the person I thought of. What should I do?"

"Tell your parents—that's what you have to do."

"Oh, Cassie, I can't."

I put my arm around her and drew her to me. "Let's walk back to town. Clear your head," I told her. She nodded, and we walked to River Bend, neither of us saying a word. But when we got to Elrod's, Emily said, "Okay, if you'll come with me, if you'll be there, I think I can tell my mom and dad. Think I can."

"Of course I'll come with you," I answered. *Stag Applebee is a predator, and someone has to do something about him.*

37

An Upper Crust Girl Punks Out

It's hard to believe, having lived in River Bend all my life, but like I said earlier, I had never been inside a Snob Hill home, not even Taylor's, even though I'd been invited. As I said before, I just didn't feel comfortable. But there I was being introduced to Emily's UC parents, introduced by Emily, who was going to drop a bombshell on them any minute. I looked around at the high cathedral ceilings, fine wood floors and furnishings, and at the baby grand sitting in the living room.

"We are very glad to meet you, Cassie," Emily's dad said, extending his hand. Mr. Lutker firmly grasped my hand, informing me that he'd heard so much about me, had even rooted for me at the meets. I nodded and said thanks. A big Airedale bounced up to me, and Emily led the dog away then quickly returned.

Mrs. Lutker wasn't nearly as enthused about my presence as Mr. Lutker seemed to be. *UC through and through.*

The father gestured for me to sit on the sofa. I was actually afraid to—afraid I'd get something on it—then Mrs. Lutker would know for sure that this commoner wasn't *fit* for her palace. But I sat down anyway, taking one more look around before Emily broke the news. *My God, either these people have a lot of dough, or like Dad says, they're in debt up to their butts.*

"Can we get you something to drink?" asked Mr. Lutker.

"No, I'm good."

The mother gave me the stink eye.

All of these preliminaries were actually annoying me. I had a purpose for being in this Snob Hill house, and it wasn't to make chitchat. I looked at Emily. "Were you about to say something?" I asked her, prompting Emily to tell her parents what had happened with Stag—and Destiny.

Emily quickly said, "No, I wasn't going to say anything." Then she looked at her parents, who studied both of us carefully. She looked back at me. "We had a great run. Didn't we, Cassie?"

Dumbfounded, I stared at Emily, and then said, "Yeah, it was good while it lasted."

Then, Mrs. Lutker turned away and went to a bar in the corner. With her back to us, she poured a drink as she said, "Emily, I know you say you get something out of this cross country, but I can't imagine what it is."

"Oh, for God's sake, let her alone about it," said her father.

The mother pivoted and snapped. "Well, I think her time could be better spent doing something like…"

"Like what?" interrupted Mr. Lutker.

It was as though Emily and I weren't even there. Emily had

a look on her face that seemed caught somewhere between disgust and humiliation.

"I don't know, something different, something more . . . Oh, forget it." Mrs. Lutker turned away with a snort.

I don't want to be in this house any longer. "I have to go," I told Emily as I stood. But before I left, I thanked the Lutkers for inviting me in. Mr. Lutker apologized for the "scene." I acted like I hadn't even noticed. Mrs. Lutker didn't say anything; she had her face stuck in her drink. But I just couldn't leave without saying something to her. "Mrs. Lutker, I just want to let you know that Emily is a really good runner."

Emily's mother held her left arm across her chest, hand wadded into a fist and tucked under her right elbow, the glass gripped in her right hand. "Oh, she is, is she?"

"Yes, she is, Mrs. Lutker." I walked out of the living room of the big house with its high ceilings, fine floors, and pricey furnishings. Emily followed me to the front door, and as I walked into the autumn sunlight she said, "Cassie, I'm so sorry. I thought I could tell them, but I just couldn't." She hung her head. "Just couldn't."

"I know you couldn't," I answered. "See you at practice tomorrow."

"Okay, see you tomorrow. I hope you understand."

"I understand perfectly," I answered. Then I left. One thing I knew for sure. A girl didn't have to live in a shack by the Mississinewa to have a screwed-up home life. But there was still Destiny. She'd been handed a raw deal. Emily had dumped on her—and dumped the whole tale on me; now it was my burden to try to make it right for Destiny. I didn't even have to think about it; I headed for Coach's place.

38

Confessing To Coach

By the time I got to Van Winkle Estates and found Coach home, the sun was dipping in the west. Night would be coming on, and I didn't want my parents to send a search party out for me, so I didn't beat around the bush. Standing beside her as she sat at her desk, I raced through the whole story, emphasizing two things: Destiny had literally saved Emily, but Emily wouldn't do anything about Stag Applebee.

"You're sure about all of this?" Coach asked, a grim expression on her face.

"I'm positive. I believe Stag Applebee tried to rape Emily." I hesitated. "He'd do that kind of thing because . . ." My voice trailed off into silence.

Now I knew how Emily felt; it was painful to tell Coach what Stag had tried to do to me. Made me feel weak and vulnerable.

She must have sensed something coming, because she got up from the desk and touched my shoulder. "Cassie, what is it?"

I looked into Coach's eyes. "Because he tried to rape me."

Coach took me by the arm, led me to the sofa, and sat down beside me. She put her arm around me. As I gently cried, I told her what Stag Applebee had tried to do to me two years earlier. When I was finished, Coach picked up the portable phone, went into her bedroom, and shut the door. I couldn't hear the conversation, but she wasn't on the phone long. When she came out, she said, "Are you willing to go to the police?"

I nodded that I was. "But Emily won't tell the police. She won't even tell her parents."

"Have you told yours?"

I glanced down and shook my head.

"Then, after we've located Destiny—told her that she's back on the team—we're going to your house and you're going to tell your mom and dad what this guy tried to do to you."

39

"I'll Kill Him As Sure As Our Name Is Garnet"

As we drove to Destiny's, my mouth was dry and my pulse raced, but I knew that I was doing the right thing. Destiny was home by this time. Her mother's man-for-the-night was gone, and apparently, Mrs. Berry was dead to the world.

Destiny stepped out onto the porch. "I don't have anything to say—told you that this morning, Cassie."

"We don't expect you to say anything, Destiny," Coach responded. "We just came to let you know that I'm going to fight to get you back on the team."

Destiny gave us a skeptical look. "Just like that, no questions asked?"

Coach smiled. "That's right. No questions asked. I'll go see both the principal and superintendent tomorrow and make the best argument I can for you."

"And they'll listen to you?"

"I'll sure try to make them listen."

"We need you," I interrupted. "The team needs you."

Destiny burst into tears as she embraced Coach; she hugged me, too.

Coach said, "We know what happened with Emily."

Quickly I explained that Emily had told me the whole story that afternoon.

"Will you tell the police what happened?" asked Coach.

Destiny looked off toward the Mississinewa and nodded. "But it won't do any good."

"Yes, it will," said Coach. "You were there. You saw what he would have done to Emily if you hadn't helped her."

Destiny turned back toward us. "They're not going to believe me. I can tell you now that Emily won't rat on Stag. She's too afraid. So it will just be my word against Applebee's. Then, when Emily claims she's got no idea what I'm talking about, it will be my word—" She looked at Coach and me. "—and my reputation against a couple UCs from Snob Hill. No one will believe me."

Except for the slapping of the Mississinewa against rocks, there was silence, and then I said, "She's right. Emily won't budge."

"But Emily has the truth on her side. What's she afraid of?" asked Coach.

"Take your pick," I said. "Her mother, Stag Applebee, what people will say or think. Maybe she doesn't know why she's afraid. She's just afraid. But she will not own up to what happened. Destiny will look like a liar."

Coach's lips tightened. She nodded. "See you tomorrow, Destiny?"

"Yeah, I'll be at school early," Destiny answered. Then, we got into the car and drove away.

The ride home was miserable. Now, I knew how Emily felt. Telling my mom and dad what Stag Applebee tried to do to me was going to be hard, even if it was two years ago. I also felt guilty. Not because of the thing with Stag, but because earlier in the day I had thought less of Emily when she'd backed out. Talk's easy when you don't have to do the walk. Now I had to do the walk, and I felt like bellying up just like Emily. But I didn't.

With Coach sitting beside me at the dining room table, and Mom and Dad sitting across from us, I told them Stag Applebee had tried to rape me two years earlier. As I told it, I could see my Mom's eyes narrow with that get-even look and rage start to build in my dad until it had nowhere to go but out.

"Damn him to hell!" he yelled, jumping up from the table. He grabbed his car keys and started for the door. Mom got in front of him, and Coach helped her hold him back. "I will kill him sure as our name is Garnet!"

Now, I was crying. "Please, Daddy—nothing happened. You're scaring me. Please, don't get in trouble over him." He turned and took me in his arms, and I felt like a little girl again.

We went back to the table where he sat quietly for a spell, Mom with her arm around him.

Then, Mom asked, "Has he tried this with anyone else?"

There was no way that I was going to break Emily's confidence any more than I already had. Coach spoke up. "Yes, he has. But the other girl is not willing to come forward."

Mom studied the tablecloth and asked, "Did he get his way with this other girl?"

"No," Coach answered. "Someone—another girl—came to her rescue."

"Good," Mom said softly.

Now, Dad spoke. "How about the police?"

"That's up to Cassie," Coach answered, sitting back down at the table. "But coming forward two years later weakens the case. I know that much about the law."

"I'm willing to do what it takes to see that Stag Applebee gets what he deserves," I answered.

"No," said Mom. "No, Cassie, I'm not going to let you go through that."

"Something ought to happen to that thug—damn criminal!" Dad declared as he pounded his fist onto the table again.

Coach pushed herself away from the table and stood. "I think I can do something. Play a little game of poker." The three of us glanced at each other, then at her. "Tomorrow I meet with the administration. I'm not going to mention any of the girls' names, but I'm going to bring up Stag Applebee's name and things I've heard—and what I plan to do. I have a feeling that Cassie and this other young woman are not the only ones he's assaulted, and if that's the case, I have a feeling the principal or the superintendent—maybe both—have heard things, too. Just maybe I can do something about him." Then, she thanked Mom and Dad, gave me a hug, and left.

That night I lay awake until after midnight. Finally, I drifted off and got a solid six hours.

40

A Kick In the Crotch

Coach had her plan and I had mine. Next morning I waited for Stag in the parking lot. He pulled in and I marched over to his red Corvette. The *reptile* saw me and crawled out awkwardly, probably hurting from Destiny's thumping. But he still had his cocky swagger.

"Hey, Cassie, baby."

"Don't you 'Cassie, baby' me," I sneered, ramming my right index finger into his chest and glaring into his ugly mug. "Stay away from the girls on the cross country team."

He took a move back. "Yeah, well, I'll do whatever I want."

That was it. I drove my right foot squarely into his crotch.

"Ugh," he moaned, grabbing his privates, bending over, then dropping to his knees. We had been alone, but now a crowd was gathering.

A girl's voice said, "Ooh, Cassie clipped Stag in his big brass ones." Others joined her with an assortment of comments. I paid them no attention.

"You try another stunt like you did with Emily—or any other girl in River Bend—and I'll snap your antlers so far off we'll be calling you Bambi."

"Oh, yeah?" he groaned, looking up at me as he held himself. I leaned down and put my mouth close to his ear. "I'll tell people that you tried to rape me on that so-called date we had."

His breath smelled of liquor.

What a drunk. Even drinks his breakfast, I thought.

He snarled, "You know you wanted it." I held my ground and moved eye to eye with him. "I told you no, and if I hadn't gotten the door opened, you'd have kept right on." I whispered, "Just try me. When I'm finished you won't be able to get a date with a sow."

I straightened and stood over him. "Take it easy, Stag—baby."

The crowd was quiet, and they stepped aside as I marched to my first period class. On my way, I spotted Coach coming out of the principal's office. The superintendent followed her.

At lunch, Destiny sat down at the table and slid over to me. "I just saw that pervert and his old man leaving school," she said under her breath. "His old man looked mad, and Stag was trying to act cool. He's a lousy actor. Wonder what's up?"

I laid down my slice of pizza. "Don't know." I started to say something else, but decided against it. "I don't know."

41

A Poker Bluff Before Facing
The Top Team

Coach's "poker bluff" worked. No one has seen Stag
Applebee since that day. I heard he's at a prep school in
Massachusetts. Sure, Coach got rid of him, but he didn't get
what he deserved. I mean, it turned out great for River Bend, but
it's not so good for Massachusetts—like spreading a disease.
But at least he was gone.

I kept wondering what Coach said to the principal and
superintendent. *Had to be quite a speech she made in there*, I
told myself. Coach must have told the principal and
superintendent about Destiny coming to the rescue of one of
Stag's victims and put up some argument, because Destiny was
back—our team was together again. I would have loved to be a
fly on the wall.

The week after the regional, my routine was to come home from practice, do homework, then lie around tired and bummed because I lost the patch. It wasn't until the Thursday night before semi-state that my quick step returned. Even so, Ky beat me over the team course during practice. Sure, I wasn't 100 percent, but she was also getting better every time out. That made me glad. However, she was wearing my patch and that pissed me.

Going to the semi-state would be a brand new experience for River Bend. The only team of any kind from RBHS that had gone to semi-state was the boys' basketball team. But if the Lady Coyotes could get out of our semi-state meet, it would be, well, like a fantasy. We'd be going to the state finals. No River Bend team in any sport had ever done that. Surprisingly, there was a lot of chatter about our cross country team. I could hardly believe it. People in River Bend were actually excited.

As I said earlier, Marion High hadn't been in our sectional or regional. Weird, seeing how Marion's just upriver. But it was a good thing—a miracle—because they would have knocked us down to sixth for sure. Somebody must have been looking out for us. But our charmed life was over—Sarah Rothman and the Lady Giants were in our semi-state.

Rothman has a reputation throughout the state for being unbeatable. Nothing but first places. In fact, the whole Marion team has a reputation. They'd won every single meet. What's more, the news got worse. The semi-state was being held on Marion's course at Matter Park.

When we stepped to the line that Saturday, my mouth was so dry from nerves that I could have spit cotton. We jostled for position in our lane. Coach wanted us to try and stay with Marion. "Run as a team as much as possible," she advised us.

When the starter fired the pistol, all seven of us Coyotes broke fast. Ky and I glued our eyes to Rothman's back and went with her as we passed some tennis courts and headed up an incline and down the other side. There was a lot of nudging and elbowing as we raced to get to the bottom of the hill. I prayed that none of our team would take a tumble.

Ky reached the bottom before me. She was right on Rothman's shoulder. I sprinted after her, about two steps behind.

We raced up another hill—a big one—and when we got to the top, there were Dad, Jake, and Leon Hendrix—Ky's dad—yelling. They were with a mass of spectators, but my ears were tuned to pick out their voices. "Hang with her, Cassie . . . Kyesha!" yelled Dad. Jake yelled for us to drive our arms forward and run tall. Then, I heard Mr. Hendrix yell Destiny's name—for her to move up with me and Ky. *Good God*, I said to myself, *three of us are up front.*

Down the hill we came, our feet thudding hard, trying to keep our legs under control. We roller-coastered over three little hills—up and down, up and down, up and down. The course reminded me of ours—hilly, even had a stretch beside the Mississinewa—but nothing like Monster Hill. Fine with me.

At the sixteen-hundred-meter mark, three of Rothman's teammates pulled alongside Ky and me as we headed for the narrow path winding beside the river. The coaches, except for Coach Simon, were packed there. As usual, she'd positioned herself well down the path. Ky and I sprinted toward her as we trailed Rothman, while two of Rothman's teammates tried to pass us.

We shot by Coach. "Five forty-one! Five forty-two!" Then she was quiet. In my head I was counting my strides, and when I reached twelve, I heard Coach yell, "Five forty-eight!"

Destiny told me earlier in the week that while she was off the team, she still worked out hard over the course—twice a day—just to relieve her nerves.

Five forty-eight must be Destiny's time, I thought. *We have a chance.* I picked it up, moving ahead of Ky and just behind Rothman. I glanced to each side, spotting only Kyesha. The other Marion runners weren't there. Ky pulled up to me, and we dueled as we chased after Rothman. Then, purple jerseys suddenly surrounded us. Now, three of Rothman's teammates edged past as runners from other schools pulled even with Ky and me. I knew that if I faded, Destiny and maybe even Ky would fade, too.

I figured it was now or never. Rothman was about ten yards ahead—still within striking distance. But a lot of other runners were grouped with us. "Let's go," I gasped to Kyesha. She and I picked a side and sprinted past the three from Marion. God, I hurt so bad, but I still had that quick step. Footsteps thundered behind me. I had to hold them off.

As we circled a yellow flag, we raced away from the banks of the Mississinewa into an open field where I picked out Dad, Jake, and Leon Hendrix. They had sprinted to another spot on the course along the fence and were mixed in with a mob of crazed parents and coaches. Ky and I shot past them then down a hill. We picked it up. My legs were wobbling but holding up. The finish was in sight. Rothman was closer. *Maybe I can catch her*, I told myself. I let it out a notch. Ky came with me. Rothman was flying. Ky went to another gear and passed me. I chased her, but a second Marion runner went by us both. We dashed past Mom and Mrs. Hendrix; they were screaming like maniacs.

Coach was sprinting just beyond Mom and Mrs. Hendrix. She was yelling for us to hang on. We dashed by her. Both of us crossed the finish line and went into the chute at seventeen thirty-six. Ky had edged me out by a step. I had to settle for fourth, and she still had the pink patch. But I didn't care. How did the Lady Coyotes finish? That was the important question.

Sarah Rothman had set a new course record—seventeen sixteen. She'd blazed the last mile in just a little over five minutes, and so had one of her Marion teammates who passed us in the stretch. As runners straggled in, we discovered that Destiny had fallen off the pace after the sixteen-hundred meter mark, coming in fifteenth. And Samantha Peters didn't have the race she'd had in the sectional, placing back in forty-fifth. However, Taylor and Emily ran side by side the entire way, and their places of twenty-three and twenty-four put us in good shape. Only Muncie and, of course, Marion had better scores. River Bend High School's girls' cross country team would be heading for the state championship meet in Terre Haute.

42

Coach Confides In Cassie

The bus is pulling out of a rest stop. We had to pee. Nerves.

A horn is honking. I'm looking out the window. My parents and the Hendrixes speed by in the Hendrixes' van. "Hey, Kyesha, there go the old folks." The whole team waves. They'll beat us there."

Five miles to go.

Who would have thought it? When we girls met in the chemistry lab last spring, all I hoped for was a better than ordinary season. No big dreams; couldn't even imagine we'd get to state. Who would've thought it? Coach—she thought it. She believed in us.

It's been a weird week. Monday and Tuesday Coach worked us until we dropped. We raced the course, and Ky edged me each time. She still has *my* pink patch. Then Coach worked us up and down Monster Hill. Finally we ran the Indian run. Did all

219

of that both days. The next two days, we did a few wind sprints, stretched out good, and then we went home and relaxed. That was it. Yesterday, we never even had practice. Coach said the rest would charge up our batteries. Seemed bizarre that we weren't working out hard every day—state and all. But if Coach says rest, then we rest. Her word is gospel.

Last evening—Friday evening—Jake wanted me to go out with him. He said it would relax me to go, but I told him I needed some alone time. He didn't pressure me—seemed to understand. After supper I threw on my jacket and headed out of the house. Dad wanted me to stay in, but Mom told him to let me be—let me go.

At first I just wandered around town with no particular destination in mind. At least consciously I was going no certain place. Subconsciously, though, I must have known where I was heading, ending up over at Van Winkle Estates to see Coach.

The two of us talked a little strategy, but mostly we gabbed about other things: what a great season it has been and how we had toughened up.

"I don't want to pry, Coach. But I'll ask. Your poker bluff—what did you do that forced Sherman Applebee to send Stag away?"

Coach nodded. "I told Mr. Applebee and the superintendent that several girls had confided in me about Stag—what he had attempted to do to them. What he *did* do to them. Assaulted and molested them. I described in detail for Applebee and the superintendent what he'd done. But I never spoke your names. They tried to get me to divulge your names, but I wouldn't budge."

"And that's all it took?"

"No, Sherman Applebee called me a liar. He swore that Stag would never do anything like I had accused him of. So I told them I had friends at the Indianapolis papers and the New York

220

papers. I looked Applebee and the superintendent in the eye and asked them if they wanted to run the risk of a story like this getting out. If they wanted the Associated Press or other wire services to get hold of it—spread it all over the country. The superintendent turned pale when I threatened that. Terrified of the horrible publicity."

"And Applebee, what about him?"

"I thought he was going to explode. His face puffed like a blowfish and turned crimson. Called me—well, a 'lying bitch'—said I couldn't do anything to him. So I showed them a hard copy of an e-mail I got from my reporter friend at the *Indianapolis Star* saying that the *Star* was 'always interested in stories about Indiana school districts.' Of course, I didn't tell them that my query wasn't about Stag and the menace he presented. It was about you young women—the bond you'd developed. "

"And they bought it?"

"Swallowed it whole. It's amazing how putting some fear into evil can do some good. By the end of the day, Sherman Applebee was withdrawing Stag. But before he left the school, he had to get in a parting shot. Sought me out and threatened me."

"Coach, Sherman Applebee is a powerful guy around here."

"I don't care how powerful he is," was all she said.

I shook my head. "Man, this whole story gets more and more fantastic—more and more incredible."

"Cassie, let's forget about all that. It's behind us. We have more important things to talk about." Coach looked at me and smiled. Then, the smile left her face. "I hope you understand what I'm about to say. She hesitated. "Realistically, the team doesn't have much of a chance to finish first tomorrow." I tossed her a look. I mean, this was bizarre. Reality and Coach were like oil and water; they never mix.

"Don't take that the wrong way," she said. "Everyone on the team should try her hardest, but we're a couple years away from even finishing in the top five at state."

Coach came over to the couch where I was sitting. I scooted over and she sat down and put her arm around me. "Cassie, tomorrow," she spoke softly, "I want you to run for yourself, not for the team. Don't wait for anyone—Ky or anyone. You have more in you, and I want you to let yourself go."

I swallowed and looked down. All season it had always been about *the team*, but now she was saying that the most important meet of the year was supposed to be about *me*. She tightened her hold on me, pulled me closer. I looked at her. "Don't worry about any of your teammates. Relax and reach for your limits. Their day will come—tomorrow should be yours." I started moaning about team spirit when she stopped me. "Cassie, you have one shot. Take it."

We sat there, her arm around me, total silence surrounding us. I should have felt like an immature idiot with my cross country coach hugging me, but I didn't—I felt good. And we sat quietly on the couch like that for a while.

Finally, Coach removed her arm and broke the silence. "Cassie," she began, and then paused, looking into space. She continued. "I don't know if it matters to folks in River Bend any longer, but for quite a while people wanted to know what brought me here."

"Ah, Ms. Simon, no one cares about that anymore—no one that matters." And that was pretty much the truth. Sure, it was a question that used to race through my head, but over the past few weeks it hadn't even entered my mind.

"That's good if most people in town truly don't care why I am here. I'm a private person. They will never know—unless you tell them."

I looked at her. "What?"

"I want you to know why I came here."

"Ah, Coach, it's none of my business. I..."

"Listen, Cassie, I don't have anyone—absolutely no one—no siblings, no mother or father, no one—to whom I can talk in confidence—really talk—except you."

I nodded. "All right."

Coach rose from the couch and walked to a chair across from me. She sat down and paused again, taking a deep breath before she launched into her story. "I wasn't fired from my job at the pharmaceutical company, like some people suspect. Although I didn't like some of my coworkers much. And the management, well, that's a tale for another time. Mostly the company was good to me; I could still be working there if I wanted." Now a tiny smile crossed her lips. "And I'm not running away from anything, nor do I have a secret love life in Indianapolis."

I hung my head, embarrassed and ashamed for River Bend.

"Yes, I've heard all the stories. None of them is why I left."

I looked at her and nodded. Not just to be polite either; she had sparked my curiosity.

She chuckled. "And I wasn't running from the law either, as certain individuals in town have speculated."

"Ms. Simon, you don't have to explain..."

"Cassie, I want you to know. Sometimes you just need to tell someone, and you're the one person on whom I can count."

"Okay, why then?" I said. "Why would someone give up a really good paying job to come teach here for peanuts?"

"It's simple—and not really very interesting. My conscience got to me." She read the puzzled look on my face. "That job wasn't for me anymore. I couldn't work on drugs that were supposed to help people, but then the drugs cost so much that people can't afford them. Deliberately priced high so rich people could get richer." She paused. "And there were some drugs that were worse than the diseases they were supposed to be curing."

223

She looked me squarely in the eye. "That's why I quit to teach here. It's as simple as that."

As simple as that. Her conscience was guilty, so she had to quit—had to make it right.

When I left Coach's, I went straight to bed, and my brain worked overtime, rerunning what she'd said to me about why she had come to teach in River Bend—and about me and the state meet. Excitement and doubts sprinted around the inside of my skull. At last I slipped on my earphones and let the music turn off my brain. Next thing I knew, Dad was rapping on my door to get me up. I felt for my earphones, but they were gone. Mom told me this morning that she slipped them off after I had fallen asleep.

43

The Race Of A Lifetime

Now, our bus has exited I-70 onto a two-lane highway leading into Terre Haute. Out the window I see fields, some plowed, others covered with corn and bean stubble. My teammates have stirred, and they're running their mouths nonstop. Anxious, I guess. Freshmen are naive. Samantha just told Taylor we're going to kick butt and win state. I know better. I fought it at first—team concept and all—but Coach is right. The team is about two years away—then watch out.

Mr. Borgman is wheeling the bus down a long lane. Off in the distance I see other buses—lots of cars, too. Three really good teams will be here that we haven't run against this year: Richmond, a Catholic school from South Bend, and Evansville. Good individual runners, too. Marion is still the team to beat though. But I'm not going to even look at Rothman. For a change, I'll just run my race and not worry about her.

225

Mr. Borgman is stopping the bus. He parks. We're filing off. LaVern Gibson Course is packed. Nothing to compare to basketball, mind you; still, it's nice to see so many Indiana folks out for cross country. How about that? There's Mr. Bouton talking to the Hendrixes and my parents. Hey, the Elrod brothers are standing by the starting line. Jeez, Clarence must have closed the garage and left Mrs. Anderson by herself to run his Quick Mart. That makes me feel so good. I give them a little wave and they wave back.

Now, Mom and Dad and Leon (that's what he insisted we call him) and Mrs. Hendrix walk over and start talking to the Elrods. Mr. Bouton smiles at me and nods. I nod back.

Jake stands beside me. I look up at him and smile. My teammates continue to rattle on, but I keep quiet—don't feel like talking. Jake doesn't say anything either.

The state officials sent Coach a map of the course. She and I went over it earlier this week. Now, she's telling me to jog the team over the course. We begin trotting together in our sweats. Lots of other runners are going over it, too. It's hilly. That makes me smile.

"Hey, there's Rothman," Ky tells me. She and the other Lady Giants jog past us. I nod to Ky and pick up the jog, keeping my word not to set eyes on Rothman. Up and down little hills. Up and down a couple big hills. *Nothing like Monster Hill*, I tell myself. But the course has a little bit of everything: woods, plenty of trees and bushes, a bridge over a creek, its share of turns.

When we get back, I suddenly have to pee—suddenly the whole team has to pee. *Remember the Hoosier Classic?* Can't help but recall Kayla—how she stood guard for the rest of us. I'm grinning; then I think of Kayla wrestling the kid to the ground, and I giggle.

Mr. Bouton is staying put, but the rest of the River Bend

fans—Mom, Dad, the Hendrixes, and the Elrod brothers—are heading our way. But I have to take care of business in one of the portapotties. I'll make sure to get right back.

Out of the portapotty I come. They're waiting for us, and other parents have joined them. My teammates are excited, and they chitchat with different ones, but "hi" is all I say.

"We have to loosen up," I tell the team. We begin stretching as I look out at the starting line, then back at the swarms of people all up and down the course.

Jake is beside me as I'm extending my hamstrings.

Dad and Mom come over. "Just run your best, honey," Dad tells me.

"Okay." I keep stretching.

Mom is patting and rubbing my back as I bend and touch my toes. She is asking me if I slept well. I am nodding.

The rest of the team's dads and moms—except for Destiny's and Emily's moms—neither have come—are encouraging them. Even Kayla's grandmother is here. Emily's dad is talking to her. But I'm paying the parents no mind. I'm done stretching. Jake wraps an arm around me. We don't say anything, just walk off together to see Coach. My heart is slamming against my chest.

"Cassie, just relax," Coach says. "Stretched out well?" I nod. The rest of the team comes up to us. Coach is pulling me aside. "Just run your race—not anyone else's race—yours. It's there for you, Cassie. Breathe deeply, relax—you have to relax—and take it."

I want to believe what Coach Simon says, but I'm still fighting off negative feelings—feelings of doubt—as I attach the timing chip to my shoe.

As I peel off my sweats, I whisper, "Where is Mr. Bouton's sense of peace?"

"Did you say something?" Jake asks. I am shaking my head no.

It's nippy. You know how a November is in Indiana—frost on the pumpkin and all that stuff.

Under my uniform I have on tights and a light long-sleeved competition shirt. To chase away the chill, the whole team is wearing yellow tights and shirts under our blue jerseys and shorts. I glance over at Ky as she secures *my* pink patch onto *her* jersey. I adjust the number Coach Simon pinned on me.

We are being called to the start. Runners in their school colors create a spectrum along the line, like the giant box of crayons I had back in kindergarten. Dad, Jake, and Leon are on the right, about a hundred meters down course from the start. The Elrod brothers, my mom, and Mrs. Hendrix stand even to the starting line along with Mr. Bouton. Parents of runners have spread out along the orange mesh fence beside the course. Some have even disappeared into the woods.

I jostle for position. I search for Coach. There she is in her bright red sweat suit—about a quarter mile away—near the first flag. I'm fighting off the urge to look for Rothman. Ky is on my left, and then I see purple out of the corner of my right eye. I know it's Rothman; I don't look at her. She's so close I could spit and smack her flush. Now it hits me: *Maybe she wants to keep me close; maybe she's scared of me.* Calm floods me.

"Run Rothman's butt into the ground," someone whispers. I turn. Ky looks me in the eye and says it again. "Run her butt into the ground, Cass."

The gun is up. No movement. Only quiet. I take a deep breath. Bang! A thundering herd. Rothman is sprinting to the front along with a runner from Evansville—a tall girl—and another, shorter runner from South Bend. I have to go after them. I sprint. An electric cart with a large digital timer is traveling in front of us. *Blistering pace.* The frosty air makes my throat and lungs feel like they're being turned inside out. We're rounding the yellow flag where Coach stands.

"Go to the front and make them run your race, Cassie!" she yells.

I'm picking it up as we start up a little hill. Out of the corner of my eye, I catch Ky coming with me. I'm reaching for a little more. Now, I don't see her. Maybe I've left her. My breath is coming hard and fast and deep. I'm passing the runners from Evansville and South Bend. *Dear God, I'm beside Rothman*—a prayer, not just an empty thought. She gives me a glance as we're coming down a hill and entering the woods. Our legs are churning like windmills in a tornado. She's trying to let it out another notch—burn me off. I turn it over even faster. *Stay with her.* I hit a rhythm. Now, my breathing is coming easy, and the chilly air feels good. I'm driving my arms and matching Rothman stride for stride. Behind me I hear other runners. Is Ky there? I won't look back to see.

We sprint into and out of a grove of trees, racing toward a good-sized hill. People are screaming. Dad, Jake, and Leon are yelling. Leon says, "That's it, Cassie!"

Dad says, "Drive those arms!" As I rocket past, I hear Jake yell my name, then his voice trails off. I don't catch the rest of what he yells. It doesn't matter. Where is Coach? Monster Hill enters my mind. I lean into the incline, digging just ahead of Rothman. *She's straining*, I tell myself. I still hear other runners, their feet pounding, lungs sucking air. But the sounds are growing more distant, getting lost in the spectators' roar; it's Rothman and me out in front of them all. Now at the top. Now racing down. There's another gang of frantic people at the bottom. Around a red flag I go; Rothman follows. God, I'm feeling so good. I let it out another notch, but she matches me.

I reach down and grab an extra deep breath and send it out through fluttering lips. We are along a tiny stream; we fly over a wooden bridge. *Plunk! Plunk! Plunk! Plunk! Plunk!* shout the boards. We race off of the bridge. I'm listening and counting.

One-thousand-one, one-thousand-two . . . five . . . At *six,* I hear other feet hitting the wooden planks. The nearest runner to us is about six or seven seconds back. Good God, my insides are trembling. Another big hill. At the bottom is the sixteen-hundred-meter mark. Coaches and spectators are strung all up and down the incline, along the orange mesh fence.

Coach Simon waits at the top, having sprinted over a shortcut to catch us. She yells down the hill, "Keep it up, Cass!" The digital timer on the electric cart flashes 5.14! My adrenaline surges. Up I start, bearing down with short, quick strides. Rothman lengthens her stride. *She's making a mistake. She should run the Monster; she'd learn a thing or two about hills.*

There's Rothman's coach. He yells for her to pick it up. He looks worried. "Burn her out, Sarah—burn her out!" he shouts behind us. She tries to pass me as we shoot upward. I'm gobbling up the hill using quick, choppy strides, moving a couple steps ahead of Rothman.

Coach stands at the top. She's not yelling—not even looking at her stopwatch. She leans over the fence and advises, "Breathe deeply—lift your knees—drive your arms forward."

Rothman and I are even. Now I'm nudging ahead. Down the hill we are going; my legs are about to run out from under me. We hit the bottom. Passing a blue flag, I head back into the woods. I glance to one side, then the other. I can't see her.

Dried leaves rustle and twigs crunch under my feet. I listen—three, maybe four seconds pass before I hear steps behind me. I pick up the pace more. *Am I really going this fast? Legs turning over this fast?* Puffs of air burst from my mouth, shooting clouds out and then behind me.

Out of the woods I dash toward a mass of people. Dad—jacket off—sweating. Jake's there. Leon, too. All about to stroke out. All waiting for me.

"Hang tough, Cassie! Hang tough!" Jake screams.

Now, Leon lifts his arms, spreading them so that his hands are about a foot apart. He shouts, "Keep on keepin' on! Cassie, you've got ten yards on them."

Them? Has Rothman fallen back? Is more than one runner making a move on me?

"Ten yards!" shouts Leon again as I fly past him, and then past Jake and Dad. I hear them screaming behind me. Up a little hill I sprint. At the top. Over the top. Racing down. Coach is there. *She cut from the other side of the course—sprinted*, I tell myself.

Now, she's yelling, "Lose them in the woods! You're going to do it!" She bolts in a blur.

Around a red flag I fly. Into the thick woods a third time. The path broadens. It winds around a clump of trees to my left, then slingshots straight ahead toward an opening. I am racing to that opening. My skin is coated with sweat. Fatigue has caught me. *God, if I can only hold on.*

Out of the woods and into a field I come. The people are scrambling to find spots. There is Coach again—hair all frazzled, sweat suit looks like she slept in it. Dad, Jake, and Leon are soaked with sweat. They are yelling, but I only hear Coach. "Keep your form! Lift your knees! Drive your arms! Don't give in! Relax—let your conditioning do the work!"

I kick it out, legs struggling to move even faster. Past Mom, Mrs. Hendrix—the Elrod brothers are like lunatics, screaming in an alien language. Mr. Bouton—Emily's dad—even Mr. Borgman—yelling!

People screaming. A coach is shouting encouragement. Is Rothman catching me? But it's not the Marion coach. I've never seen this coach. I sense someone. I glance right. Evansville—the tall girl. *Oh, God, she seems fresh. One stride equals two of mine. So tired. How important is winning? Is it that important? Do I want this? Second is good—better than ordinary,* I'm telling myself. *But it's not first—not my best.* So now I am reaching down to stay with her. We're racing up a long, steep incline, the final stretch to the finish. People are packed in a long line along the edges of the course. Their voices uniting into a single roar. She has a step on me. *Force yourself! Another gear!*

I lean into the hill, drive my arms, and kick it out up on my toes with a hundred meters left. Now, we are even, but she is coming with me. My chest is heaving; my lungs are ready to explode. Sweat soaks me. *So tired! My last notch, my wad.* I burst toward the finish. I have a step on her as I dash over the finish and sprawl headfirst into the chute.

44

Northern Indiana University Nibbles

Officials are helping me up. One on each side holding me. I pull away from them, raising my arms so that I can support the back of my head on my intertwined fingers, elbows jutting out in opposite directions. My breath is still coming hard and fast. It doesn't seem real; I know I won, but I still can't understand that I won. You'd think I'd be strutting all puffed up and bragging, but I have no desire to wallow in glory.

Ky is crossing the finish line. I just heard Coach say "ten." I walk to Ky and we wrap our arms around each other, proud and exhausted. Now, I'm surrounded—Mom, Dad, Leon, Jake—the others from River Bend. They're chattering, but I don't hear them. Mom, Dad, and Jake are hugging and patting me on the back. I break free, turn and look toward the finish.

Emily is coming in, and Coach says, "Thirty-one." I stand,

hands on hips waiting for the other Lady Coyotes and listening for Coach to yell out the places. Taylor and Destiny finish together. "Sixty-one and sixty-two," says Coach. Finally, Samantha strides across the finish line. I don't hear her place because Mom is jabbering as she hands me a bottle of water. I guzzle it.

Kayla is nowhere to be found.

Coach—smart phone in hand—is calculating our total score. She finishes and everyone crowds around as she speaks. "Cassie, when your first place is added in with our other top four finishers, it could be good enough to put us in the top ten as a team—maybe."

I think, *Okay, it's not first. Never expected our team to win anyway. But top ten in the state? Better than ordinary.* Now I think of Coach's words. *"Cassie, when your first place is added in . . ."*

"It must be real," I whisper, "because it hurts when I pinch myself." Still, it's hard to grab hold of. People—people who must be from Marion—are gathered around Sarah Rothman. I hear one tell her that it was a fluke—my winning and her losing was a fluke. But I won't let it bother me because I know better. And all the people who count know better, too.

Coach puts her arm around my shoulder and draws me to her. She doesn't say anything, just holds me. A woman accompanied by a man packing a camera is introducing herself. "Reporter from the *Indianapolis Star*," I hear her say. I didn't catch the name. The photographer is snapping pictures. Coach walks away.

"Did I expect to win?" Before I answer the reporter's question, I glance at Coach in the distance as she double checks her figures, then I answer. "I expected to do my best. That's all, just do my best. Coach Simon," I point at her, "got me ready and I did my best."

"A picture with my coach? I would like that." I am calling for Coach Simon. She comes and stands beside me as runners straggle in. We put our arms around each other, and the photo is taken. People from River Bend are taking pictures, too. Now, the reporter is talking to Coach, but I don't listen. Sarah Rothman is being interviewed by the Marion paper. I hear the reporter say, "...an *off* day." So I move closer and eavesdrop.

Rothman is plenty pissed. I move closer. "Garnet from River Bend took me out of my race. I admit it, she set a pace over the hills that I couldn't handle today," she tells the *Chronicle-Tribune* reporter. Rothman didn't even get third; she got fourth.

I am pulling on my sweats; now slipping the hood over my head. Someone is touching my shoulder. When I turn, there she is—Sarah Rothman. We stand in silence for a couple seconds. Then Rothman says, "You were great today."

I nod. "Thanks."

Again, awkward silence.

"You a senior?' she asks.

"Yeah."

"Me too. Who are you going to run for next year? Where are you going to college?"

"Don't know. No one's...I don't know about next year. How about you?"

"I plan to sign a letter of intent to run at UCLA. Want to leave the Indiana winter for the California sun. They're offering me a good deal. Hope today doesn't screw it up." Rothman scrunches up her face in a puzzled look. "You really don't have any idea where you'll be running next year?"

"Nope."

"Cassie, after today, your phone's going to start ringing off the hook."

"Yeah, maybe." Then I tell her, "You pushed me—Sarah—you pushed me. It was my day, but you pushed me."

She reaches out her hand, and I clasp it. Sarah smiles slightly. "Cassie, you were just great. On those hills, you were just great." Then we hug.

I study her as she drags herself to her coach. *She's spent—really tired—and bummed. Her only loss all year—and in the state championship. Has to hurt.* It's weird—I feel sorry that she lost, but not sorry that I won.

The last runner has come into the chute. It's not Kayla. Ky is telling me that she dropped out. No matter. Kayla hasn't figured into the scoring all season. Never has counted anyway.

The officials mount stairs leading to a stage. A guy stands in front of a microphone. He's telling what a success the state meet has been. Now, he's ready to announce the team winners. I already know from Coach's tally that Marion got third. The Catholic school from South Bend second. Evansville won.

The announcer starts with "tenth," "ninth," eighth…." We got sixth—sixth in the whole state of Indiana. The Lady Coyotes, and even Coach, are hugging each other and slapping high fives. We mount the stage and team medals are hung around our necks. We are handed the sixth-place trophy—not gigantic, but pretty big. As a team we raise it high above our heads. The crowd is clapping, politely, but the fans from River Bend yell and cheer. The team descends, and we gather with Coach to have our photo taken.

Now, they are announcing the individual winners—fifth, fourth, third, second. Then my name is called. The River Bend folks cheer loudly. I walk up and stand on the stage. The first place medal is draped around my neck. I grip it and look at it. Then hold it up for the crowd to see. I descend the stage with my feet seeming not to touch the stairs.

A woman stops me. She introduces herself as the women's cross country coach from Northern Indiana University. "What year are you?" I tell her I am a senior. "Where are you going to college?" she asks.

"Haven't even thought about college," I tell her. "Figured that maybe I would go to community college—or maybe not go at all, just get a job."

"You have got to be kidding," she says. "You just won the state cross country championship."

I just shrug. I mean, what does a person say to that?

Coach Simon comes over. The Northern Indiana University coach introduces herself, then says, "I was just telling Cassie that I hope she gives running for Northern some consideration."

I nod politely.

Coach Simon tells her that I will give it a lot of thought.

"Have you taken the ACT test yet?" the Northern coach asks.

I tell her no, but I have signed up to take it before the winter break.

Coach Simon says, "Don't worry. Cassie will score better than the minimum required."

Coach lets her know that my grades are okay too. She and I already checked my GPA. It's a 2.67. It should be even higher after this semester because my first quarter grades were really good—four A's and two B's. Better than ordinary, I'd say. Better than ever, in fact.

Now, Mom and Dad join us. They introduce themselves. They listen as the Northern coach says that if my grades and ACT score are good enough, she might be interested in me running for the Lady Trappers. Dad is excited. It's a Division I school. He says I should jump at the offer, but Coach pulls us aside.

"Mr. and Mrs. Garnet, Cassie is going to be getting more offers from colleges. My advice is to see who gives her the best deal. If Northern is the one, that's fine, but let's see what develops. Besides, if you noticed, the Lady Trappers' coach said she '*might* be interested' in Cassie running for Northern. She's not being very definite—not a firm offer. Let's play hard to get and see what other offers Cassie gets. Make Northern squirm a little." Mom and Dad agree.

Now, Coach is asking the Northern coach to step over by a big oak tree, where they visit for a few minutes, and then shake hands. Coach heads our way as we wait for her near the start.

Everyone is leaving; the cars are pulling away. Cross country runners are loading onto their buses. Coach is telling us it's time to go. I am going through the open bus door and climbing the steps. I take a seat. Jake sits beside me, and I scoot close to him. He puts his arm around me, and I sink back so that my whole body is supported by his chest and shoulder. Everyone is loaded on. Mr. Borgman fires up the bus and we ramble down the road we came on.

Ky leaves her seat at the back of the rumbling school bus and wobbles down the aisle. She eases herself in front of Jake and me and swivels on her butt so she faces me, her legs resting straight on the seat so that her feet dangle over the sides. Then she reaches up and unpins the pink patch. "Cassie, it's all yours now," she says, extending the brass-colored safety pin and piece of cloth toward me.

"No, it's yours, Kyesha. Keep it." I look around, and tip my head at the teammates who will be returning. "Let one of them try and take it from you next season."

Ky smiles, nods, and pins the pink patch back onto her warm-up suit, then slips on her earphones and sinks back, propping herself against the corner where the seat meets the window.

For the first few miles, my teammates jabber, but exhaustion takes over and most go to sleep. Only Kayla and I are awake.

Both of us continue to gaze out of the window, looking at nothing really. My guess is that my other teammates will sleep until the bus pulls into some fast food joint so we can eat. Kayla looks over at me. I smile. Now she looks back out the window.

I gaze out the window, too. The billboards and the harvested fields on the opposite side of the road from the one we came on blur past. Now, I look at Coach Simon entering *data* into her laptop. *Logging times to use as a comparison for next season —for next year.*

Hey, I should admit it: I wasn't being honest with that Northern Indiana coach when I told her I might not go to college. I don't know why I told her that. Maybe it is because I'm p.o.'d at myself for not trying harder in school all those years—I was a little scared because everything seems so uncertain. Truthfully, I'm still scared.

45

Ephemeral

Ephemeral. A word I learned in English lit. A word that describes my winning the Indiana High School Cross Country Tournament. It came and went so fast—seems so long ago. Exactly thirteen days—312 hours—have slipped by since I lunged over the finish line in first place—to be better than everyone else—to be better than ordinary at cross country.

So much has happened over the past two weeks. It's been like a wild ride on a really steep roller coaster: up and down, down and up—joy and anger, anger and joy. And most of that ride had nothing to do with my winning—or even with cross country.

For a couple days I couldn't go anywhere in River Bend without people making over me. Gradually, though, the excitement died down. All the backslappers faded away, and as usual River Bend resumed its obsession with its true love—basketball—with Jake Nader. But for a few hours, I wallowed in all the attention.

Our bus arrived back in River Bend in the late afternoon that Saturday of the state meet, and the word had spread—texts, e-mails, social media. When we pulled into the parking lot of RBHS, a crowd was there to greet us. Mostly cheering and shouting my name.

"It was the whole team, not just me," I kept saying over and over.

I have to be honest, though: In spite of all my talk about *the team,* hearing people shout my name sent a chill of excitement shooting through me that I had never known before. It was the only time River Bend High had won state in anything, so the people were going to share the glory with me, even if it wasn't basketball. And the town council gave a major boost to my ego when it held a special session that very evening and voted to spend money on fancy signs to put up on every road leading into town: **Welcome to River Bend, Home of Cassie Garnet, Indiana High School Cross Country Champion.**

Really, the signs are all that's left to remind people of that Saturday in Terre Haute, now almost 313 hours ago.

After a while, it all began to wear thin. Yes, I appreciated it, but it became a little embarrassing. As I worked it over in my mind while lying in bed the next day—Sunday morning after the state meet—I kept asking myself if the value of this season was about more than me winning—about more than the team—about more than cross country.

The next day, Monday, Mr. Broadneck—the guy who had reamed out Coach for talking to us about menstruation— called an assembly for the whole school. Everyone gathered in the gym where Jake would be playing his last year of Indiana high school basketball—where he would score 47 points in the first home game of the season that coming Friday.

Broadneck hoisted the team's trophy, which now rests in the trophy case, high as our schoolmates cheered. He said the name of each of my teammates. Everyone clapped. Then he announced: "And the number one cross country runner in the entire state of Indiana, River Bend High School's own Cassie Garnet!"

Before the assembly, Broadneck wanted my medal, so I reluctantly gave it to him.

What's he gonna do with it?" I had asked myself, as I watched him stuff it into his suit coat.

Then I knew. The principal removed it from his pocket, dangled it high for the student body to see, and then hung it around my neck like *he* was presenting it to me for the *first* time. The gym erupted in cheers, whistles and applause. Then, someone started chanting my name, and everyone joined in. I sighed and thought, *Is this a school assembly, or a political rally?*

When everything quieted down, Broadneck told me to "say a few words." I took the microphone and said, "The whole team did great." Then I looked over at Ms. Simon and nodded. "We did great because of Coach Simon." She smiled and nodded back. At that moment, I realized that my relationship with Coach was what made this season special—what gave it value to me. Without even thinking, I went to her and we embraced as the gym exploded in more shouts and cheers.

But, while walking back to my seat, I saw that not everyone was thrilled. My eyes spotted Sherry Dumont burning a hole through me. I looked away. *Consider the source. Just blow it off.*

Anyway, that's what I told myself.

46

Eavesdropping On Really Bad News

Mrs. Anderson was behind the counter absorbed in a tabloid as I headed for the cooler planning to get an orange juice. From the open door leading to the garage I overheard Henry say, "Knew right off there was trouble brewing; figured it had something to do with Miss Simon . . ."

Glancing over at Mrs. Anderson, face still buried in the tabloid, I stepped close to the door leading to the garage. "Four of 'em slitherin' into the principal's office like snakes last Friday. Knew they were going to take turns biting hunks out of her," Henry continued.

Then, I heard Clarence ask, "You got an inkling what went on in there—specifically?"

I kept myself hidden around the corner, my eyes on Mrs. Anderson, my ears eavesdropping while the Elrod brothers discussed River Bend's latest news, but all I could hear was metal colliding with metal, then Clarence said, "Dadburnit!" Then a loud *clang*!

Mrs. Anderson looked up just as some grade school kids wanting candy and a guy paying for gas came through the door. I pretended to be browsing the rack of chips. She took everyone's cash, returned to her tabloid, and I went back to listening.

"What's the matter?" asks Henry.

"The nut's on too tight," Clarence groaned. There was silence, and then he said, "Go on with this situation over at the school."

"'Got an inkling'? You bet I do," says Henry. "I didn't want them to think I might be listenin' in—especially with Mrs. McGrady there. She'd know right off what I was up to if she saw me, so after they all got in there . . ."

Who's "all of them—they?" I asked myself.

". . . and closed the door, I slipped out from around the corner with my dust mop and stood in a spot where you can hear pretty good if you tilt your head just right."

"Well, what was it all about?" Clarence asked. More clanking, but duller than before, and I took another peek over at Mrs. Anderson, still reading. "Got it!" I heard Clarence declare. "Hell's bells—alternator's shot."

Henry continued. "Well, you know how it is when you get four snakes together in the grass—they usually squirm around before they figure out who's the head rattler. Anyway, after a minute of silence, I heard Mel Dumont's voice . . ."

"Dumont," I whispered.

". . . tells 'em he's become real disturbed . . . ."

"He's real disturbed, all right." Clarence laughed.

Henry laughed, too, and then went on. "Like I was saying, Mel Dumont told everyone that he's become real disturbed over things his daughter has told him . . ."

"Sherry," I whispered.

". . . went on to say that he's discussed it with Betty McGrady at church and she'd told him that he didn't know the half of it—that Miss Simon had given Jarvis trouble, too."

"Hand me that wrench," said Clarence.

"Prissy Butt has had it out for Miss Simon right from the get-go," continued Henry.

"Threatened by her I reckon. Besides, she and Max Jarvis don't like Miss Simon because she's a Jew."

I set my jaw, glanced at Mrs. Anderson who was reading, and edged my head around the corner. Clarence came out from under the hood of the car and stared at his brother. I ducked back out of sight. "You mean to tell me that Prissy and Mad Max hold that against Miss Simon?"

"Yep! One mornin'—early, when they didn't know I was around the corner—Jarvis was complaining about Miss Simon bein' so aggressive, and Betty says, 'Well, that shouldn't surprise you. We all know how members of *that tribe* are. Don't need her kind around here. Like to help her pack and buy her a ticket out of town.' And old Mad Max pipes up and says, 'Yeah, like to Israel.' Then, they both laughed like hell."

"Well, of all the low down . . ." Clarence paused. "Are Prissy and Mad Max spearheadin' this mess?"

"Nah, they're all snakes in the grass," Henry said. "Why, from the time Mel Dumont kicked open the door, those other three, including the girl..."

"Sherry?"

"Yeah, her. She jumped right in with her two cents worth every chance she got, just like the others. You wouldn't believe the things she accused Miss Simon of."

I peeked around the corner again. Clarence tossed the wrench with a clunk onto the work table and stared at Henry. I turned toward Mrs. Anderson who looked up and smiled at me. I picked up a bag of corn chips, pretending to study them. She raised the paper to begin reading. I started to place the chips back, but a woman with a little kid came in. She strolled around the store getting stuff to eat—a hot dog, a large drink, and a bag of cookies—at the same time yanking things away from her kid that he kept pulling off the shelves. She paid for the food and left. Mrs. Anderson looked back at me, and I continued pretending to study the chip bag.

She lowered her eyes to the paper.

Placing the chips back on the rack, I peered around the corner. Henry started to look around. I jerked my head from view and heard him mumble something to Clarence.

Boy, whatever Henry told Clarence must have been juicy, because he hardly ever whispers anything, and hard as I strained to hear, there was only low talk. Then, Clarence blurts, "What! You don't mean it!"

"That's what they accused her of. Of course, I don't believe it."

I wish I could have heard what Henry had told Clarence—heard what it was those four snakes, to use Henry's words, had accused Coach of.

Henry was talking again. "Principal says that he'll make sure the superintendent gives this item top billing on the agenda for the next board meeting. He says the superintendent is gonna go through the roof."

"Yeah, well, I hope they don't get rid of Miss Simon. The way she worked with those girls and had them runnin'—the whole team—but especially Cassie Garnet and that black girl —the Hendrix girl. Saw it with my own eyes almost every day this summer. Hell, it's no secret to me why Cassie won the state

248

championship." Clarence stopped talking. Silence—and then, "Miss Simon has to be a bang up coach—and I like her, what I know of her."

I could tell from the muffled sound that he was back under the hood of the car.

"Yeah, she's a good gal. Kids say she's a real good teacher, too," agreed Henry.

Suddenly Mrs. Anderson said something, and I jerked around. "What?"

"Can I help you find something, Cassie?"

"No, guess not." I chuckled nervously. "Guess I'm not as thirsty—hungry—as I thought."

She nodded slowly, paused, and then lowered her eyes to the tabloid.

Like I said, I'd come to the convenience store for a juice, but when I heard Coach was going to be offered up as fresh meat for Prissy Butt, Mad Max, and the Dumonts, I wasn't thirsty anymore. I shoved open one side of the double glass doors and hurried across the concrete surrounding the gas pumps. I rushed, but didn't know for sure where I was going; anger was driving me. Coach was the best thing that had ever happened to our team—to me—and I wasn't going to let the Dumonts or Prissy Butt or Mad Max or anyone mess that up.

As I took long, quick strides away from Elrod's Quick Mart, I keep asking myself what it was that old Hefty Hips Sherry and the Three Stooges had accused Coach of, and the more I stewed about it, the more my blood boiled. At last, I decided the best way to find out was to ask Coach. That was, if she knew.

47

"Inappropriate Behavior"

There was a stinging chill in mid-November air. Last year we had an Indian summer about this time, but not this year. I tugged the collar of my jacket up around my neck as I shuffled through fallen leaves. I was not quite sure how I'd bring this up, but I figured it made more sense getting it directly from Coach—horse's mouth and all that.

As I turned the corner, I saw a dim light in her apartment. I mounted the cement steps slowly and stood for a spell at her door debating whether or not this was a smart move. Guess I was scared to find out what the accusations were. Besides, maybe she hadn't even heard about it yet. But I doubted that. After all, Henry Elrod said River Bend's *morals police* had met with the principal Friday, so I was sure that Broadneck had called her in today, this being Monday. *Yet, she didn't seem upset when I stopped in to see her after school. Of course, nothing rattles her.*

At last I got up the nerve and pressed the doorbell. The chimes rang. They're pretty loud. It seemed like an eternity, and I was about to leave when the door opened. There stood Coach, and she'd been bawling. Jeez, to know she'd been crying made me feel funny, and I wished I hadn't come. But I couldn't just walk away.

"Hello, Cassie." She hesitated. "Come in out of the cold."

She was trying hard to act chipper—put on the tough act. I walked past her; she stayed a moment at the door, looking outside. There was an open box of Kleenex on the table beside the couch, and the lamp next to the tissues cast a weak light.

"Sit down. Let me take your jacket."

"I'll just lay it here," I told her, pulling my arms out of the sleeves, and then draping it over the back of a chair that I sat down in. Her body collapsed into the couch across from me.

Everything went silent—and uncomfortable. *Coming over here was a dumb idea—bad timing.*

"You girls were outstanding this season, and you were a great captain, Cassie."

But she wasn't fooling me; she had more important things on her mind than cross country.

"Yeah," I answered. More silence. Then, without thinking —and glad that I didn't think or I would've clammed up—I said, "Coach, what's wrong?"

She didn't answer right off, but turned her head and stared out the window into the dark. Jeez, I felt so sorry for her, and the silence was murdering me.

After a while, she said, "Cassie, some people in town have accused me of things."

My blood ran hot. "The evil quartet?"

She looked at me. "You've heard." She seemed disgusted

and disappointed all at the same time. "Word certainly travels fast in River Bend."

"I went to Elrod's for a juice. Wasn't trying to be a sneak. Clarence and Henry just didn't know I was around." I explained that I'd overheard a conversation between the Elrod brothers—that she was accused of "something" by the Dumonts, McGrady, and Jarvis. I didn't know of what, though. "I came straight over to your place—haven't told a soul." She smiled but her body was still tense. I went on. "What kind of things are they saying about you? If you don't mind me asking."

More silence, then she blew her nose into a Kleenex. "This afternoon," she began, "I was going to my car after school, and Mr. Boardneck approached me and told me that I was to come to his office." She laughed softly. "I was thinking I must really be in trouble being called to the principal's office again." She stopped laughing. Quiet. Then, "I had no idea how much trouble." A shudder raced through her, and she bit her bottom lip as tears rolled down her cheeks. "Inappropriate behavior." She'd said it like I wasn't there; she sobbed into her hands.

It was weird. Suddenly I didn't feel uncomfortable anymore. You'd think I would—Ms. Simon acting so different, so shook up—but I didn't. I couldn't help myself. I got up and went to her—sat down beside her and wrapped my arms around her. "Don't you worry, Coach, we're not going to let those slugs get away with this." I started bawling and hugged her tightly.

Jeez, it seemed peculiar—me trying to comfort Ms. Simon. I mean, she's so strong and everything. Besides, I was not at all sure who "we" were, or how "we" were going to keep the vultures from picking Coach's bones.

I asked, "Do you think one of them has been sending you those e-mails?"

She shrugged. "I don't know. Probably. But how can I prove it?"

"I don't know how to prove it. But I got to tell you, that one e-mail I read sounded an awful lot like that nut job, Mel Dumont." There was quiet for a moment. "Coach, I haven't gotten any e-mails, but. . ." I looked at my hands and then at her.

She studied me. "What is it, Cassie?"

"Right after we won the sectional I received a note stuck in the morning paper. It said . . ."

"Go ahead, tell me if you want to."

"It said that neither our team nor you would last."

She laughed quietly. "Well, we showed them, didn't we?"

"We sure did—we really showed them."

Coach leaned back against the couch, hung her head, and said, "What a nightmare. What a nightmare." She dabbed at her red and swollen eyes. "Excuse me," she said. "Normally I'm not a crier. But the idea of giving up something I've come to . . ." Her voice trailed off as she covered her mouth, stifling a sob.

"Hey, that's all right. Everyone has to have a good cry now and then. Coach, I kept the note if you ever need it."

She nodded and gently wrung the Kleenex. "Cassie, Mr. Broadneck and the superintendent..."

"The superintendent was there, too?" I interrupted.

She nodded. ". . . wouldn't specify what all the allegations are. All he said is 'Inappropriate behavior.'" Coach stopped crying and sat quietly. "Let's just say that life isn't fair and some people make unkind accusations." She drew in a breath and let it out in a sigh. "It seems that a few of those people live here in River Bend." She sniffed and wiped at her nose, and then gazed out the window into the dark. She spoke as though she was thinking out loud: "'Really, why did you leave your position in Indianapolis to teach chemistry in River Bend?'"

"What?" I asked.

Coach's head turned away from the window. "Sorry, Cassie—daydreaming. That was what Mr. Broadneck asked me.

Why I left my job to come here when I'd make a lot less money."

"Isn't that something he should have asked at your interview?"

"Well, like I told you, he didn't—neither did the superintendent," Coach answered.

"Apparently, they were so anxious to fill the chemistry position they just didn't care back then. Now, though—" she sniffed and bit her lip, "now, it's become an issue."

The memory of why Ms. Simon gave up a big money job to teach chemistry in River Bend fluttered around my skull, and I felt really good—honored—that she confided in me that night before the state meet—told only me. "Oh, BS!" I snapped. "It's no one's business—doesn't matter. You're here now—doing a super job. I'll never ever tell anyone, even if you say I can."

Coach forced a smile. We hugged each other tightly. Then, her body shuddered as she sobbed, "I can't believe this is happening."

I held her close. We embraced for several seconds as she got hold of herself, then she let go of me, wiped at her eyes, and blew her nose into the wadded, frayed Kleenex, then set it on the lamp table. I continued to pat her on the back. She reached over and jerked a couple more tissues from the box and ran them under her eyes. "The principal and superintendent knew all about you students coming over to my apartment. They gave me orders that I wasn't to let you visit anymore. But I refused to agree to that; I'm not going to allow those two—or anyone else—tell me whom I can and can't have in my home." She set her jaw. "There is nothing inappropriate that goes on here."

Coach's voice was determined, but I was wondering if maybe the stress was screwing up her judgment. "Jeez, Coach, maybe I better get out of here. I mean, I don't want to make it worse for you." I started to stand. "They're probably spying right now."

"No. Don't you dare. I'm not giving in to them—to those witch hunters." She paused and examined her hands. "Besides, it couldn't get any worse." Then she almost whispered. "They certainly know a lot about you kids coming over here—even about the track meet last summer. Apparently, one of them—maybe all four—have followed my every move." She sniffed and looked down at the freshly wadded Kleenex. "Who knows what they've done?"

"Everybody pries into everyone else's business in River Bend, but to try and ruin someone is a bunch of fu. . ." I stop before the word slipped out.

"I'm not afraid of people knowing my business," she said. "What I'm afraid of is that some people in town don't put a premium on the truth—they're determined to ruin me, no matter what it takes. As far as my reason for leaving my job, that's a personal decision that I won't share with them—just won't. Especially now that they have made it a part of their inquisition."

Any one of the four who met with Broadneck had a motive. But at that moment, I believed Sherry was the one who'd spied on Coach—had stalked her.

"The superintendent said the board was going to discuss this with all the parties involved at a closed hearing. He said there were other charges, but wasn't more specific just that they are serious." Coach thought for a moment. "The only thing keeping him from terminating me right now is that I teach chemistry."

"Fire you!" I jumped to my feet. "That is all fu—all messed up!"

She looked up at me, smiled, and then patted the top of my hand, which I'd rested on her shoulder. "'Don't want to go through that again—if I can help it,'" Coach sarcastically repeated the principal's words. She looked toward the door and spoke. "The superintendent said if I can't satisfy the board that I'm not guilty of all this—whatever *horrible* thing I've done—then I would be let go immediately. They'll hear both sides at the next board meeting."

Damn, I could strangle them all!

"I can bring witnesses on my behalf."

"I'll be there," I assured her. "I'll make sure the whole team's there." The two of us were quiet for a while. It was time for me to go. I stood, we hugged again, and I left.

I bawled all the way home. Although I tried to hide it, Mom and Dad could see that I'd been crying. Mom thought it was about Jake—we'd broken up again or something. I didn't answer her—didn't say anything, but went to my room.

After a while, there was a knock on the door. It was Mom. I blubbered the whole story. I could tell she was really pissed. A scary look was on her face. The same look she got when a former neighbor, Bill Foster, called her a liar over a property line dispute. Mom and Dad sued. They proved in court they were right. Foster had to give back a hundred and twenty square feet of *our* yard that he'd been claiming as his. Not an angry look, but that get-even look.

She left the room and came back with Dad. I told him the whole thing, and he blew his cork. I won't repeat his choice of language, but take my word for it, he had some very colorful names for those four fools—and for River Bend's school administration, too.

48

"Citizens Against Immoral Teachers"

Everyone took sides. The next afternoon my heart jumped into my throat when I spotted a couple cars go down Main Street sporting bumper stickers that said, *Citizens Against Immoral Teachers*. I didn't have to be a rocket scientist to figure out what that was about. These were the "decency" people. Like any town—small or big—River Bend has a "decency" crowd. Poor fools who were bound and determined to "save" us from Ms. Simon. With them, if she was accused she was guilty, and don't confuse them with facts.

That evening, Mom and I were grocery shopping at the Pig 'n Whistle Supermarket. Mom got into a big argument with Edith Baldwin, one of that decency bunch. Mom doesn't like Mrs. Baldwin anyway, so when she mentioned the "courage" of the Dumonts and the other "good" folks who were "protecting" our children from "that woman," Mom fired back.

"Have you met Miss Simon?" Mom asked Mrs. Baldwin.

"Well, no."

"I have. We're personal friends. And I'm proud to say she's my daughter's coach—mentor. She's a wonderful woman and a great teacher."

"How great can she be?" asked Mrs. Baldwin. "If she was a great teacher, she wouldn't be under investigation—have all those accusations made against her. She'll destroy education in River Bend—corrupt our children."

"'Accusations'? Lies are what they are," snapped Mom. She was getting loud. People were stopping their carts by the meat case, pretending to look over the loins. But I didn't care how loud she got or who heard, and Mom kept it up. "Lies from four people who would accuse the Lord Himself." I smiled. A pinch of religion was the perfect ingredient.

"Really," said Mrs. Baldwin.

Wow! What a comeback.

Then, Mom threw the knockout punch. She set her jaw, looked Mrs. Baldwin in the eye, and said, "Everyone is an expert on education because they've either been to school or know someone who has. You're the last kind." Snickers all up and down the aisle. Mrs. Baldwin's mouth hung open like a black hole, and we headed for the checkout lane.

"Great work," I mumbled. Mom looked straight ahead and rolled her cart to the counter.

On the way home from the store, Mom and I turned the car off of Main Street onto Broad Avenue, and the big billboard on the corner screamed the message *SAVE RIVER BEND'S CHILDREN* above the silhouettes of a little boy and little girl hanging their heads. I slowed the car and we looked at it as we rolled by.

Bumper stickers—billboards? "Mom, all this stuff these Ms. Simon haters are putting on billboards and their cars has to cost money. I wonder who's paying for it."

She shook her head. "I don't know. I just now asked myself the same question."

What we did know was that we had to do more for Ms. Simon than just toss out some witty comebacks to people like Edith Baldwin. We had to fight.

Later that night when I was wrestling with my thoughts, trying to fall asleep, I heard Mom talking to someone on the phone. They talked for a long time, but I couldn't catch the drift of the conversation. Then, she hung up and for the next hour or so, she and Dad talked; I couldn't make that out either. God, I'm such an eavesdropper and would have killed to know what they said.

All the talk at school the next day was about Ms. Simon's trouble. Before class took up, a big crowd gathered outside the building. Most of the kids thought she was getting a raw deal. She had become really popular. Oh, there were a couple royal jerks. Fat Nick Luttrell and Joe Skall really pissed me off. Dork-faced Joe said Coach was loose and Fat Nick agreed. God, I was so steamed. I ripped into them. "In your dreams, creeps!" I yelled. "You're both full of it! Coach Simon is a great person!" All the time I jabbed the middle fingers of both hands into Joe's sunken chest, and the rest of the kids urged me on. Doofus Joe and his fat friend didn't hang around to find out what was coming next. Their butts just kept getting smaller and smaller until they disappeared around the corner of the building.

I got discouraged at lunch, though, when I heard a group of chemistry students sitting at the table next to me discussing whether Coach was in River Bend because she was running away from something in Indianapolis—because she had messed up somewhere else. It frustrated me that I couldn't set them straight—tell them really why Ms. Simon came to teach in River Bend.

49

The Dynamic Duo

The whole town turned out to see if Coach would lose her head. The school board room was way too small, so the meeting was moved to the high school gym. It was jammed.

Although I hated that Coach had to face this dork court, it was nice to see so many people pack the gym for something besides a basketball game. Of course, if they'd come to gobble up all the juicy details, they'd be disappointed. That sideshow wasn't open to the public. Only the school officials, Ms. Simon, her witnesses, and the four jerks who'd stirred up all this trouble were supposed to be allowed into the hearing. The audio-visual room would be used for that.

There had only been a few days between the time we'd found out about Coach's trouble and the hearing, and we'd worked like lunatics to get the town behind her.

Weird, Dad was pissed—cussed and shouted—but Mom was

the one who really got involved. I don't know whether it was the billboard or that argument with Edith Baldwin, but she was obsessed with saving Coach Simon, and God help anyone who got in her way. When I think about it, that doesn't surprise me; like I've said, Mom doesn't get mad—she gets even.

The other person who jumped in with both feet was Leon Hendrix, Ky's dad. And believe it or not, Mom and Leon teamed up. When they got together, it was like he and Mom created a third personality that was possessed. First, Leon organized what he called a "phone army." He told Mom that talking and texting on the phone came naturally to teenagers, so he enlisted Coach Simon's chemistry students, the team—including Jake— and any other interested kids to call people in town to get them behind Coach. Kids phoned and texted, telling everyone that Coach was getting railroaded and asked them to support her. A kid named Tyler Jaslope—a real computer brain—created this really cool Facebook page. Coach's supporters posted information there, and a lot of kids kept Instagram fired up with photos of Ms. Simon teaching and coaching.

Kids in Leon's "phone army" asked people to spread the word and to show up at the board meeting. Boy, when people in River Bend found out Jake Nader was backing her, a lot of fence riders hopped off to Coach's side.

The next thing Mom and Mr. Hendrix did was go old school and print up petitions. The petitions told the board and administration that they'd better let Ms. Simon stay on as a teacher and as cross country coach or face the consequences. The petitions didn't specify what the consequences would be. "Keep them guessing," advised Leon Hendrix. Adults passed the petitions around—you know, registered voters and all that. People like my dad and even Mr. Bouton carried them around. Many folks were happy to sign, although a few arms had to be twisted. But not everyone would sign. Old Mr. Van Winkle wouldn't. He told Dad, "I'm not interested." Then, he disappeared into his office at the snack shop and slammed the door.

It really pissed me off that Van Winkle refused to sign the petition, considering Coach being his renter and all. "What's up with that old fart?" I asked Ky.

She shrugged. "I have no idea. Thought my dad had scared him straight."

"What do you mean?"

"Remember when I told you he wouldn't wait on me and my brother?"

"Yeah. What changed him? Seems to like you now."

"My dad went in and told him our money was as good as anyone's, and my dad expected him to serve us just like anyone else in River Bend."

"That made him see the light?"

"Not at first. Next time I tried to buy something, he was really unfriendly. He waited on me but wouldn't place the change in my hand—just tossed the coins up on the counter for me to pick up. I went right home and told my dad. He marched me into the store, looked at old man Van Winkle like he was drilling a hole through him, and told him he'd better stop disrespecting our family or Dad would get a lawyer—sue him for discrimination."

"That did it, huh?"

"Yeah, no more throwing change at me. Now, he seems happy when I come in."

"Can't figure out why he wouldn't stick up for Coach," I said.

Ky shrugged.

Van Winkle not signing pretty much sealed it for me that he was putting up the money for the campaign against Ms. Simon.

I started boycotting the Snack Shop, and so did a lot of my friends.

Thanks to Mom and Leon, people like Edith Baldwin and Van Winkle were a minority. The "Dynamic Duo" got adults to call school board members, send e-mails, and send letters by snail mail. Leon and Mom even set up Twitter accounts. Believe me, Twitter was tweeting nonstop in River Bend; Mom about wore her thumbs out. Leon Hendrix called this "positive pressure." And the board was feeling the heat. One board member told Dad down at the barbershop that Coach's supporters hadn't given him a minute's peace. All Dad said was, "That's good."

Mr. Hendrix really raised a stink about Coach not knowing all the accusations against her. He tried to get a meeting with the superintendent, but couldn't get past his secretary. Hardly anyone ever sees River Bend School District's super-intendent—in or out of the office. There have been more sightings of Elvis.

But Leon did corral Broadneck. He caught him at the end of the day while he was trying to beat us kids out the door.

Leon told Broadneck that "inappropriate behavior" wasn't specific enough. "How is she supposed to mount a defense?" Mr. Hendrix asked. But Broadneck wouldn't budge. Of course, the rumors were flying. The decency people kept spreading the same old crap as to why Coach had run away from a mega-bucks job to teach chemistry for peanuts: "Got fired," "Did something unethical—even illegal," and the theory that made them buzz like bees: "Has a secret lover in Indy." In the barbershop, at the beauty parlor, between the aisles of the Pig 'n Whistle, and of course at the churches, they debated the question: "Married man or even an under-aged lover—maybe a lesbian underage lover?"

Some of the latest talk involved Jake and me and all the time we'd spent over at Ms. Simon's place. That made me feel uncomfortable. But Clarence Elrod set me straight. "Did you do anything wrong?"

"No."

"Then give it the brush off. People with good sense will recognize a pack of lies—and those with dirty minds will just keep tellin' lies." After Clarence said that, I didn't worry so much.

But to top it off, the day of the big meeting the *River Bend Bugle* came out with a headline that screamed *TEACHER JEOPARDIZES STUDENTS!* Below the headline was an article that most people thought was more like an opinion, not just reporting the facts. It said that "Many citizens of River Bend are concerned about the influence of a certain River Bend High School teacher on the character of our community's students." The article didn't mention a thing about the people supporting that "certain" teacher. My dad was so mad, he went straight into the office of the *Bugle's* editor, Mark Gotchum, and told him that he was a "Damn poor excuse for a journalist" and "You're the one that ought to be run out of town." Gotchum didn't answer back—and he didn't move from behind his desk either. Dad's not big, but as a young guy he was a Golden Gloves boxing champ, and Gotchum knew he'd get the crap knocked out of him.

Dad said a lot of other things to the editor that day, but they are definitely not repeatable. After he had blasted Gotchum, Dad canceled our subscription to the *Bugle*—and so did other people like the Hendrixes.

As I said, Leon got really pissed when the school administration refused to be up front with Ms. Simon about the charges. He said it was a violation of her civil rights. "You should sue the board members, the principal, the superintendent, and those three half-wits," he told her. I guess he thought Sherry was too young to be sued.

Anyway, when the night of the hearing rolled around, Dad told Mom as we were leaving that he was proud of her; that she'd done everything but stand on her head in a dress without undies.

"Now, we've got to speak up for Ms. Simon at this meeting—this is what really counts," she said as she adjusted the bundle of petitions she was lugging with both arms. Dad agreed. I was sure, though, that Mom wouldn't do much talking; speaking in front of more than three people practically makes her pee her pants. She was putting faith in Leon to do the talking.

50

Zero Hour and Where Is Leon?

The board sliced through a bunch of baloney during the first part of the meeting. Boring! I was a nervous wreck. Being bored and nervous at the same time is no fun. I mean, all the yakking about lawn mowers and school buses, and whether they should charge a buck more or only a half-buck more for lunch at the grade school. Good God! And I wasn't the only one.

People kept squirming. Checking their watches. Yawning. I kept glancing over at Coach, sitting down one row of bleachers to my left. She seemed as cool as a rock in winter. To this day, I don't get how she could have been that calm.

What really worried me—and I know it was driving Mom crazy—was that the Hendrixes were nowhere to be found. Not even Kyesha. Mom was constantly looking around, the gob of petitions hugged against her chest. And, of course, every girl on the cross country team was dying to hear Leon Hendrix unload

269

both barrels at the board and the administration. He gets to the point like an ice pick. Also, I knew Mom *had* to have Leon there.

I kept sneaking peeks at Sherry Dumont to my right. She and her doofus dad were sitting in the first row like they just couldn't wait to get at their dirty business. To this day, I don't know where Mel Dumont's better half was. Before the meeting, I'd have bet my driver's license that Muffy Jo Dumont would be occupying three front row seats, wearing a bright muumuu with her beehive hair stacked to the sky and her mug plastered with Mary Kay Cosmetics. But she wasn't there to see Coach Simon led to the slaughter. Maybe Muffy's heart couldn't stand that much fun all at once. Whatever the reason, only Sherry and Doofus Mel were representing the Dumont household.

As for Prissy Butt McGrady and Mad Max Jarvis, they were sitting directly behind us, and believe me, I could feel the daggers being tossed at my mom. Henry Elrod told people down at the Quick Mart that the day before the board meeting Prissy had been fuming about all of Coach Simon's support. "Some people would rather cause trouble than make sure their children aren't being corrupted," she spouted.

I didn't have to think twice about who she meant by "some people."

Finally, the school board president announced that they were going into a "closed hearing with approved parties" to discuss an important personnel matter. Everyone came alive, running his or her mouth like electric motors. The board president banged her gavel a half dozen times to get them settled down. Zero hour—and the Hendrixes still hadn't shown. Thought we'd have to sedate Mom. Dad told her, "Just relax," but her body was actually trembling.

Most of the crowd was left behind in the gym, and to a person they stayed put. Coach's trouble had generated nearly as much excitement as a trip to the state basketball tournament —nearly. The rest of us headed for the audio-visual room for this inquisition. We were about to round a corner in the hall when in walked Ky with her mom and little brother—but no Leon. Mom rushed over to Mrs. Hendrix. Jake and I scurried up to Kyesha.

"Where is your dad? Mom's about to have a nervous breakdown," I asked.

Ky shrugged, and then pushed up her glasses. Her face was worried. "I'm not sure. He told Mom he had to meet someone. Left before dinner. We waited as long as we could."

"I hope he gets here quick," said Jake. "We're deep into the fourth quarter on this thing."

"I know," answered Ky as the three of us hustled through the double doors of the hall leading to the audio-visual room. "Just don't know why he's not back yet or who he had to meet—tonight of all nights."

Before they herded us in, the superintendent himself made us sign in, and then checked our names against a list of witnesses. *So that's what he looks like.* Inside the audio-visual room there are long rows of lecture desks with attached seats on levels that descended toward a large screen on the wall.

The board members took their seats at long tables that had been placed on the ground floor in front of the screen. I parked right next to Coach. Jake sat beside me. There was an empty chair to Coach's left, and Mom started to sit there, but Coach said, "Mrs. Garnet, I'd better keep this seat open."

For who? Leon? Jake and I gave each other a glance.

Mom packed the petitions up to the front and set them in front of the board president, who studied them for a second, then pushed them aside.

Mom looked discouraged as she plopped down on the other side of Jake. Dad sat next to her. All of us front and center. Then the president banged her gavel. Coach Simon's future—and in a way mine—was about to be decided. And we were also in for more than one big surprise.

51

Shock And Awe

When we first walked into the AV room, I didn't notice him. But after getting settled, I looked around and he caught my eye. There he was, sitting in a dark corner at the back of the room, all dressed like some guy who'd just stepped off of Wall Street. Sherman Applebee, Stag's old man, leaned forward so that his face came out of the shadows. I studied him. When he saw Coach, he looked her up and down, and then he turned his eyes away, smirking and slightly nodding as if he were saying, "I warned you."

I had been wrong. All along I thought it was old man Van Winkle paying for the billboards, the bumper stickers, and sending the "decency" people door to door with fancy colored handouts calling for Coach to resign or be fired. *Cassie, you should've guessed it wouldn't be Van Winkle. He's a money grubber. That's the point. He wouldn't drive away a regularly paying tenant. It takes a UC like Stag's old man to have enough meanness to kick up this much trouble. But why didn't Van Winkle sign the petition?* I didn't have an answer.

Some of the others in the room noticed Applebee; others didn't. No one asked him why he was there. *Guess they figure he's Sherman Applebee, banker and big shot UC from Snob Hill. Should I say something—challenge him—ask what he's here for?*

"Miss Simon," the president read from a paper. (Really pissed me off that she called Coach "Miss.") Anyway, she went on to say that serious charges had been made against Coach, and "Miss" Simon was there to prove her innocence. The lawyer for the school board stopped her and whispered something.

"Why doesn't he say it so we can all hear?" Jake said under his breath.

I agreed.

Then, the president corrected herself and said Ms. Simon had a right to offer evidence to contradict the allegations. Blah! Blah! Blah! The whole spiel made me sick. The president made it sound like everyone in town was complaining about Ms. Simon. I got the impression she'd already made up her mind that Coach was guilty, which made me boil.

Mom kept glancing over her shoulder at the doors. Once I caught her looking back at Mrs. Hendrix, who shrugged as if to say, "I don't know where he's at." Then, Mom caught sight of Applebee, and her face turned bright red. Her eyes drifted to the floor, and she breathed heavily as she bit her lower lip.

The president droned on for about five minutes, and then the door to the AV room creaked open. Everyone turned. In walked Leon, and with him was another black man—a really distinguished-looking guy—older with a few gray hairs around his temples. He had a frown on his face, like he was really pissed at someone. Mom let out a sigh of relief; her whole body relaxed. Applebee leaned forward and narrowed his eyes at the two black men.

The sight of the two caught people off guard. The superintendent studied the man with Mr. Hendrix, and then asked, "Do you people have some direct involvement in this business?"

Leon answered, "Yes, we do. I'm Leon Hendrix—here as a witness on Ms. Simon's behalf. And this gentleman . . ." He motioned toward the other black man, but before Leon could introduce him, the man interrupted.

"I'm Nigel Patterson. I've been retained as Ms. Simon's attorney." Then, he marched to the front and sat in the empty seat beside Coach Simon. Leon Hendrix followed him and sat nearby.

The room buzzed like bees. The board president banged her gavel and asked for order. A scowl seemed cemented on Patterson's face.

The first person who was called to tell why Ms. Simon should be fired was Mel Dumont. He was told to come to the front where he took a seat at a long table perpendicular to the ones where the board was sitting. Right off he started whining about all the "trauma" his daughter had suffered because of Coach Simon's "ways." I couldn't decide whether I wanted to puke or kick him in the privates.

After going on and on, repeating the same old crap, the school board's lawyer stopped him. "Mr. Dumont, be precise. Give us examples that *you* have witnessed."

About time, I thought.

Coach Simon scooted to the edge of her chair. Patterson studied Dumont, waiting for a response.

"Well . . ." Dumont hesitated, looking toward Ms. Simon, but not directly at her. "Well, she—Miss Simon—told the girls on the cross country team that they were old enough to have sexual relations."

"That's a lie!" I blurted.

Everyone looked my way. The president rapped her gavel against the table. "Cassie, you'll get a chance to speak your piece. Right now, just be quiet until we're ready to hear from you."

Jake put his arm around me. At the same time, Coach turned and looked at me, gently shaking her head, encouraging me to keep my cool.

"As I was saying," continued Dumont, "she encouraged them to fornicate and to use protection—you know, *contraceptives*." (Yes, he actually used the word "fornicate," and he said "contraceptives" like it was a terrorist plot.) "Said she would get it for them—get birth control," continued Mel Dumont.

"She did not!" "Never said it!" came objections from most of my teammates. I didn't dare say what I thought; it would have gotten me in big trouble.

The president banged the gavel again, telling them to be still.

Coach Simon whispered to her lawyer. Patterson nodded, glared at Mel Dumont, and then stood. "Excuse me. I want to ask this gentleman some questions."

"*Gentleman*? He obviously doesn't know Doofus Dumont," I whispered to Jake who smothered a snicker.

At first, the board president wasn't going to let Patterson say anything, but after the school board's lawyer whispered something to her, she told Patterson to go ahead. Patterson turned to Dumont. "Did *you* hear Ms. Simon tell the girls on the cross country team they should have sex and she'd get contraceptives for them?"

Dumont hesitated then said, "Well, no. But my daughter heard her and told me.

"Where's your daughter?"

276

Dumont tipped his head toward Sherry. "Right over there."

I looked over at Sherry squirming in her seat.

Patterson stared at her. "Young lady, did Ms. Simon say that to *you?*"

Sherry turned red—then got snotty. "Yes, that's exactly what she said."

"You heard her?"

"Yes, I did."

"Sherry, you're lying!" I blurted. Some of the other team members chimed in.

The president pounded the table. "Quiet!" Patterson ignored the board president and went right on. "You heard Ms. Simon encourage the girls on the cross country team to have sexual intercourse, and that she would assist them to get contraceptives? *You* heard her?"

The gavel fell and the president interrupted. "Mr. Patterson, should you really…"

The board's lawyer touched the president's arm. "I want to hear her answer."

You could've heard a mouse fart, it was so quiet.

Patterson turned back to Sherry. "Did she encourage *you* to have sexual intercourse and say she would provide *you* with contraceptives?"

Wow, talk about being candid.

"Yes, she did."

"When was this? Where was this? Who was there?" Patterson rifled the questions at her. Sherry hesitated, then stammered, "Well—well . . ." Every eye was on her. "At our cross country practice."

"That's interesting. You're Sherry Dumont, aren't you?"

Sherry drew out a "Yes."

"Didn't you quit the team after the first meeting last spring? You haven't practiced with the team since then, have you?"

Out of the corner of my eye, I spotted Mom glance at Leon Hendrix. A smile had broken out on his face.

"I thought you told us that Ms. Simon said those things directly to you."

"Hey, just hold on, mister!" Mel Dumont jumped to his feet. The president gaveled, telling him to be quiet. Dumont ignored her. He pointed his finger at Patterson. "You just hold on. My daughter's not the one on trial."

The board's lawyer broke in. "No one is on trial here, Mr. Dumont. This isn't a court of law. We're just seeking the truth, and as her attorney . . ."

Again Dumont pointed his finger at Patterson. "Well, he acts like it's a court of law!"

Suddenly, a voice came from the back of the room. "Court of law or not, we want the truth."

We turned to look.

Not a soul had heard him slip in, but there he was. Old Mr. Van Winkle.

"Mr. Van Winkle—" The superintendent hesitated. "We're glad to have you with us—are you—are you a witness in the matter?"

"No, but I pay more taxes than most people in the town, and I want to make sure my money is used the right way. What's more, it's also my money that's paying for Attorney Patterson there. I don't think any of you good people would take issue with an accused person being defended. Would you?"

There was silence for an instant. Van Winkle turned and glared at Sherman Applebee, sniffed, and looked toward the front. "Got as much right to be here as Applebee, don't I?"

Sherman Applebee clinched his teeth.

The president turned to the superintendent and board's attorney for advice. The board's attorney said, "Well, as Ms. Simon's lawyer, Mr. Patterson has a right—an obligation—to ask questions on his client's behalf." The board's lawyer peeked up at Applebee and looked back at Van Winkle. "And if you are paying for Mr. Patterson, then you may stay."

"Then, let's get on with it," said Van Winkle as he took a seat, shooting Sherman Applebee another glare. Applebee refused to look at Van Winkle. He leaned back into the shadows and seemed to be staring straight ahead. In the darkness, I couldn't see his face.

"Mel, you sit down, too," said the president. Dumont sank into a chair.

I gave Jake a look, and then glanced at Mom. Dad just shook his head, astonished at this turn of events. The rest of the people in the room were too stunned to move. Old man Van Winkle paying for Coach's black lawyer—who would have even imagined it?

Patterson thanked the school board's lawyer and the board members. He turned back to Sherry. "Did Ms. Simon encourage *you* to have intercourse and tell *you* she would get *you* birth control?"

Sherry glared into space. "No, I didn't actually hear her."

Everyone in the crowd started talking. The president of the board and the other board members listened.

"You're repeating hearsay—repeating what someone else said, aren't you?"

Sherry didn't answer at first. She looked away; every eye in the room was on her. Then she said, "One of my teammates told me."

The team looked at each other—except for one, who stared at the floor. I looked at Sherry. I was really pissed at Dumont, yet I also found myself feeling sorry for her. I mean the way she had said it: "'One of *my* teammates.'" Sherry didn't get it. She still thought of herself as part of the team. There had been a quiver in her voice; her eyes were wet and red.

"Who is this other girl?" asked Patterson.
The room waited for Sherry's answer.

52

The Cabal Exposed

"Kayla Thomas."

Kayla's head shot up. "I did not!"

The president banged her gavel. Every eye was on Kayla.

"You did too!" Sherry yelled back. "You told me that Miss Simon said it was all right to have sex as long as you used condoms."

The president continued rapping the table, calling for order.

"For once why don't you just shut your big fat mouth!" screamed Kayla. Again, the gavel fell. Kayla's grandma, sitting beside her, tried to settle her down. Sherry went right on. "She spied on Miss Simon's apartment. Told me Jake Nader and Cassie Garnet were always over there."

"What?" Jake and I said.

Kayla looked up at me, and then hung her head. The rest of the team glared at her.

Patterson turned to the board and pointed at Sherry. "This young woman didn't hear Ms. Simon say anything about sex or condoms. She recants and now says she got the information from this young lady—" He pointed to Kayla. "Who apparently has stalked Ms. Simon and. . ."

Kayla jumped to her feet and gestured at Mel Dumont. "He talked me into spying on her—showed me how to send those weird e-mails with a fake name." Then, she pointed at Sherry. "And you put that note in Cassie's newspaper."

I set my jaw. *Knew it was one of them. Makes sense that it was Sherry.*

"Kayla, sit down." Her grandma pulled her back to her seat.

"Please, girls—order," said the president.

What a soap opera.

Now, Mel Dumont was on his feet. "Kayla is—uh—confused." He swallowed. "I—uh—I simply said that she and Sherry should—uh—report anything that was—improper—about any of the teachers—not just Miss Simon."

"Improper? Spying? E-mails? What are you, self-appointed guardian of morals around here?" Patterson asked.

A nervous chuckle rippled through the room.

The president banged the gavel. "This is no laughing matter." Then, she buried her face in her hands, muttering, "I can't believe this is happening—just can't believe it."

Another board member consoled her while the rest of the board and the school superintendent stared at each other, stunned speechless.

Now, Mel Dumont bristled. "Well, a good citizen has to make sure that young people are not being corrupted."

The board's attorney spoke up. "So you decided that the way to do this was to dupe your daughter and her friend . . ."

"She's no friend of mine," said Kayla.

"You're not mine either," answered Sherry.

"That's enough out of both of you," said the school board's lawyer. "Did you counsel Kayla to spy on Miss Simon and to send anonymous e-mails to her?"

Mel Dumont's face was beet red. "Well, I wouldn't call it spying," he sputtered. "Besides, several of us were—we were concerned about Miss Simon's lifestyle."

"Her lifestyle is none of your business," said Patterson. "And who is 'several of us' anyway? Who are the others?" Silence. Patterson turned to the board members. "This is nothing but a conspiracy of lies."

"Betty McGrady and I . . ." Dumont stammered.

McGrady stood. "May I explain?" We all looked at Prissy Butt, then back at Dumont, and then back at Prissy Butt, who went on. "What Mr. Dumont is trying to say, is that he and I had a discussion at church about good morals. Certainly, I never suggested that anyone—students or adults—should spy on or send any kind of threatening e-mails to any of the teachers. I know what the law says about that kind of thing."

"I'll just bet you do," remarked Patterson. McGrady ignored him.

I glanced behind me. A smile stretched clear across Leon's face. Mom grinned back at him. This was starting to unravel right in front of our eyes. But McGrady was cool and collected. And old Mr. Van Winkle? He was reared back in his chair taking it all in.

"My involvement in all of this was not to sabotage Ms. Simon." Prissy Butt looked at Coach Simon. "I simply raised with Mr. Dumont—" she turned and looked off to the far corner of the room, "—and also with Mr. Applebee—concerns expressed to me by these young ladies." She looked first at Sherry, and then at Kayla, who was now seated. "Girls, you remember that day you confided in me about Ms. Simon? Let's see, it was—" she removed a pocket calendar from her purse and studied it,—"September fifteenth at four-thirty in the afternoon. The conversation ended at four forty-three." She closed the calendar. "Oh, just for the record, I told Mr. Broadneck, too. And I have that documented if you would like to see it." She glanced at the principal then looked squarely at Mad Max. "Perhaps Coach Jarvis would like to shed some light on all of this."

McGrady sat down, her lips pressed tightly, her nose up so high she'd drown in a drizzle.

Mad Max had been lying low; now he looked like he'd been kicked between the legs.

The superintendent spoke up. "What about it, Coach Jarvis? You had quite a bit to say when we all met."

Jarvis glanced at McGrady as he stood slowly. But she kept her eyes on the board members. He looked up toward Applebee, then at the board. Mad Max seemed tongue tied.

"Coach Jarvis?"

"What?"

"We want to hear from you," said the superintendent.

"Well . . ." He hesitated. "Well . . . I just think Miss Simon's . . . well, she's gettin' these kids' heads all turned around."

Patterson bent down as Ms. Simon whispered to him.

Jarvis started to sit, but Patterson stopped him dead. "What does that mean, 'getting their heads all turned around'? Give us examples." Patterson waited in silence. Finally, he said, "Let me help you. Let's see—" he studied a yellow legal pad that he'd removed from his briefcase, —"you're the football coach. Right, Mr. Jarvis?"

Jarvis dragged out a "Yes."

"Coach Jarvis, isn't it true that you got involved in this crusade because Jake Nader decided not to go out for your football team and instead assisted Ms. Simon with cross country?"

Mad Max hesitated, and then he bellowed, "Messin' up the way we do things! That's what she's done! Why'd she come here anyway?"

The president slammed the gavel against the table and started to speak, but Patterson beat her to it. "Sir, that's none of your business. As I understand it, you're not a native of this community. Why did you come here?" Patterson looked at Prissy Butt McGrady. Leon touched Patterson's arm, and the lawyer leaned down to listen to Leon. Patterson looked up at Applebee hiding in the shadows, and then back at McGrady and said, "To do other people's dirty work? Is that your purpose for being in this town?" Prissy glared at Patterson.

Jarvis sat down without an answer.

Patterson pointed at Jarvis. "Ladies and gentlemen, silence is agreement."

Mad Max was like a teenager who just got caught wearing his mother's underwear. He looked toward McGrady for help. She stared straight ahead.

Slick as ice. Remember when Mrs. Anderson, the old lady who works for Clarence at the Quick Mart, said McGrady was neither smart nor good looking? Wrong. McGrady is definitely smart. She's one of those people who can tumble ass-backwards into manure and come out smelling like a rose. Know the kind? It was plain to me that she had played old doofus Mel Dumont and Mad Max Jarvis like cheap violins. Set up the whole thing, along with Sherman Applebee. I only had one problem. Sherry, her dad, and the other three—Prissy Butt, Mad Max, and Applebee—I understood their motives, but why Kayla? *What is she so pissed about?* I wanted to ask her, but Coach got to it first.

She stood and faced Kayla. "Kayla, I consider you an

important part of the team. Is Sherry telling the truth? Did you watch my apartment and send those e-mails? Did you lie to her about what I said?" Coach appealed to Kayla's grandma. "Mrs. Thomas, Kayla was as much a part of this team as any of the other young women." Kayla's grandma didn't answer, just stared at Ms. Simon, then turned her eyes away. Kayla sat with her teeth clenched, pouting, eyes pasted on the floor. "Kayla, you know I never said for you—for any of your team members—to do anything wrong. Why did you say that I did?"

"You said if we had sex, we should use condoms," she mumbled.

Now Ky was on her feet. "Coach said that she would rather we didn't have sex, but if we were going to, to use a condom." The president raised the gavel; the board's lawyer placed a hand on her arm, stopping her. "That's no more than we're told on television every day," Ky continued. "But it means more when Coach says it. We're more likely to listen."

A chorus of "That's right!" and "Yeses!" came from the team and Coach Simon's supporters. Ky sat down.

Ms. Simon continued. "You're a part of our team, Kayla. Why did you twist what I told you?" Then Coach sat down slowly, like a weight was on her shoulders.

Kayla simmered, and then she sprang to her feet and pointed at team members. "Because of you! And you! And you! And you! You run away, leaving me behind in practices. Ignore me when I run in meets. You all think you're so great with your *Coach Simon* and all the bragging she does on you to the papers and all. You don't even thank me when I stand guard while all you *big stars* go pee in the woods!"

Kayla's grandma continued to look straight ahead. The president slammed the gavel against the table. "Young lady, that's enough out of you."

It seemed like Kayla had gone wacko. Mind you, I wasn't mad at her—I pitied her. But I was also ashamed because I knew there was some truth to what she'd said. Some of my teammates sent her a shocked look, others hung their heads.

Ms. Simon left her chair and came to Kayla. She slipped her arm around her shoulder, but Kayla jerked away.

I had to say something. "Kayla, we didn't mean to leave you out. We . . ." But my words were useless.

"And especially you, Cassie—" She flung her right index finger at Jake. "—and your lover boy!" She turned back to Ms. Simon. "And you—setting everything up for them." She gave a snort and snarled, "*Coach.*" Then she buried her head in Ms. Simon's shoulder and sobbed as I watched Sherman Applebee get up and leave.

53

"Good Teachers Are Too Hard To Come By"

It didn't take long. We were all sent back to the gym, and the board went into a closed meeting. A few minutes later the superintendent announced Coach would be staying. The crowd went nuts. You should have heard the hooting and hollering. Should have seen all the hugging. And I couldn't believe it—Coach actually cried again.

Right after Kayla's meltdown in the AV room, her grandma had taken her home, so she wasn't around for the big news. But Sherry and her dad were. The expression on their faces was a mixture of disappointment and hate. Mad Max Jarvis hid out like a criminal up in a far dark corner of the bleachers. Prissy Butt McGrady? Well, she plopped down in the middle of the crowd smirking like she was waiting to be handed a trophy. No conscience.

Oh, yeah, Mr. Van Winkle? He didn't wait around for the board's decision. He slipped out as quietly as he'd come in. What a story that turned out to be.

Before they went into the closed meeting, Patterson had each member of the team, except Kayla, tell that Coach had never once encouraged us to to have sex. He had Ms. Simon explain that she was just trying to do the "prudent" thing—the right thing.

Marge Johnson, a board member, asked Coach why she'd brought up sex at all.

Coach answered, "With all the sexually transmitted diseases and out-of-wedlock pregnancies, I'd be remiss not to advise the young women. Of course, I'd rather they weren't sexually active, but to assume that every young person in River Bend is going to abstain and doesn't need to know about options would be irresponsible. I'd be negligent as a teacher not to inform them."

"But is that the school's job?" another board member asked.

"Certainly, it's better if parents take the responsibility. But we can't assume that all parents will talk with their children. I told the young women on the team that I'd discuss it further with them if their parents wouldn't. But I first put it into the hands of the young women and their parents."

Everyone on the team backed up what she said.

Patterson had her explain that Jake and I were just coming over to deliver cross country statistics, and that she'd treated us to a track meet in Indianapolis—with our parents' permission. Other times we went to her place to get advice—her counsel.

Jake explained how he and Ms. Simon had talked about school and chemistry and how she had helped him have more confidence. They really liked that part. Probably figured it would make him a better basketball player. Jake and I both told them that everything was *kosher*, as Ms. Simon says when

290

things are cool. I told about how she got me interested in reading and writing poetry. Then I asked if I could say something else.

"Go ahead, Cassie," the president said.

I cleared my throat. "I just want to say that Ms. Simon is the best coach—best teacher—I've ever had. She helped me believe in myself. Believe that I could be really good at something—be good at a lot of things—if I tried."

My teammates agreed.

I looked over at Coach. She looked back at me like she was about to burst out crying.

Then before we were sent to the gym, the school board president let Patterson make a statement on Ms. Simon's behalf. He told them that her accusers had been completely discredited. That their accusations were nothing but vindictive hearsay and malicious fabrications. He reminded them that every other girl on the team, plus Jake, had contradicted Ms. Simon's accusers.

Finally, Patterson spoke like he was chatting across the kitchen table with each board member. "All of these young people," Patterson motioned toward the team, "have spoken tonight about what a positive influence Ms. Simon is. What's more, you must not really want to let her go, otherwise you wouldn't have granted a first-year teacher—as she is—this kind of hearing." He stepped closer. Board members listened carefully. "We can't afford to lose good teachers—a teacher of C.R. Simon's caliber—not a single teacher of her caliber. Good teachers are too hard to come by. You can't afford *not* to have her teach your children." Patterson sat down. We clapped, and that's when we were excused to the gym.

54

Staying!

Anyway, after it was announced that Coach would be staying, that freak Mel Dumont dragged his rear end off the bleachers and slinked out of the gym. Sherry right behind. Nigel Patterson wanted Coach to press charges against him for putting Kayla up to the stalking and harassment, but she wouldn't do it. As for Sherry Dumont, she marched right back to school the very next day like nothing happened. Can't believe it. No shame.

Henry Elrod told us at the convenience store that he listened to the principal and superintendent take turns giving McGrady a good "butt-chewin,'" as he called it.

"When the door opened, I glanced up from my sweepin' and out came Betty, dabbing at her red, swollen eyes and red nose with a lace hankie. Sniveled like that all day. Every time I came into the office, she was either bawlin' or blowin,'" said Henry.

Believe me, it didn't last. A couple days later, I went into the office and Prissy Butt had her snout back in the air, barking orders and darting all around. The tears had been a show.

"Funny thing," Henry told us, "as mad as they were at Betty, neither the principal nor the superintendent uttered the word *fired*."

That didn't surprise me. Prissy Butt doesn't have anything to worry about. They'll yell at her, but they won't fire her; they're afraid of her—and I don't know why. Everyone in town's been whispering that she's got dirt on someone important. She must. How else could she get off scot-free?

But clueless Mad Max Jarvis didn't have the leverage that McGrady has. He turned in his resignation before they could fire him. River Bend's looking for a new football coach.

Somehow Patterson discovered that Prissy and Mad Max had made cracks about Coach being Jewish, so he met with the school board's attorney. When the board's lawyer heard about the anti-Semitism, the crap hit the fan. The latest news has it that he told the superintendent and the board members they'd be lucky if Coach didn't sue the district and win a bundle of cash. They don't have to worry about that; Coach won't sue. That's not her style. In fact, Coach lectured the whole team on not being bitter. But I can't help it—considering all the trouble those freaks caused her.

Sherman Applebee? After I thought about it, I wasn't surprised that he was involved.

As for Kayla, the school officials were determined to expel her. I felt sorry for her. I mean, yeah, she did the spying and e-mailing, but she was just a pawn for the Dumonts. Ms. Simon went to the board and stuck up for Kayla—told the board members that Kayla had been exploited. Coach must have put up quite an argument, because they voted four to three not to expel her; she did get suspended for three days, though.

We—the team—tried to be nice. Told her we wanted her to

hang with us. But she must really be pissed off—or ashamed—or depressed—or all three. Except for school, none of us see her much anymore. She has no friends, and apparently doesn't want any. It's like she figures she's an outcast, so she'll act the part. That's sad. I mean it, it's really sad.

Nigel Patterson's a legend around town. When I'm old and wrinkled, people in River Bend will probably still be blabbing about the black lawyer who came to town to rescue the Jewish cross country coach.

But the real heroes are Leon Hendrix and old Mr. Van Winkle. Unbelievable. Who would have ever thought they'd wind up working together. See, Patterson is an old friend of Leon's. He said that Patterson worked a lot on civil rights cases when he was a young lawyer way back in the day, and he's always defending the underdog. Anyway, you remember when old Mr. Van Winkle didn't sign the petition—walked my dad off and slammed the door to his office? Come to find out, he phoned Leon. Imagine that? Old Mr. Van Winkle told Leon he knew Coach was getting a raw deal, but signing a petition was a waste of time, ink, and energy—they needed to take real action. It had stuck in Van Winkle's head that Leon had threatened to sue him over not treating Ky and her brother right, so he figured Leon must know a good lawyer. Which, of course, he does. Van Winkle said that he would put up the money, if Leon would get a hold of the attorney. So Leon got Coach Simon a meeting with Patterson. The three met in Indianapolis. Patterson said he'd take the case pro bono. But Leon said that wasn't necessary because Mr. Van Winkle would pay the retainer. On the night of the big meeting, Leon waited at Clarence Elrod's Quick Mart to direct Patterson to the high school. But Patterson got lost, plus they moved the meeting from the board office to the gym. That's why they were late. But they made it—just in time. And as they say, the rest is history.

Oh, yeah, my mom—I'm proud of her, too. So is Dad. He didn't say it right out, but I could tell by the way he treated her when they walked to the car after the meeting. You know, putting his arm around her and stuff. When they got into the car, he pulled her over to him and kept his arm around her, holding her tightly all the way home.

55

"Like *Mediocre*, The Word *Ordinary* Is Not In My Vocabulary"

It's weird how one person can change things for another person. Coach getting me to read those books by Dick Francis and write poetry gave me a whole different view of life. And if it hadn't been for Coach motivating me and encouraging me, I wouldn't have won state. But I did win—not just better than ordinary but the best. Funny thing, even if I hadn't won, I think I'd still have confidence. It's like this: I won state because I believe in myself, I don't believe in myself just because I won state. But until Coach Simon came along, I lacked confidence, and she helped me find it—find it right here inside of me. I tell her that she's changed my life, but she says that's silly—that *I* changed my life—that *I* decided to make the change.

I still worry a little about how I look—my figure and all. But not very much, really. Maybe someday I'll catch up to C.R. Simon in that respect. Yeah, right. Ah, who cares if my body will never be like hers anyway? A year ago I figured the answer to that question was that men care. But I'm placing my bets that not all men will hold it against me that I don't have a body like C.R. Simon's. I don't think Jake cares.

Something else has changed: I shoved aside my discomfort and accepted an invitation from Taylor to spend the night with her next weekend. Coach and I talked, and I decided it's important that I get past my prejudice towards UCs.

As far as college, yes, a few coaches from colleges have contacted my parents or Coach Simon showing interest in me running for them. But, no, the phone hasn't been ringing off the hook, like Sarah Rothman predicted. I guess, though, that some interest is better than no interest. And, as Coach said, if the Northern Indiana coach is really interested, then she'll offer me a good deal. She's already called me once. One thing I like about Northern, it's not far from home. I would rather not be too far away. But Coach is right, wherever it is, I should take the best deal—the one that will give me a good education and cost Mom and Dad as little as possible.

Maybe Indiana University will show interest in me, too. Jake always wanted to be an IU Hoosier, and they're dangling a full ride in front of him to play basketball next year, depending on how this season goes—and so far he's doing great. But I'm not sure it's such a good idea for Jake and me to be at the same college. I mean, even as much as we like each other, I think we need some breathing room to see what our relationship is made of.

One thing's for sure. No matter what college I end up running for, or what I decide to study or what happens between Jake and me, like the word *mediocre,* the word *ordinary* isn't in my vocabulary anymore.